Fortress

L. G Campbell

DEDICATION

I am dedicating this book to a woman who wasn't perfect, but she had the biggest heart.

To the woman who would tell you how fabulous you are, when you just a little child dancing around and being silly.

To the woman that joined in our games, wore our homemade flower petal perfume and embraced our crazy childhood dreams.

To the woman who told you that you could have it all and be the best at whatever or who-ever you wanted to be.

To the woman who made me love to eat corn beef hash and faggots. Still to this day I've only ever ate yours.

To the woman who opened her house and heart to me.

For the wonderful fun loving woman that gave me her time, her last penny and her love.

You played a huge part in my life growing up as a child. I am forever grateful and honoured to have had you in my life.

Heather you were one of a kind. You will be missed, but you will be forever be in our hearts.

PROLOGUE

As I stand here watching Carter propose to my baby sister, a wave of happiness and pride fills my chest. Seeing how far she's come and how strong she is, seeing her finally get her happily ever after, I can't help the empty feeling that settles in my gut. I can't help the slight wave of jealousy I feel towards my two sisters.

Downing my glass of champagne I head outside for some fresh air. I feel the light evening breeze. I take a deep breath and curse myself for feeling this way. I chose to be alone, I chose not to let anyone in. It's safer this way, I can't get hurt again. I have to be the strong one for Caden, it isn't just about me and my feelings.

I don't hear him approach, but I know he's stood nearby, watching me. It's as though my body senses whenever he's nearby and I hate that it does that.

"I'm not interested Rip, I just want to be on my own. I'm not in the mood for your shit. So please...just leave me be...okay?" I say, keeping my back to him and looking straight ahead.

"You know you could have that too, one day. You could have that happiness if you just let someone in." Rip states.

I spin round to face him, anger building in me. But I won't admit to myself that it's because he's absolutely right. I refuse to ever admit that to him, so I'm certainly not going to admit it to myself.

"Don't. You don't know a single thing about me. You have no idea what you're talking about. Why don't you just go find some girl to fuck and leave me the hell alone?!" I seethe.

Rip walks towards me, his ice blue eyes pinning me. I step back until my back hits a tree. Only when I'm cornered does Rip stop. He's so close I can feel his breath across my lips.

"I know a lot more than you think sweetheart. I know you've built this wall to protect yourself, except it ain't protecting you, it's stopping you from living your damn life. You act like you don't have a care in the world when in reality, you're fuckin' terrified. You're terrified to feel again, terrified you'll get it wrong and your heart will be broken." Rip says, placing his palm over my heart.

My whole body shivers from his touch. I hate that he causes this reaction in me. I swallow and shake my head.

"So let me guess, you're going to be that guy, are you? You're the one that's going to fix me!" I say sarcastically, rolling my eyes.

Rip smiles, leaning in closer, his hand moving from my chest up my neck to cup my face. He pauses, his lips just grazing mine.

"I see you're finally getting it sweetheart." He whispers before his mouth is on mine, kissing me.

I have no control when it comes to Rip. My body responds to him. Placing my hands on his chest I kiss him back, he lets out a low growl and deepens the kiss. I gasp and he takes advantage, sliding his tongue across mine. He nips at my bottom lip, and continues kissing and caressing down my neck and across my collar bone. I'm completely gone, my body is his.

Rip's cellphone rings. We both ignore it, but it doesn't stop. It carries on. Frustrated I reach into his pocket and grab it, not looking at the screen I answer.

"What?" I growl into his phone. I feel Rip's lips smile against my neck as he continues kissing and nipping.

"Rip, baby, is that you?" A feminine voice asks.

I tense, Rip notices and his head comes up, his eyes searching my face.

"Who's calling?" I ask.

"It's Candy. Listen, can you tell Rip he left his wallet here last night? Oh and ask him to call me."

I pause, close my eyes and take a deep breath.

"Sure." I disconnect. I hang up and kick Rip in the crotch and throw his phone at him. I lay into him, I don't hold back.

Then I storm off. I'm so angry at myself for letting him in, even if it was just a small part of me. I need to get out of here. I need to get as far away as I can, right now. The way he makes me feel petrifies me. I can't let him near my heart, he's a player looking for a good time. I can never be that girl. I was right to trust my instincts, it's just me and Caden against the world.

CHAPTER ONE

"Now, are you sure you're going to be okay? I've left my number on the fridge, and Wes is about usually if you do need anything. I've updated the insurance on the truck so feel free to use it. I thought it'd help you and Caden to get about. Daisy is also about...um...." Lily pauses biting her thumbnail.

"Darlin', Rose is a fully grown woman, I'm sure she will cope. Now Mrs Stone, get your fine ass in the truck, or we will hit traffic." Blake says. Smacking Lily's arse he walks past to load the last of the luggage. Lily just grins.

"Listen to your husband, bugger off and have a fantastic honeymoon!" I pull her in for a tight hug and then push her towards the door.

"Okay, okay! I'm going! Love you, love you

Caden!" Lily shouts, Caden engrossed in playing on the games console just grunts. I wave them off and close the door.

"Hey bud, what do you say to going out for some lunch? Maybe we could go see the sights and have a look around the town?" I ask Caden.

"Sure Mum, just let me beat the boss and then I'm good." He says, his eyes never moving from the tv screen.

I roll my eyes and head to the kitchen. I sit down with a bottle of water and flick through a magazine. I sigh, the silence is deafening. I've never told Lily this but her moving over here was hard on me. Living with her filled the void, it stopped me from being on my own.

When she left, it was just Caden and me. When he was at his dad's or in bed it was just me. I'd try and fill the time by going out or going over to my parents house, but that wasn't always possible. Lost in my thoughts Caden comes barrelling in.

"Hey Mum, let's go. I kicked that bosses ass like a champ!" he beams.

Quick to hide my sadness I plaster on a smile.

"That's cool buddy, but stop saying ass." I say while grabbing the house keys and my purse.

We jump in the truck and it takes me a while

to adjust the seat and learn where everything is.

We make it to town and pull-up outside Jeanie's diner. Both Lily and Daisy have said how nice this place is, so I figured it's probably the best place to start.

As we're about to enter Jeanie's there's a loud rumble of motorcycles approaching. I try to ignore it and head inside the diner, but Caden is instantly excited to see if it's Rip and the guys.

"Hey Mum! Look! It's Rip and the rest of the Satan's." Caden shouts excitedly.

I tense as I hear the bikes pull up behind us. I ignore the way my skin breaks out in goose bumps and my heart rate picks up just because I know Rip is watching me. I turn, smiling down at Caden, and scruff the hair on top of his head. I wave at the guys, avoiding looking in Rip's direction.

Khan, Rubble, Big Papa and Wheels or Max as I was introduced to him, pull up alongside Rip. Max has a trike, and it's beautiful. He reaches round the back and grabs his wheelchair. With practiced ease he has it open to the side of him and pulls himself into it. He flashes a smile and a wink. This time my smile is genuine.

"Hey Caden, my brother! You getting some lunch with your ma?" Khan asks, walking toward Caden and giving him a fist bump.

"Yeah, you guys want to join us? That's cool,

right mum?" Caden asks. I smile and nod. Caden cheers and runs inside with Khan and the others following.

"Sweetheart, you got a minute?" I pause my body tenses. I push my shoulders back and cross my arms over my chest. I watch as Rip walks towards me, stopping just a foot away. God he looks good. He's in a pair of worn jeans, a black t-shirt that stretched across his broad chest, with his Satan's Cut over the top. He reaches up and sighs, running his hand through his messy black hair. He takes off his sunglasses and pierces me with his ice blue eyes. My face is void of any emotion, I don't want him to see the effect he has on me.

"Look, sweetheart, I know things went down the other night and I'm sorry about that. I didn't mean to hurt you. It just...shit...I ain't good at this. What I'm trying to say is that Candy was nothing, just a one night thing." Rip states and shrugs.

I can't help but smile and shake my head.

"Well that's okay then. Christ. Here's the thing Rip, I got caught up in the moment with you. Twice actually. But that's all it was: a moment. it was never more...and it will never happen again. I have my son to think about, I am not a 'candy' type of girl, and I won't be treated like one. So your conscience is clear, I won't hold a grudge against you. You're free to go get as much

'Candy' as you like." I say with a smile and spin round and head into the diner, leaving Rip stood on the sidewalk. I take a seat next to the guys and smile, grabbing a menu.

"Where is Pres' going?" Khan asks, watching Rip back out of the spot and ride off.

"Maybe he went to get himself some candy." I murmur, looking at the menu. When I look up Max is watching me like he knows exactly what I'm talking about.

"Hey y'all. Hey you, you must be Rose! Welcome to our town honey, what can I get for you today?" Jeanie greets me, waiting to take our order,

"Hi, that's me! It's nice to meet you. I will have the cheeseburger and fries with a chocolate milkshake please, Lily says they're to die for." I smile. Jeanie smiles warmly at me. She crouches down next to Caden.

"And what will it be for you young man?" Caden holds the menu up in one hand while holding his chin with the other as if he is pondering his choice.

"I would like a cheeseburger with fries and a chocolate milkshake. Thank you Miss." Caden hands her the menu. Jeanie takes it from him, holding back a laugh.

"I'm guessing you boys are having your usuals?" Jeanie asks. All of the guys nod in agreement.

"Okay, I'll be back in a jiffy with y'all drinks." Jeanie turns and leaves.

"So what are you guys up to today?" I ask. They all exchange a look, but it's Max that speaks up.

"Just over seeing some business darlin', gotta make sure all runs smoothly. What about you two, anything fun?" Max asks.

"Mum said we're going to have a look around the town for a while, then we'll probably go home where Mum will open a bottle of wine because its five o'clock somewhere. We'll probably eat sweets and watch a movie with a guy in it, Mum will say she wouldn't mind having a bit of him. And after all that she will put me to bed and sit alone for the rest of the night." Caden lists off without coming up for air. I feel my face turn red and I face plant the table in embarrassment.

"God Caden, way to make me sound like a lonely alcoholic mother. Geez." I sigh, wishing the ground would swallow me up.

The guys all laugh.

"Dude, word of advice, don't talk about things that make women look bad, they don't like it. Believe me brother, you don't want that ball ache." Khan says. Caden nods like he understands and agrees completely.

"Are all women a ball ache?" Caden asks honestly. The table erupts in laughter. I can't hold back my own laughter.

The chair opposite me is pulled out, I turn my head and Rip sits down, his eyes on me. Those damn eyes are my kryptonite.

My smile falls off of my face.

"What you doing here? I thought you left?" I ask.

"There was something I really wanted here, so I came back." He replies, his eyes never leaving mine. I swallow, my mouth going dry.

"Yay! Rip, you came back! I'm having the cheeseburger, what are you having?" Caden shouts excitedly.

Rip smiles his panty-melting smile. Oh bollocks! Maybe his smile is my kryptonite.

"I'm having the same as you buddy! It's the food of champions. Only the really cool guys get the cheeseburgers." Rip answers.

"I'm totally cool man!" Caden answers, trying to be a cool guy. I smile at my boy and lean over and kiss his head.

"Mum! No kisses! I'm a cool guy, and cool guys don't get kissed." Caden grumbles.

"Actually little dude, if your mum's handing out kisses, I'm a cool guy. I'd take your mums kisses any day." Khan says wiggling his eyebrows at me. I laugh and lean over, giving him a kiss on the cheek.

"There cool guy, just for you." I chuckle. Rip almost lets out a low growl and pins Khan with a look that has Khan smiling and holding up his hands in surrender.

Jeanie arrives at our table with a tray full of drinks. It breaks the tense situation between Rip and Khan.

"Right, here we go! Rip, I guessed you'd come back so here's your soda. I'll be back with all your food soon." Jeanie says with a smile and walks off.

"So Rose, how long are you planning on staying?" Max asks. I feel Rip watching me, waiting for my answer.

"Well I'm only supposed be over here for a few weeks, and then head back, but I lost my job recently and its Caden's school holidays. So we have time to stay a little longer. I'll see what happens I guess, it's nice to just get away from London." I answer honestly.

"Sorry to hear about your job darlin', but it means you have a few extra weeks to kick back and relax." Max says with a wink.

I smile and take a sip of my milkshake. I can't help the moan that escapes my lips.

"Oh! Now that is a bloody good milkshake." I

say drinking more.

Jeanie arrives a little while later with our food, and it tastes amazing. Probably the best burger I've ever had.

"Good to see you're enjoying it sweetheart." Rips smirks. I pause from eating and look up at him.

"Huh?" I ask with a mouthful of food. Rip reaches out and runs his thumb across my lower lip. I watch as he places his sauce covered thumb in his mouth.

"You missed a bit." He says smirking. I stare, completely stunned, not moving or doing anything, just sat holding my burger in front of my mouth.

"Rose, breathe." Rip says softly. I shake my head and look away. The table has gone silent. I look up and they are all watching us and smiling. Even Caden is smiling.

I feel myself blush. I quickly look away and continue eating my burger. After we've all finished, I order Caden a hot fudge sundae. I take a picture of him on my phone and laugh at the state of him. He has chocolate sauce everywhere!

Jeanie places the bill on the table, and I grab my purse. Before I can put any money down Rip takes the bill.

"Put your damn purse away." Rip orders. I frown.

"I am quite capable of paying for mine and my son's food."

"I never disputed that, put your purse away." Rip argues back.

"No, I'm paying our share." I bite back.

"Woman, stop arguing back with me. I'm fucking paying, end of story." Rip growls.

I'm about to argue back, when Max places a hand on my arm.

"Darlin', I taught my boy to treat women right and to always be a gentleman. I know he doesn't always act like a gentleman, so make the most of it and let him pay." Max says with a wink. I smile and nod.

"Fine. Thank you Rip." I grumble. Rip just grunts in reply.

"Come on Caden, let's head back home to chill out for a while and leave these guys to do what they've got to do." I stand and Caden reluctantly follows.

"Say bye to the guys." I tell him.

"Bye, see you later." Caden says, moping.

The guys all say bye and give him a cool guy chin lift.

In the truck on the way back, my mind is

consumed with Rip. I need to lock that down. I mentally build my wall. I won't let anyone in, especially not a guy like Rip.

CHAPTER TWO

The next day I'm sitting on the back deck enjoying my morning coffee in my over-sized night shirt. It has a big picture of Jareth the Goblin King on it.

"Hell, I don't think I've ever found anyone sexy in a David Bowie t-shirt until this very moment." Wes whistles, sitting next to me in a pair of fitted jeans and a white t-shirt that stretches across his broad chest.

"Good morning to you too Wes." I say smiling.

"Damn! Shut down by a beautiful woman, that's my day ruined." He says with mock despair.

"Sorry, Wes I'm not on the look out for any man, don't take it personally. Besides, I already have a man in my life, and he's got my un-divided attention." I say, looking at Caden who is currently running through the sprinklers. It's 7:30am, how he can do that this early in the morning is beyond me.

"Not what I've heard. Something about a certain cousin of mine." Wes nudges me, wig-gling his eyebrows.

I roll my eyes in response and drink my coffee.

"Look, nothing is going on. It was a drunken kiss, that's all. I'm not interested. So you can for-get that rumour."

"Whatever you say darlin'. Listen, I'm off to work at the Den tonight, I won't be back until late, you guys alright on your own?" Wes asks.

"Of course, I thought I'd take Caden to the park and apparently there's a lake not too far from here, right? I might take a picnic down with us and go there."

"Okay, well I've got a few errands to run, so I won't catch you guys until tomorrow. If you get bored come for a drink in the Den." Wes stands, kisses my head and shouts bye to Caden.

I sigh, why do all the guys have to be so good looking here. More to the point, why am I attracted to the one that's the biggest player?!

Caden has a blast at the park, his energy

levels don't seem to die down. So after the park we head off to find the lake. After a few wrong turns we eventually find it. It's fairly busy with families, lots of kids are splashing and playing in the lake. I smile looking at the place. It's stunning and the perfect place for Caden to play with the other kids while I read.

We sit down and eat the small picnic I made. Caden is eating almost without chewing, he is so desperate to get in the water and play.

"Right, remember, do not go in passed your knees. Do not wander off and remember where I am sat. Be nice to the other kids. Make friends and, most importantly, please don't embarrass me." I warn him and he just smiles and runs off.

"I will be good!" he shouts over his shoulder.

I watch as Caden dives in head-first, scaring the crap out of me. I am ready to run if he doesn't surface. The little sod comes up and stands, turns, smiles and gives me the thumbs up. That will be another grey hair to add to the rest. As if he hasn't bloody well given me enough over the years!

I pick up my kindle satisfied, he isn't about to drown trying to do dangerous stunts.

I get quite engrossed in my book when a shadow casts over me. I squint my eyes and look up to see a guy smiling at me.

"Can I help you?" I ask.

"Sorry, I didn't want to interrupt you, it looked like your book was getting interesting." He says pointing to my kindle.

"Um, yeah it was." I say, still not sure what he wants.

"Sorry, I'm Owen. I'm here with my son, Zack. It appears your son and mine have made friends." He says pointing to the two boys, they're laughing and splashing around in the lake. I smile.

"Hi Owen, I'm Rose, and my son is called Caden." I put my hand out in greeting. He shakes my hand softly. It's funny what your parents teach you. My dad always said you can tell a lot by a handshake, if it's too soft and limp it can mean they are nice, but maybe a bit boring and a pushover. I know it's just one of my dad's quirks but it's something that has stuck with me ever since.

"Listen, I'm sat just over there by myself, and I have a cooler with a couple of beers in if you want to come and join me while the boys are playing." Owen asks nervously, I guess Dad's handshake theory was sort of right. Not really wanting to sit with him, but also not wanting to be rude, I agree. He helps me grab my things and I follow him over.

"I'll just tell Caden where I am." I say as I walk off to the lake.

"Caden! Come here a sec buddy." I call. He wades over soaking wet with the biggest grin on his face.

"Hey Mum, we're not going yet are we?" he asks.

"No bud, I'm just telling you I've moved. I'm now sat with your new friend Zack's dad, just over there. Okay?" I turn and point.

"Okay! Cool! We're playing water monster serpents, the idea is to try and swim unnoticed and touch people's ankles. It's so funny mum, I made that big guy over there scream like a girl and he ran out of the water." Caden says bent over laughing. I can't help but giggle.

"Caden maybe you should play a different game, you could upset a lot of people." I say hoping he will actually listen and take my advice.

"Okay, gotta go!" He ignores me and heads off. I sigh and just pray that he stops and doesn't embarrass me.

I take a seat next to Owen and he hands me a beer.

"Thanks."

"So Rose, it's obvious you're not from round here. What brings you to Mufftown? I mean it's not like it's a big tourist hot spot." Owen asks taking a pull of his beer.

"Oh, my sister lives here. Well, actually,

both my sisters do now. It was my sister Lily's wedding a couple of days ago. I'm just staying here for a few weeks." I say with a shrug.

"I see, was that Blake Stone's wedding?" Owen asks. I look to him puzzled, how he could know that? Frowning I nod.

"Don't panic, it's a small town. Everyone knows Blake Stone and that he married an English girl." He smiles.

"Ah, I guess I will have to get used to the small town thing while I'm here. It's certainly not like this back in London. So, what is it you do?" I ask.

"I'm a physiotherapist. I work in the rehabilitation centre at the hospital a few towns over. What about you?"

"I'm a nurse, currently on the look out for a new job though. Had a bit of a shitty time back at the old job." I answer honestly.

"That's a darn shame. So, how are you finding Mufftown so far?"

"Quiet, peaceful and friendly." I smile.

We sit and chat back and forth. It's nice, easy. Owen seems to be a nice guy. He's not ugly. He's attractive with mousey brown hair, brown eyes, and a clean shaven face. He's also neatly dressed.

We spend about another hour or so sitting here while the boys play just chatting.

It's time to pack up and go home, and as I'm loading the bits into the truck, Owen walks over.

"Listen, I had a great time this afternoon, and well, I was wondering if you fancied meeting up again, with or without the boys?" Owen asks, clearly nervous, his hands in his pockets.

I smile.

"Sure, write down your number and I'll give you a call."

Owen writes his number down and hands it to me.

"I really hope you call Rose." He leans in and kisses my cheek then turns and walks back to his truck. I jump in the truck and put his number in my purse.

"Is he your boyfriend now mum?" Caden asks from the backseat.

"No, why on earth would you think that?" I ask, laughing.

"Because he kissed you, but then I've noticed a lot of the guys have kissed you." Caden adds.

I freeze, hoping he didn't witness me and Rip.

"Like who, bud?" I ask, as nonchalantly as possible.

"Wes, Khan, and now Zack's dad." I sigh, relieved he hasn't mentioned Rip.

"Oh honey, they are just being friendly. Come on, let's go home and order pizza!" I say. Caden cheers. I laugh and shake my head, that kid has always been easy to distract with food.

I pull up to the house and notice a couple of bikes parked up alongside Wes' truck. I frown in confusion, I thought he said he would be working all night. I turn to tell Caden and see he's passed out, asleep in the back. I groan, he's such a heavy lump to carry, especially when he's asleep and a dead weight. I jump down from the truck and manage to get Caden in my arms. I waddle to the steps, cursing.

"God sake kid, how can a skinny little boy like you weigh fifty bloody tonnes when you're asleep? God I need to pee so bad." I huff to myself.

Someone coughs, I look up to see Rip smirking, staring down at me. He walks towards me, takes Caden from my arms and carries him with ease up the steps into the house. Reminded I need to pee, I run up and straight to the bathroom. After I've taken care of business I head into mine and Caden's room. I watch as Rip tucks him in. I ignore the warm fuzzy feeling in my heart.

Rip turns and stalks towards me, he never just walks towards me, it always comes across as predatory. I stand my ground and cross my arms over my chest. He stops just in front of me,

I tilt my head up, keeping my emotions hidden. He reaches forward and tucks a strand of hair behind my ear.

"You've caught the sun, sweetheart." He says softly.

"We took a picnic down to the lake, thanks for carrying him up." I reply.

He doesn't say anything, he just stares at me for a moment. His gaze becomes too intense. I look away. I step back, needing to put distance between us. I clear my throat.

"I'm going to get the rest of the stuff in." I mumble and then walk away as fast as I can without running. I take a deep breath when I reach the bottom of the stairs. I hate that he seems to have this power over me, it's his eyes, his smile, his stunning face, and his body. Even his damn smell has an effect on me. I shake my head, giving myself a mental slap, I turn and look back up the stairs. Standing at the top is Rip, he's watching me. I move quickly out of the front door to the truck and grab the bags and cooler. I lug it up the stairs and into the kitchen.

I see the guys out the back deck huddled over something. Figuring I should go say hello I walk out to see them.

"Hey guys, good to see you." I say before turning to Wes. "What you doing home Wes? I thought you'd be working all night?" I ask. They all jump slightly at my presence, apart from Rip. Khan makes quick work folding the papers up.

"Hey darlin', I'm just on break for a few hours. Gonna head back out there in an hour or so. You go to the lake?" he diverts.

I nod.

"Yeah, Caden made a friend and crashed right out." I say with a smile.

"I promised Caden pizza, so I'm just going to go shower, then order some in. Let me know if you guys want anything."

I turn to head inside, when I overhear the guys.

"That was close brother, we don't want the women knowing about any of this until we got it locked down. Clear?" Rip orders. The others reply with grunts.

"So you got it bad, huh? And she ain't making it easy for you either." I hear Wes chuckle.

"Fuck you man, you don't know what you're talking about." Rip answers.

"Whatever you say, but I ain't fucking blind and neither is anyone else. Remember, she ain't no cheap pussy, you're actually gonna have to work at this one." Wes warns.

"Alright fuckin' Dr Phil, enough of the advice. I've never had any problems getting women before." Rip boasts.

"That's where you're making your damn mistake, Rose isn't just any woman." Wes finishes. Hearing them all move and start to get up, I quickly run upstairs. I grab my things and jump in the shower.

I get out and change into a pair of ripped jean shorts and a white tank top. I leave my hair wet and head downstairs. I can hear Caden's voice chatting away.

"So then we played monster serpents and freaked all these people out by touching their ankles." Caden roars with laughter, clearly still finding that game hilarious. All the guys are sat round listening to him and laughing with him.

"It was so much fun, Zack's dad gave mum his number so I can see Zack again. He kissed mum too, it was gross." Caden makes a gagging sound. All the guys heads turn and look my way.

"So darlin', seems it wasn't just Caden that got some fun at the beach." Wes says wiggling his eyebrows.

"Bugger off. He was just being friendly, nothing more. Now I'm going to order pizza, am I ordering for you gossip girls too?" I ask sarcastically.

"Yeah, meat pizzas, no veg." Khan orders.

I go to the kitchen and hunt for the menu in the draw. Lily showed me where all of the menus were kept.

I pull it out and grab the phone and start dialling.

"He kissed you." I lift my head and see Rip stood in the doorway, arms crossed over his chest, looking pissed.

"Err, yeah." I answer confused.

"You kiss him back?" Rip asks.

I shake my head.

"Not that it's any of your business, but no I didn't. Like I said, it was just a friendly kiss." I snap back.

Rip moves toward me and grunts. I turn my back on him and continue to place the pizza order. The guy asks for my card number, I reach for my purse and open it. I grab my card and chuck my purse on the side whilst reading my details to him. It takes all my concentration to do this while I can feel Rip is close. I hang up once that's done. Turning I see Rip holding a piece of paper in his hand, he looks pissed. It takes me a moment to realise what it is he's holding. I then immediately get pissed.

"Did you just get that from my purse?" I ask angrily.

"Owen, just being friendly, happened to give you his number too?! He's just a real friendly guy, ain't he sweetheart?" Rip growls back at me.

"It's none of your damn business! Give it back to me." I bite back.

"You know he just wants to get in your fucking panties, sweetheart. He ain't being friendly, he wants to fuck you." He seethes.

Now I am beyond pissed off.

"So what?! Maybe, just maybe, I want to fuck him! Maybe I want him in my panties Rip. Did that ever occur to you? Did it ever occur to you that maybe I'd want someone else to fuck me and that I just don't want you!" I shout.

I watch as Rip snaps, he moves quickly, pinning me with his body against the kitchen counter. I can feel every hard inch of him, I gasp.

"You keep telling yourself that sweetheart, but you see, your body betrays you."

He runs his hand along my neck, over my erratic heart rate, moving slowly down to the swell of my breasts. My nipples harden at his touch. Rip just smirks.

"You see sweetheart, you want me just as much as I want you. You can keep denying yourself this fact but believe me, you're mine. Your body knows it, you just need to stop being scared and hiding behind those walls you've built up." Rips states, my heart feels like it's about to leap from my chest. He leans in, his lips grazing my neck. I shudder at the light contact.

"I'm a patient man, sweetheart. When you're ready, I am taking what's mine." Rip whispers and nips my ear.

He steps back, his eyes never leaving mine. He smirks and walks back out of the kitchen, screwing up the bit of paper with Owen's number on and chucking it in the trash as he walks past.

I just stand there, wide eyed and stunned. More to the point, I let him do that, if that was anyone else I would have completely chewed them out. Apparently when it comes to Rip not only does my body lose all control, but my mind does too. I mentally add another brick to my wall.

CHAPTER THREE

After last night's events I try and keep myself busy, and out of the way of Rip. I head over to visit Daisy and see how she's getting on with her plans to build a centre for domestic abuse victims and their families.

I pull up and Caden jumps out and runs to the house.

"Hey tough guy!" He yells. Carter smiles down at Caden.

"Hey dude, listen, I've got to work right now so I will have to catch up with you another time." Carter informs Caden, his little face drops. Carter sighs. I try and give him a look to say don't fall for it, Caden is playing you, but unfortunately for Carter, he doesn't look my way.

"How about, if your mom says it's okay, you come to work with me for the afternoon?" Carter asks. Caden's head whips round to me, his eyes alight with excitement. I sigh and nod.

"Woohoo! I get to build stuff for the day! Do you have power tools? Can I play with the power tools?" Caden asks, bouncing with excitement. Before Carter can answer I interrupt.

"No power tools, for the love of god. No! Remember what happened to Grandad's shed when he let you use the drill?" I remind him.

"Why? What happened?" Carter asks, Caden looks away sheepishly.

"Someone here didn't listen to instructions and thought he would help by cello taping the power button on the drill down." I say, giving Caden the eye.

"It was to help Grandad, so he didn't have to keep pushing and holding it on while trying to drill holes." Caden defends.

"Yes, but you were only building a cabinet, and Grandad was supposed to drill the holes, not you. By the time you were finished with it, the only thing it was good for was being a giant bloody colander it had that many holes in it!" I remind him.

"Well Grandad shouldn't have left me alone with the tools. I'm just a child." Caden mutters under his breath.

"Caden." I warn.

"You sure you still want him to come with you." I ask Carter. He smiles and laughs.

"Sure, just make sure you do as I say bud, can't have you cutting an arm off." Carter adds.

Caden runs off to Carter's truck and hops in, both of them give me a wave as I head into the house. I call out for Daisy, she shouts that she's out the back. When I reach her, she has the plans all laid out across the table.

"Hey, what's all this?" I ask, taking a seat.

"Oh it's from the architect. There are two different plans for the centre, and I'm supposed to pick which one I like the best. But they're both great. I just can't decide." She huffs. I take a quick look and pull one out and hold it up to her.

"Here, this is the one." I say.

"How can you decide that so quickly?" She asks.

"Easily, this one has big open windows, it will be brighter, more inviting." I say on a shrug.

"Damn it! You're absolutely right. Well, that's that sorted. Where's Caden?" she asks, looking around.

"Your future husband has taken him to work this afternoon." I state. Daisy raises her eyebrow in question.

"I know, I warned him. Don't blame me if he comes back traumatised."

Daisy just giggles. She suggests making some lunch and having a cheeky glass or two of wine, of course I happily oblige. After a delicious lunch and a fair amount of wine we're sprawled out on the sun loungers in the back garden.

"Rose, there's something I want to ask you. I want you to really think about it and consider it." I look at her and nod for her to continue.

"When the centre is open. I'd like to offer you a job as a full time nurse there. What do you say?" Daisy asks, nibbling her bottom lip, something she's always done when she's been nervous.

"Hell yes! I'd love too!" I cry out, smiling. Daisy claps her hands in excitement and pulls me into a hug.

"There's only one draw back. The job probably won't be available for another six months, maybe more. The building hasn't even been built yet. I know that means you having to wait but I figured it would give you enough time to maybe do temp work when you go back to London. You could sell up some of what you don't need and then come on over. I know Lily and I would both love to have you close to us." Daisy beams.

"Sounds perfect. Gives me time to inform dick too." I say.

"Oh, yeah. Do you think he will let Caden leave London?" Daisy asks.

"Don't think he has much choice, do you? As soon as I tell Caden about moving here he will be packing up his stuff straight away. A fresh start over here will be exactly what Caden and I need."

I smile, actually looking forward to it. I will have to sell the flat and look for a place over here but that shouldn't be a problem. I can put it on the market as soon as I get back. The only thing that has my stomach twisting is the thought of being permanently closer to Rip. Maybe I can buy somewhere and try and keep it from him. At least I can avoid him that way.

Me and Daisy drink more wine, as she's decided that I can get a lift home from someone or spend the night at their's. Sat giggling we don't hear Carter and Caden return.

"MUM! It was soooo cool, Carter let me hammer in nails and saw some wood. I got a big splinter too, look!" Caden shouts, shoving his splinter in my face.

"Glad you had a good time, and no injuries or hospital visits, so a good day overall!" I say smiling. Carter lifts his hand, it's covered with a bandage.

"What on earth happened? How did you get that?" I ask, dread creeping in.

"Don't worry, he just slipped with the saw and, well, the hammer too." Carter says holding up his bandaged thumb on his other hand. I groan.

"I am so sorry Carter." I apologise.

Carter just shakes it off.

We all sit down to dinner later on and Carter suggests Daisy and I continue to have drinks down at the den. He says he will look after Caden.

"Wait a cocking minute, not only have you looked after my hellion of a son all afternoon, you're now offering to sit with him tonight too so I can go out?!" I ask, dumbfounded.

Daisy and Carter both laugh.

"Hey Mum, you said I'm a lovely boy. Why wouldn't Carter want to spend more time with me?" Caden asks, feigning hurt.

"No offence sweetie, but you are a little excitable sometimes." I say pinching his cheeks.

"I'd say I'm awesome, not excitable. My teacher at school says I have over enthusiasm, I do all task with the enthusiasm of ten people." Caden boast proudly. Carter and Daisy just smile.

"What do you say Daisy? Are you up for continuing the night out?" I ask. Daisy just smiles and clinks her glass with mine. We head indoors to freshen up she sends a group text to Evelynn,

Suellen, Louisa, Trudy and Raven.

"Right, you can borrow this dress, I'm wearing the halter neck one. Oh and Raven can't make it because she's working, but Trudy said she will swing by, pick up Caden, take him back to Lily's for you and babysit him there. That way Carter can drive us and be our personal taxi." Daisy grins.

I'm overwhelmed at people's kindness here, you wouldn't get this back in London. Some of my family would, but not people I've only known a short while. It's not like Trudy is just anyone, she's Blake's family, so I know I can relax and trust her. Plus she did have to raise three boys, so I know she can definitely handle Caden.

I pick up the wine coloured wrap dress that Daisy has picked out for me and hold it up. It wraps completely from the bust down and ties at the side. I shrug and put it on, it's a bit tight around the bust area as I'm a little bigger in that department than Daisy. It hugs my curves, if it wasn't for the wine I have already drank, I would be feeling a lot more self-conscious. I haven't worn a dress like this in a hell of a long time. The only clothes I wear are either my work uniform or what ever is comfy and clean. I don't go out back home, because I just don't have the time. I'm either working or I have Caden. I pinch some of Daisy's make-up, just keeping it light. I don't normally do make-up either. I keep on my wedge sandals on as they match well.

I turn and look at Daisy, looking beautiful in her pale blue halter neck dress. It clings to her waist then loosely flows to mid-thigh.

"Let's go!" Daisy says with a grin. We head downstairs and Carter spots Daisy, his eyes admiring every single inch of her. As soon as she reaches the bottom step he pulls her into his arms and kisses her passionately.

"I'm thinking I'm going to have to hang around the bar tonight babe, make sure no one tries to make a play for what is mine. Fuck, you're beautiful." Carter growls.

"Enough, stop being all alpha. Is Trudy here yet?" Daisy asks.

"She'll be here in two minutes."

I turn to find Caden and make sure he's okay with being with Trudy.

"You sure you're going to be okay?" I ask.

"Sure Mum, she said we will watch some movies and she will make me cookies and ice cream. You look pretty." Caden says smiling. With that sweet comment I grab him and give him a great big kiss. Of course Caden pushes me away, with his face screwed up in disgust.

A few minutes later Trudy arrives.

"Well don't you girls look beautiful. Now Caden, I've got cookie dough and ice cream and I promise you can pick the movie, is that a deal?" she asks.

"Hell yeah!" Caden yells, running straight to the front door.

"Bye Mum, love you, have a good night!" he carries on shouting over his shoulder, running to Trudy's car.

"Um, are you sure about this? He can be pretty full on." I ask.

"Of course! Go have fun, from what your mom said, you don't get out much back in London so this will do you good. We will both be just fine." Trudy says. Suddenly the car horn starts beeping.

"Come on Trudy, the ice cream will melt!" Caden shouts from her truck. I cover my face in horror. Thankfully Trudy just laughs it off.

"That's my cue to go. Have fun." She waves over her shoulder and heads out. Daisy and Carter both laugh.

"Come on. Let's get you a stiff drink." Daisy says pulling me out of the door.

We arrive at the Den and see that Wes is working. He gives us drinks on the house for most of the night. Evelynn and Suellen join us halfway through the evening and poor Louisa can't make it as Eliza is running a slight fever.

"So I said to him, honey if you touch my ass one more time I'll whip you like a redheaded stepchild." Suellen says, pausing to take a sip of her drink.

"And then do you know what he did, he bent over and said whip me mama. I proceeded to kick him hard right in the ass, he stumbled and fell forward. Honestly, he is so dumb, he couldn't pour piss out of a boot with a hole in the toe and directions in the heel!" Suellen hollers, laughing.

I'm crying with laughter. "I have absolutely no fucking clue what you're on about, but you make me laugh, so it's all good." I say downing the rest of my drink.

I stand up and head to the bar to get another round in. I can't wipe the smile off my face, this is just what I needed. I haven't laughed this much in a really long time.

As I'm waiting my turn I hear my name being called. I turn and see that Owen is walking towards me smiling.

"Oh hey Owen!" I say, feeling a little tipsy.

"My god. You looked beautiful down at the lake, but right now you're beyond stunning." Owen says as he leans in, kissing my cheek.

"Oh now, stop it." I flirtily slap at his chest.

"I was hoping I'd see you, when you didn't

call I thought that was it, that you weren't interested." Owen says shyly.

"Oh I would have called, but I err...lost your number. Plus I know Caden definitely wants to see Zack again." I say smiling, as Owen is about to answer the bartender comes to take my order. Owen offers to pay but I tell him that's not necessary, as we've been getting them free.

"Ah of course. The Stone brothers are your family now. So, anyway, I have something that might interest you, a temporary nurses position is about to come up. It's covering someone's maternity leave, and I know you're in between jobs. So would you be interested?" He asks.

"Oh fuck yeah!" I squeal and jump up, hugging him. He wraps his arms around me, and I swear I feel him sniff my hair, but I ignore it, not wanting to go there. I step back and calm myself.

"I mean, yes, thank you." I say, a little embarrassed by my outburst.

"Are you free on Wednesday morning, say, ten?" He asks. I nod eagerly.

"Great! I will meet you at the hospital entrance and take you to meet my aunt, she's on the hiring committee. You guys can have a chat and hopefully you'll have a job after." Owen says smiling. He really is just a nice guy. I lean up on my tip toes and kiss his cheek.

"Thank you." I say smiling.

"You're welcome, so, can I take you out for lunch afterwards?" He asks.

"No you fuckin' can't asshole!" is boomed from behind Owen. I jump and Owen spins on his feet to see who said it. A very familiar pair of ice blue eyes are staring angrily at me.

"Errrr...I'm sorry...I wasn't aware you we're in a relationship with Rip." Owen says.

"I'm not!" I growl back.

"You're mine." Rip seethes back and I mock laugh.

"Oh you're funny! I don't remember agreeing to any of that." I turn to Owen

"Ignore him, we're nothing. He is just delusional. I would love to go to lunch after the interview. I will see you Wednesday, thank you Owen. I lean up purposefully pushing my breast into Owen and kiss him again on the cheek. I turn and grab the tray of drinks and walk back to the girls, making sure my hips have a little bit of extra sway in them. I tell myself it's for Owen but deep down I know it's for Rip's benefit. I flick Rip the bird over my shoulder as I reach the table. The girls all burst out laughing, of course they've watched the whole showdown.

"You need to sit your ass down and tell us what the hell that was all about." Evelynn demands.

I roll my eyes and bring them up to speed with what's happened. When I'm finished Evelynn and Suellen both sit back and smirk.

"Well you sure are in trouble honey, because both guys haven't taken their eyes off you." Suellen states. I try to subtly look, I see Owen looking at me, he gives me a small smile when his eyes connect with mine. I smile back. I look the other way and my eyes collide with Rip. His gaze is so intense my breath gets caught in my throat.

"Holy fuck." I mumble.

"Holy fuck is right, but can I just say for our sake, please just go for one ride with biker boy over there, because damn he's one fine looking man! Let's face it, we all want to know if he knows how to use his throttle." Evelynn states. I snort back my laughter.

"Well you'll have to wait for someone else to tell you I'm afraid, this girl will not be revving his throttle any time soon." I say, taking a large swig of my drink. They all throw their heads back laughing, not believing a word.

We start on the shots and poor Daisy just can't handle anymore, she fell asleep in her chair about five minutes ago.

"Okay, my go! Donald Trump, Pee Wee Herman, Putin? Fuck, marry, blow job? You have to choose." I slur laughing. Both Suellen and Evelynn make gagging sounds.

"Fine. I will go first. I would blow Pee Wee Herman, fuck Donald trump and marry Putin." Evelynn gags.

"You'd fuck Trump?!" Suellen asks in disgust.

"Well yeah, but it would have to be with him behind me, so I didn't have to look at him. Why?! What the hell would you do?" she asks.

"I'd blow Pee Wee, I'd fuck Putin and I'd marry Trump." Suellen states.

"Ewww how could you marry Trump? I mean sure, Putin isn't great either but at least I don't gag when I'm looking at him." I say with a shudder.

"Because, my dear ladies, what you are forgetting is just because we are married doesn't mean I have to sleep with it." Suellen states.

"Well damn it! You're right! Evelynn hoots.

I stand and wobble on my feet a little.

"Ladies, excuse me. I have to pee!" I bow, they all laugh at me. Daisy suddenly wakes and stands.

"Hold up, I'm coming too." She links her arm through mine as she supports me and I support her to the toilets.

After taking care of business I wash my hands. Daisy is stood next to me laughing at my drunken state as I play with the fancy taps that have a sensor on them.

"And Rose said let there be water! And boom! There's water." I cackle to myself like an amused child.

"And now ladies and gentlemen, for my next trick…" I pause, as Daisy nudges me.

"What?" I ask and she nods her head towards the door. I turn and see Rip standing there, arms crossed over his broad chest, his tattooed muscled forearms tensed. God damn it! He even has beautiful forearms. The bastard.

Rip's lips twitch and Daisy giggles. I turn and whisper to her.

"Did I just say that out loud?" Daisy nods smiling.

"Daisy, give us a minute." Rip orders. She just nods and leaves.

"Traitor! You are no sister of mine!" I yell after her.

Rip moves towards me and pins me against the sinks.

"Can you read?" I ask.

"Yeah." Rip replies frowning.

"Well obviously not very fucking well. This is the ladies. Unless your dick has dropped off and you now have a vagina you're in the wrong room bucko." I say. Rip throws his head back laughing. God damn it! He even laughs sexy. I can practically feel my panties melt away.

Rip stops laughing and leans in close, his face millimetres from mine.

"You said that out loud sweetheart. Also, I'm liking you drunk, it's like a truth serum for you." He whispers low across my lips. I hitch in a breath.

"Why are you in here?" I ask. Trying my hardest not to react to his presence.

"To speak to you." Rip answers.

"I have nothing to say to you." I answer, all breathy as Rip slowly grazes his mouth across mine.

"Oh sweetheart. I think we do, you seem to keep forgetting you're mine. I keep having to re-mind you, you will not be meeting up with that jackass Owen." He growls. I lean back, slightly pissed off.

"For fuck's sake Rip! I am not yours! You don't bloody own me, I am not a possession. We are not together. I can talk, kiss or fuck who ever I damn well please!" I yell angrily.

Rip doesn't say anything, instead he crashes his mouth on mine. I gasp and try to feebly push at his chest. My body caves within seconds and instead of pushing at his chest I'm clawing at his shirt. Rip's hands cup my behind and he lifts me so I'm seated on the sinks and he's positioned between my legs. I moan into his mouth when he presses himself against me. Our hands are frantic, my body can't get enough of him.

My hands move to his belt and his jeans and I start to undo them. I pull them down slightly freeing his impressive, thick, hard length. I take him in my hand.

Rip lets out a low moan in his throat. He moves his hand up my thighs and wraps my legs around his waist. I grip the side and circle my hips up and down his hard length. Rip growls, moves my knickers aside and positions himself at my entrance. He pauses, looking at me, almost asking if I'm sure. I don't answer. I slide myself down his length, both of us letting out a low moan at the feel of us together. Rip grabs hold of my hips and starts to move. I moan and dig my heels into him. He growls, kissing and nipping at my throat. "Fuck. You feel incredible."

"Oh God, more, please." I beg.

Rip smiles "Hold tight sweetheart."

I grip his shoulders and his hands tighten on my hips as he fucks me hard. My orgasm takes me by surprise, hitting me with powerful waves of pleasure. I cry out, calling his name. Rip throws his head back letting out a low throaty growl as he reaches his climax.

We are both panting, Rip slowly pulls out

of me and carefully unwraps my legs from his waist. He pulls up his jeans and does them up.

Realisation hits me at what I've just done. I've just fucked Rip in the ladies toilets at a bar like some slut. Rip takes my chin in his hand and forces me to look at him.

"See sweetheart? You're mine, even if your head hasn't realised it yet, your body fuckin' has." Rip kisses me briefly then leaves.

I slowly get down off the side, and turn to face the mirror, my face is flushed and my lips are swollen. As I stare at myself a lone tear falls. I quickly wipe it away, disgusted at what I've done. For letting him get close and take that from me. For it being the best sex I've ever had, and it was a quick fuck in the god damn toilet.

I clean myself up and make sure I look okay before I head back out to the girls. I just want to go home to bed now.

They all smile at me when I return. I give them a small smile.

"Guys, I'm going to head home now, I'm not feeling too good, I just want to go to bed." I say. They all furrow their brows and look at each other in question, but thankfully they don't ask any further questions. Daisy nods and we say our goodbyes. Daisy walks to Carter who is chatting with Rip. I wait by the door. I feel his gaze on me, but I keep my head down and avoid looking at him. A few moments later Daisy, Carter and I head to the truck. As we are getting in, Rip calls my name. I ignore him, pretending I didn't hear and climb in and shut the door.

"Carter, can you just drive me back please?" I ask.

"Sure thing." Carter answers and pulls out of the parking lot. The whole way back I stare out the window at the black night sky, lost in my own thoughts and not saying a word.

Carter pulls the truck up to Blake and Lily's house. I thank them and then jump out. As I reach the steps Daisy calls outs my name and comes running up to me.

"What has happened to make you like this?" she asks, worried. I give her a small smile and sigh.

"I fucked him in the toilets, all he said after was I am his. Then he walked out." I say and shrug. "I was drunk and stupid. I let my guard down for a second and gave him what he wanted. The worst thing is, it was amazing. But after I just felt dirty and used. I felt like a slut. I knew he would have the power to make me feel this way. Why do you think I wont let him in? Guys like him are all the same. I promise you now though Daisy, I won't be letting him anywhere near me again. It's my fault. I shouldn't have let my guard down and apparently I can't shut my mouth up from speaking the damn truth after a few drinks." I rant. Daisy shakes her head and smiles a sympathetic smile at me.

"Look I don't think Rip's like all the other guys. I don't think he handled the situation well, but you can't deny there is definitely something there between you both. Now go in get some sleep because I have a feeling you'll be feeling a little rough in the morning." Daisy says, pulling me in for a hug. Then she turns to leave. As I walk in the house Trudy is sat reading a book. She puts it down and smiles up at me.

"Y'all have a good time?" she asks.

"Yeah fab time, thank you. How has Caden been, all okay?" I ask, taking off my shoes.

"Yes, he is a real character. Made me laugh a lot, you've done a good job raising him." She says, the compliment takes me back a bit because, well, apart from family no one has ever said anything like that to me. People just see Caden as a live wire, which he is, but he also has the sweetest nature.

"Thank you, no one has ever said that to me before." I say honestly. Damn it! That'll be the drink again.

Trudy pauses and places her hands on my shoulders.

"Rose, you're a wonderful mother, don't ever

doubt yourself." she says, giving my arm a gentle squeeze. She turns and grabs her cell.

"I'm just gonna text Max to come get me. He needed to use the truck earlier and said he would pick me up."

"Okay. Do you mind if I go wash up and put my pyjamas on?" I ask. She shakes her head and shoos me away with her hand.

I wash the make-up off my face, put on my pyjama shorts and tank top, piling my hair in a messy bun on my head. I'm sure Trudy won't mind seeing me in this state.

I quickly check on Caden, he's fast asleep with his hands behind his head and one leg bent. The cover is hanging off him. I bend down and kiss his head smiling and tuck him back in.

I head downstairs and find Trudy in the kitchen making a hot chocolate, her head comes up as I enter. She smiles and hands me the mug.

"It's my special hot chocolate, I used to make it for Rip all the time." She smiles, I look away at the mention of Rip. I take a sip of the hot chocolate and moan.

"This is like heaven in a cup." I say to Trudy and she smiles. We sit in the lounge while we wait for Max to turn up.

"Rose, can I be straight with you?" Trudy asks. I smile and nod for her to go on.

"My son, he can be, well, careless sometimes...but that doesn't mean his heart isn't in the right place. I know he likes you a lot, I can see it. I can see you like him too. Even when you put your defences up. Listen, please don't think I'm getting involved in what happens between you two, it's your business, but I promise you, your heart is safe with him. You don't need to hide from it." she says with a small smile.

There's a light tap on the door and in walks Rip. I jump up and look from Trudy to Rip.

"What is this? Some kind of set up? You being all nice to me and trying to talk me round and then he walks in and that's it? Problem solved? I'm like putty in your hands! Is that it? Was it not enough you fucked me in the ladies toilets tonight just to prove a point!" I seethe.

"Rip! Please tell me you didn't! You idiot. I'm sorry sweetie, I had no idea, he just said he wanted to talk." Trudy apologises.

I cross my arms and stand my ground with Rip. Neither of us saying anything, just staring at each other.

"Ma, go wait for me in the car." Rip orders. Trudy pauses for a moment, unsure if she should go. I give her a gentle nod that it is okay.

"I will call you Rose, I'm so sorry." She turns and leaves.

As soon as the door is closed, Rip walks towards me. This time I don't back down. I put my hand up, halting him, stopping him from coming any closer.

"No, I don't want you near me. Just say what you've got to say and leave."

"Shit you're fuckin' beautiful." He sighs.

I roll my eyes at him trying to lay on the charm.

"Look, I'm going to say the same shit, there's something between us, you feel it. I fuckin' feel it. I didn't mean to take things as far as I did tonight, but shit I just get near you and, well, you drive me fuckin' crazy sweetheart. I don't know whether to fuck you or put you over my knee. I know I've messed up and you've gone and rebuilt that damn fortress around yourself. Just know this, I will not give up on us, on you. I meant what I said. You're mine, your body knows it, your mind just needs to catch up and know it too. You need me to prove you're it for me, I'm going to prove it. So don't think you've got rid of me sweetheart. This is just the beginning." Rips states, I haven't realised that he's walked right up to me. His hand reaches up and cups my face. He leans forward and I instinctively close my eyes. He gently places a soft kiss on my lips.

"Sleep tight sweetheart." Rips says, then

kisses my forehead and turns and leaves. I stand there for a while, wondering what the hell just happened and thinking I'm in serious shit. I feel my fortress start to crack, just a little.

CHAPTER FOUR

Caden and I spend the next day just lounging around, I don't feel hungover thankfully. I just feel tired, I didn't get much sleep with what Rip said last night. I kept replaying his words over and over in my head. I put a movie on for Caden and I to watch, but I find myself falling asleep.

"Shhh, Mum is sleeping. I'm guessing she had a lot of special Mum juice last night with auntie Daisy." I hear whispered. I feel a blanket being laid on me and a kiss placed on my forehead. I groan and snuggle in deeper. I hear a low manly chuckle. Too tired to care, I soon drift back off to sleep.

I am woken to crashing around coming from the kitchen. It takes me a moment to awake properly. I jump to my feet and quickly run into the kitchen.

"Caden, honey...don't touch anything in the..." I pause.

Stood there at the stove with Caden is Rip. He's smiling at me. His eyes do a sweep from my head to my toes. I realise I am still in my pyjamas. I didn't see the point of getting dressed today.

"Caden, do me a favour and get the vegetables out the draw ready. Okay buddy." Rip says, Caden happily skips off to go get them. I stand there confused and a little stunned. Rip stops just in front of me.

"You sleep okay sweetheart?" Rip asks, tucking a wayward strand of hair behind my ear.

"Huh?" I ask confused.

"Shit you're cute." Rip says smiling. He leans in and kisses me briefly.

"Huh?" I say again.

"I came over, Caden let me in. You were asleep. It's nearly dinner time so Caden and I are going to make dinner." Rip says smiling down at me.

"Huh?" I ask again. Rip just throws his head back and laughs. He brings his mouth down to mine.

"Sweetheart, go jump in the shower and wake yourself up a little bit. Caden and I will take care of dinner, okay?" He turns me to face the stairs, and I walk up them.

Still confused and in a daze I get in the shower. While I'm in there I come to the conclusion I'm either still dreaming or I've fallen asleep and woken up in an alternate universe. I get out of the shower and chuck on my denim cut-off shorts and tank top. My hair still wet I walk downstairs and smell the food cooking. It makes my stomach rumble.

I walk into the kitchen and Caden comes running over.

"Mum! Come on this way! I've laid the table all nice, just for you." Caden says excitedly and pulls my hand and takes me out to the decking where he's laid out all the plates. He's even picked a flower and put it in a glass in the centre of the table.

I pull him in for a tight hug and give him a big kiss. Of course he squirms and tries to get away.

"I love it buddy, thank you." I praise.

"Sit down, dinner is served." I turn and Rip winks at me as he places a dish on the table. We sit down and Rip serves it up for us.

"Hope you like it. It's just mac n' cheese, but it's how my mum used to make it for me as a kid. We also did vegetables. Caden here cut and cooked them, he said you'd moan at him if he didn't have any vegetables on his plate." Rip winks at Caden.

Still a little stunned at what's going on, but too hungry to think too much about it, I tuck in. It tastes delicious.

"Rip, this tastes amazing." I say around another mouthful. Rip smiles and reaches across. He runs his finger across my chin, then places it into his mouth.

"You had a bit of sauce on your chin." He says smiling.

"Mum's a messy eater, she's always spilling food down her top. Grandad says we should buy her a bib." Caden says laughing.

Rip lets out a low chuckle while I give Caden the evil eye.

We finish our dinner and I offer to clean the dishes as Rip cooked. Caden runs into the lounge to switch on the Xbox.

I'm not able to contain my thoughts any longer. Rip walks in and clears the side.

"What's going on here Rip?" I blurt out while scrubbing at a pan. Rip takes the cloth from my hand and turns me around so I'm facing him.

"Exactly what I said last night. I will prove to you that there is an us, that you can rely on and trust me. this is me starting that, this is me breaking down that damn fortress you've built around yourself." Rip says gently.

"My hands are dripping soapy water all over you." is all I say. Rip just smiles.

"I don't give a shit. I know you're scared sweetheart. I will prove to you that I am worthy of winning your heart. I can promise you that." Rip states. He leans in and kisses me, and for a moment I let myself melt into his kiss. Rip feels it and he deepens the kiss. The moment is broken when his phone rings. Rip growls, pulls it out of his pocket and answers it.

"What?!" He growls down the phone. He pinches the bridge of his nose and sighs.

"Right, fuck, yeah. I will be there in twenty." He pauses.

"I'm not at home, I'm at Blake's place with Rose. Shut the fuck up. asshole." Then he disconnects.

"Sorry sweetheart, I've got to go. Club business. I'll come by tomorrow. Maybe I could take you and Caden out or something."

"I can't tomorrow, I've got a meeting with Owen at the hospital for a job." I answer.

"No fucking way, you ain't meeting up with Owen." Rip states.

"I bloody well am." I argue back, feeling myself getting annoyed.

"No you're fucking not! He orders back." Fed up I place my hands on my hips.

"Rip! Yes I am. It's for a job, he's being nice helping me out. Stop being such a twat. You can't tell me what I can and can't do." I fire back.

"Sweetheart, he isn't being nice, he wants in your fuckin' panties. You just can't see it." He replies.

I roll my eyes.

"I am going. It's important. He does not want to get in my panties and even if he did, it doesn't mean I'm going to let him, does it." I point out.

Rip looks to the ceiling and sighs.

"I ain't got time for this now. We will talk about this tomorrow." He leans in, kisses my head and leaves.

"Caden, look after your ma, I'll see you tomorrow." Rips says as he walks past Caden, giving him a fist bump.

I growl to myself, god that man is so damn infuriating!

It's soon getting late and it's time for Caden to go to bed. We're cuddled up and I'm reading him a story when he turns to me.

"Mum, is Rip your boyfriend now?" He asks. I bite my lip wondering how I should answer. it's my fault, I should have been more careful when Caden was around. I don't want him getting the wrong idea or getting too attached to Rip.

"No honey, it's err...well it's complicated. We're just friends at the moment." I answer.

"So you might be girlfriend and boyfriend one day? Because if you do, I'm totally cool with that. Rip is really cool. He's a biker and has his own biker club. He's a total badass." Caden sighs. I snort.

"Caden! Don't say badass. Just do me a favour bud, don't look into it too much okay, being a grown up it can be a little complicated."

"Only because grown-ups make it that way. It's just stupid. You like him, and he likes you. That's it. Simple. Grown ups have to be silly and make everything harder." Caden rants. I stare stunned at my very intelligent son, who has probably just spoken the most sense about adult relationships I've ever heard.

"I'm tired Mum, I don't need anymore story. Night mum." Caden then kisses me on the cheek and rolls over. I stare at him, stunned again, then kiss his head and leave him to it. Still feeling tired I get myself ready for bed. I don't want bags under my eyes for this meeting tomorrow. I jump into bed and fall asleep.

I am woken later on to the bed dipping and a hand coming around my body, pulling me back. I freeze and fling my elbow back. I'm met with a grunt and a moan.

"Christ sweetheart, take it easy." I lean forward, switch on the bedside light and turn to see Rip in bed with me.

"What in the hell are you doing in my bed?!" I screech.

"Well I'm not going to fuckin' sleep obviously!" He groans, rubbing his chest. It's then I notice he has no clothes on. His bare broad muscled tattooed chest is staring back at me. I lift the covers and take a peak, he has boxers on. I sigh, thank Christ. When I look back at Rip he's smirking.

"I can take them off too if you'd like sweetheart." He states, smirking.

"No! For god's sake why are you in my bed?!" I ask, trying to ignore that he's near enough naked.

"I couldn't sleep, I wanted to be with be with you. Wes let me in." He shrugs like it's completely normal to be climbing in bed with me.

"Uh okay, but you'll have to be out by morning because I don't think it's a good idea Caden seeing us. He's already asking questions."

Rip just grunts and lies down, pulling me with him.

"Switch the light off sweetheart." He says into my neck.

I lean forward and switch the light off. Rip

spoons me from behind. I feel his hard erection and freeze.

"Don't you dare wiggle that ass, he'll go down in a minute. Get some sleep sweetheart." He says sleepily.

I close my eyes and try to drift off but I'm too aware that I'm in bed with Rip. I lie there for what feels like an eternity. I hear his breathing even out as he falls asleep. Eventually I manage to drift off to sleep.

"Mum, Mum, wake up. Muuuuuum." I hear Caden whisper.

"Mmmm, give me two more minutes bud and then I'll get up." I mumble sleepily. I snuggle on my pillow. It's then I realise I'm not led on a soft pillow but a hard chest. My eye spring open and sure enough I am led on Rip's hard tattooed chest. I lift my head slowly and look at Caden who is giggling. Well this is shit.

"Err buddy, go watch TV for a second, okay? I'll be there in a bit." I whisper, trying to be quiet so as not to disturb a sleeping Rip. Caden nods smiling and runs out of the room. I take one last look at Rip sleeping. God, even asleep he's beautiful. I carefully move to get out of bed when strong arms circle me, pulling me back in. Rip leans over me and smiles sleepily. There goes another crack in my wall, god damn it! He just doesn't fight fair.

"Morning sweetheart." He rasps, his voice deep and husky.

"Morning, um, Caden was just in here. I told you to be gone before he woke up!" I whisper, just in case Caden has his ear pressed up against the door, I wouldn't put it past him.

"Yeah I overslept." He smiles cheekily at me. I can't help the smile that crosses my lips.

"Damn, you're fucking stunning in the morning." He says softly, leaning in kissing me, slowly and lazily.

"Why did you pretend to be asleep when Caden came in?" I ask, running my fingers through his hair.

He takes my hand and places it on his long, thick erection.

"Morning wood sweetheart. Can't very well greet the kid with this." He says smiling. His smile soon falls, and his eyes become hungry. I suck in a breath.

"You want to let go of my dick now sweetheart, or I will happily fuck you." He growls low. I gasp and let go immediately.

"Holy shit, I'm so sorry. I didn't realise I was doing it. I cover my face with my hands and let out a giggle.

"Fuckin' Christ. You're killing me sweetheart." He moans. I look up at him and smile.

It's then I remember what I'm doing today.

"What time is it?" I ask.

Rip looks up at the clock behind me.

"It's 9am, why?" He asks. I jump up and get out of bed. I run round the room to the wardrobe and start pulling out outfits.

"Bollocks bollocks bollocking bollocks. It's a bloody good job I had a shower and washed my hair late yesterday. I'm not going to have time now." I mumble to myself.

"Sweetheart, calm down! Where is it you're going?" Rip asks and I raise an eyebrow in question, wondering how he could've forgotten.

"The meeting at the hospital." I say with a sigh.

"Fuck, so you're still going then?" Rip asks with a grumble.

"Yes. Oh, could you stay with Caden and drop him to Daisy's? I'm not going to make it otherwise." I plead.

"Fine." He moans. He lies back with his hand behind his head, the cover low on his waist. I stop what I am doing and just stare, my eyes drinking him in. He smirks.

"Sweetheart, you going to this meeting or coming back to bed?" my eyes flick to his and I lick my lower lip. Tempting. I shake my head and grab my outfit.

"Close your eyes." I order. Rip just gives me a look.

"Sweetheart, I've been inside you. Why the fuck would I close my eyes?" He smirks.

The bastard is goading me, I smile because if he wants to see me naked, then he's going to see me naked. Unfortunately for him there's no time for touching. I shrug and lift off my tank top. I hear him suck in a breath. I continue to take off my shorts and chuck them out the way. I pick up my black lace thong and put it on, then I purposefully lean across the bed to grab my bra. I hear him growl and I smirk.

I'm stood in front of him in just my underwear. I decide to put my heels on next, just to add to the tease. I purposefully bend down in front of him to do my strap up. I look at him over my shoulder and smile, seeing him looking to the ceiling, clearly praying for strength. I grab my dress and slip it on. Quickly I brush my hair and spray on some perfume. I apply mascara and grab my lip gloss to put on after I've brushed my teeth. I am about to leave the room when Rip grabs my hand, pulling me back. I land on the bed and Rip lies on top of me.

"That little show, was it for my benefit? Because that was cruel sweetheart. Fuck me, I am very much looking forward to pay back." He growls and nips my neck. I laugh and he pulls me to my feet.

"Go, go meet that dick head. I will drop Caden at your sister's. I'll see you later." Rip says before kissing me passionately, leaving me breathless.

I run to the bathroom to take care of business and brush my teeth. I give Caden a quick kiss and head out of the door.

CHAPTER FIVE

I manage to find my way to the hospital with a minute to spare. I park up and run around to the entrance and standing there is Owen. He smiles, a look of relief washing over his face when he sees me.

"Hey, sorry! I overslept, which usually never happens because Caden usually wakes me up at the crack of dawn." I say breathlessly. Man, I'm really out of shape.

"No problem, we're still good for the meeting. Come on, let's go meet my aunt." Owen places his hand on the small of my back and guides me through the hospital.

Through the entire meeting I'm a massive ball of nerves. I would never normally be nervous in an interview, but I really want this job,

I really want this for me and Caden. Luckily, Owen's aunt is lovely and as it turned out, I was more than qualified for the job.

"Well, I would love you to come work for us here. You don't officially start until next month but if you could come in and shadow the nurse that will be leaving so you get to know the unit and staff, say a week before, that would be great." Mrs Tellar says smiling. I jump out of my seat and lean forward and hug her.

"Thank you, thank so much!" I sing. Thankfully she laughs and doesn't call security at my excitable outburst.

"Now if you get the paperwork sorted and back to us we can set up your visa so you can legally work here." she states. I nod and thank her again.

Owen is waiting outside for me, I skip to him smiling.

"I got the job!" I squeal and jump, hugging him. He hugs me back. I take a step back, his arms still around me.

"I knew my aunt would love you." Owen says smiling at me, his eyes drop to my lips. I gently push back out of his hold, not wanting to give him the wrong signals.

"Let me take you out, let's go have some lunch to celebrate." he states smiling.

"Um, well, it's only 11am."

"Okay, brunch then." he says smiling.

"Alright, but I can't be too long. My sister is watching Caden." I relent. Owen nods and walks us to his car.

"I will drop you back to your car afterwards." he says, opening his door for me. I climb in. I can't help but think maybe Rip was right about Owen wanting to get in my knickers.

Owen takes me to this nice coffee house and I order a cappuccino and a bagel. The conversation flows nicely, Owen is being a complete gentlemen. Maybe he is just looking for a friendship after all.

"Oh, come here, you've got a little bit of cream cheese on your cheek." Owen says reaching forward. He strokes my face and wipes the cream cheese, then licks his finger.

"Hmm, delicious." he grins.

Now I'm back to thinking he definitely wants to get in my knickers. I'm also thinking I'm a seriously messy eater as this seems to happen a lot.

"So Owen, I hope you don't mind me asking, where's Zack's mother?" I ask, taking another big bite of my bagel.

"She up and left when Zack was just six months old. Left a note saying she couldn't handle it anymore, and that she was sorry. That was it, nothing else. It has been just Zack and I ever since. I wouldn't change it for the world. Way I see it, is she's missed out on being a part of his life, he brings me so much joy. She will never get that." he states with emotion thick in his voice. I reach out and hold his hand. I give him a gentle squeeze.

"Well, you're doing a brilliant job, Zack seems like he's growing up to be a fine young man." I say, giving him a sympathetic smile.

"Thanks." he mumbles.

We carry on talking for a little while longer. I look at the time and see it's past 12pm.

"Oh shoot! I'm sorry but I really must get going and rescue my sister from Caden." I stand, placing some money on the table.

Owen hands me my money back and pays.

"Thank you." I say quietly.

Owen drives me back to the hospital and walks me to the truck.

I turn to thank him, but before I get a chance his hands are cupping my face and he's kissing me. I freeze, my brain wondering what the hell is going on. I push slightly at his chest and pull away, he doesn't back off, so I shove him harder this time and thankfully he does.

"Shit sorry, I just got carried away. Shit!"

Owen curses, his hands gripping his hair.

"Hey, it's okay. But, listen, I am sorry, but I just don't see you that way. I think we could be great friends but that's it for me. I'm sorry if I have misled you."

"No, it's fine. Look, I knew you were interested in Rip, but I just thought maybe if I kissed you, it might make you see me a little differently and maybe you would be interested in me. I know it's a stupid idea." Owen says with a sigh.

"No it's not stupid, but you're right. If things were different then maybe, but they're not. I'm sorry if I've upset you." I say as I lean up and kiss his cheek. I get into the truck and pull off. I let out a long breath. I guess Rip was right, damn it. I really hate being wrong and I especially hate being wrong when it comes to Rip.

As I drive towards Daisy's, I notice a Harley up ahead. The biker has the Satan's emblem on the back of his cut. I squint and see that it's Rubble.

Out of nowhere a black SUV speeds past me and drives straight towards Rubble. I try beeping the horn to warn him, not that there's much he would be able to do. It all happens so fast. I watch as the SUV hits the back of Rubble's bike, making it fish tale and knocking Rubble off. The bike and Rubble skid across the road, thankfully there's no oncoming traffic.

"Holy shit!" I scream. I pull over and I watch as Rubble and the bike come to a stop. I see Rubble roll to his side, relieved that he's moving. The SUV stops and out jump two men in suits. They walk towards Rubble I notice they have guns in their hands.

"Fuck me!" I breathe. Without thinking I put the truck in drive and put my foot down, beeping the horn like a crazy person. It's enough to get their attention. They both turn and look at me. I don't slow down, I head straight for them. Realising I'm not stopping they jump out of the way I slam my brakes on just in front of Rubble, skidding to a stop. I quickly jump out to get him into the truck.

"Rubble, it's me, get up. Quickly! Get in the truck! They have guns!" I screech.

Rubble slowly stands to his feet and I help him, putting his arm around my shoulders. I get him to the truck and he climbs in the back. just as I'm about to get in, gun shots are fired. They hit the truck. I scream and jump in, keeping low. I put the car in drive and put my foot down. I make the mistake of looking directly at one of the guys as I pull off. He smirks, and it sends shivers down my spine.

I drive way over the speed limit and Rubble directs me to the Satans' compound. I do a few purposeful wrong turns, making sure they aren't following us. When I am satisfied they aren't, I breathe a sigh of relief.

"Who the fuck are those guys Rubble?!" I shout.

He grunts in pain.

"Nobody darlin', just drive." he says, his voice straining. I turn to quickly look at him, holding his arm. It is hanging down.

"I'm pulling over, you need to be seen too." I say. I'm about to pull over.

"No! Just drive straight to the compound, no stops. We will be safe once we are there." he lets out a hiss of pain.

"No one my arse! Of course it's just average people who run you down then shoot at you!" I yell.

Rubble doesn't answer. I pull up to the compound, beeping my horn and flashing my lights. The two bikers on the gate walk over. I put the window down.

"It's Rubble, I've got him in the back seat, he's hurt. Open the bloody gates!" I screech. Seeing that it's me they open the gate. I drive in fast, skidding to a stop. I jump out and help Rubble out of the truck. A moment later Mammoth and Khan come out. Seeing me holding up Rubble they start running towards us.

"YO! Pres you're gonna want to get your ass

out here now!" Khan yells behind him.

Mammoth takes Rubble from me.

"Careful, I think he's got a dislocated shoulder and possible fractures."

Mammoth nods. I stop, trying to catch my breath. Rip comes out frowning. He takes in Rubble and Khan must have said something to him because his eyes come straight to mine. He moves quickly towards me, his eyes never leaving mine. As soon as he gets to me, he wraps me in his arms. That's when I let what just happen sink in. A sob bursts from my lips and my body starts shaking. Rip picks me up, cradling me in his arms. He takes me inside.

"Everyone get the fuck out! Now!" He barks.

He sits down, cradling me in his lap, and kisses the top of my head. I'm handed a glass with amber liquid in.

"Drink this sweetheart, it'll make you feel a little better." Rip says softly.

I down the drink, the alcohol burning my throat. I sit up and wipe my face.

"Is Rubble okay?" I ask. Rip cups my face and wipes my tears.

"He will be fine, you want to tell me what happened?" He asks.

I nod and tell him everything that happened. I watch as the emotions on his face change to cold and deadly.

"What did the guys look like?" He growls.

"I only got a good look at one but they both looked like maybe they were Hispanic." I say, Rip's whole body tightens at my words.

"Did they see you? Do you think they got a good look at you?" He asks.

"Yeah, one did. He gave me the chills. He smiled at me when I drove off." I shudder.

There's a knock at the door.

"What?!" Rip shouts angrily.

Khan sticks his head through the door.

"Sorry Pres, but it's Rubble. He's going to need a trip to the hospital." Khan states.

"He can't, it's too dangerous. It was the Cartel." Rip warns.

Khan's face turns to stone at the mention of the Cartel.

"Fuck. You want me to call church?" He asks.

"Not yet." He answers Khan. He then turns to me.

"Sweetheart, do you reckon you might be able to help Rubble?" He asks.

I nod confused.

"Rip, what's going on?" I ask. He just ignores me.

"Khan, call everyone in for emergency church within the next hour." He orders. Khan nods and shuts the door.

"Rip, what the fuck is going on?!" I ask .

"I will tell you, I promise, but right now I need you to see to Rubble. Okay? He needs you." Rip says, cupping my face. I roll my eyes at him avoiding my question, but I nod. Rip kisses me.

"Now I need to sort some shit out. I've got church." He says standing.

"What's Church? I'm guessing you boys haven't just stumbled upon god." I say sarcastically. Rip's lips twitch.

"Church is what we call our meetings. Usually I call them once a week more if there's shit going down." He says, pulling me to my feet.

"Oh." is all I say. He takes my hand in his and leads me to Rubble.

My mind swarming with questions and uncertainty. All I know is what ever is going down, it's not good. I'm not stupid, I've heard of the Cartel before, but only ever in movies or books. This isn't a movie or a book, though. This is very much real, and it's scary shit. All I am thankful for is that Caden wasn't with me when all of this went down, that he's safe with Daisy.

CHAPTER SIX

"Right, are you sure you're ready for this and you definitely don't want to go to the hospital?" I ask Rubble as I hold his arm, ready to pop his dislocated shoulder back in.

"Just do it, I'm not going to no hospital." Rubble grits his teeth.

"Okay, just saying, this will probably hurt like a mother effer, so don't blame the nurse. Okay?" I state.

"Mother effer?" Rubble asks, his lips twitching.

"I have a very impressionable son, remember? I have to get creative with the naughty words. Now stop distracting me and count to ten."

"Fine, one, two, three, four, five, si..... OW! SON OF A BITCH!" Rubble roars in pain as I click his shoulder back in. I give him a smile and pat him on the back.

"All done, you should be good now. Let's stitch up those wounds." I say smiling and holding up my tools. I'm not even going to ask why the Satans' had the correct equipment for stitches.

"Thanks." Rubble grunts, rubbing his shoulder.

I clean up his wounds, making him hiss in pain. I smirk. I make a start on his first wound.

"Jeez, you know for a nurse I'm pretty sure you're not supposed to smile when the patient is in pain." Rubble moans.

"Well, you're a tough biker, I'm sure you can handle it. Plus, you're not technically my patient, I'm just a friend helping out. I can laugh at you as much as I want." I wink at him and I get a small smile and a grunt in return. I carry on seeing to his wounds. Just as I'm on the last one, Mammoth walks in the room.

"Brother, when you're done Pres wants to see you to go over the plans. You doin' okay? All fixed up?" Mammoth asks.

"Yeah, I'm all good, thanks to Flo here." Rubble says pointing to me.

"Flo?" I ask confused.

"Yeah, Florence Nightingale." Rubble grunts. I snort and shake my head.

"That's it! That's your road name!" Mammoth booms.

"What? Flo?" I ask smiling.

"Sure, or we'll call you Nightingale. It's undecided. Damn, I'm usually the ones to come up with the road names. Oh well. I'll catch you later Flo!" Mammoth hollers over his shoulder.

I sigh.

"Thanks for that." I mumble.

Rubble smirks and shrugs. I bring the light in closer, so I can see the wound just on top of his head a bit better, finding it difficult to reach and see clearly, especially with him sat in like a lazy boy type chair.

"Right, don't get any ideas, and keep your hands to yourself. I'm going to have to kneel on the arm of the chair, and you'll have to move your head so you'll basically be staring at my tits. But it's the only way I can get to your wound to stitch it up properly. Just remember, I have a needle in my hand, should you feel the urge to motorboat or squeeze my arse. Do I make myself clear?" I say in the warning tone I use on Caden. Rubble winks and crosses his heart. I roll my eyes and kneel up on the arm of the chair. Rubble does as I've asked, but his head is still a little out of reach.

"Bring your head closer." I say. He does and he is that close I can feel his breath across my chest. I fight the urge to giggle at what this must look like. You certainly wouldn't get this kind of treatment in a hospital.

"Perfect. Right, don't move." I slowly start stitching up the wound on his head.

"What the fuck is going on?!" Rip yells, walking in. His loud entrance makes me jump and I wobble, jabbing Rubble in the head with the needle. He lets out a hiss of pain, I wobble so much I fall forwards, landing across Rubble's lap like I'm about to be spanked. Rubble grunts as I land. I feel something hard poking me in the stomach. I pause.

"Oh shit sorry Rubble, I didn't mean to, you know, give you that." I say, pushing myself up. Before I can stand I'm pulled back by Rip.

Rubble just smirks and shrugs. I giggle.

"You got a damn stiffy from looking at my woman?" Rip seethes.

"Oh calm down, it's not a big deal." I say laughing.

"Chill out Pres, It's not like I could help it, her tits were in my face. I tried, I really did...but, well, they're a nice pair of tits." Rubble moans.

Rip goes to lunge for him at the mention of my tits. I quickly move in front of him and place my hand on his chest, stopping him from killing Rubble, if the look in his eyes is anything to go by.

"Stop, he's already injured, it's a situation that couldn't be helped. It's not the first time the girls have caused a stir in a guys pants. I was just helping him! The poor guy had to have his face practically right on in there."

"Not fucking helping in calming me down sweetheart." Rip growls angrily.

"What I'm saying is, if you had a proper medical bed and chair, like you seem to have proper medical equipment, which, by the way, is really bloody dodgy, Rubble wouldn't have been all on up in the girls. But that doesn't matter, because it's not like I'm going to be doing this all the time, is it! It's not every day one of you gets run down or shot at." I roll my eyes and shake my head. I realise that Rip and Rubble have gone silent. I look at both of them exchanging a look.

"Oh my god. It is, isn't it? This happens a lot, doesn't it?" I ask, looking between them both.

"Rubble, leave us." Rip orders.

"Sure Pres." Rubble salutes and goes to leave the room.

"Wait Rubble!" I shout, he stops I run to him,

pull his head down towards me and quickly pull through the last stitch.

"There, all done." I smile. He gives me a chin lift and leaves. I turn back round to face Rip and go about clearing up.

"Rose will you just stop and listen to me for a second?" Rip asks. I sigh, dropping the rubbish in the bin, and turn to face him.

"Look, you should know that sometimes shit goes down with the club. I can't say what sort of things but yeah, sometimes it's bad. It doesn't happen a lot, but at the moment, it's bad. The guys you saw today were Mexican cartel, they want control of our town to deal drugs, amongst a few other things. They are trying their luck on our patch, and sweetheart, we won't have that. This has been going on a long time."

"Lily." is all I say. Realisation crosses his face and he sighs.

"What happened with Lily was because of the Cartel, wasn't it?! It was because that Ven guy had a hand in it all." I seethe. All Rip does is nod.

"Do you know, I thought that with everything she went through at his hands, I thought he must have been a complete nutcase and infatuated with Lily, but now it all makes sense. He just wanted the control of the town, liked the look of Lily and used her to get back not just at

Blake but all of you! She was meant to be a message, not from Ven but from the Cartel. I'm right aren't I?!" I ask.

"Yeah sweetheart, but Ven is dead. We are dealing with it. You don't have to worry. Trust us." Rip states, walking towards me. He tries to pull me into his arms, but I push him away and move out his way.

"They are still out there, Ven may be dead but the Cartel isn't. I can't put Caden or myself in this dangerous situation. I just can't. I'm sorry Rip, I can't do this. If something happened to Caden, I'd never forgive myself." I say swallowing back the tears. I watch as Rip clenches his jaw. He doesn't say anything, he just opens the door and walks out. I take a slow steady breath, trying to keep hold of my emotions. I turn and finish clearing up.

Mammoth comes in a few moments later.

"You ready to roll Flo?" He asks. I turn and smile at him.

"Sure, let me just grab my bag. I left it in Rip's office." I say walking past him. I make it to the office and walk in to see Rip sat at his desk, with a glass and a bottle of bourbon. His beautiful ice blue eyes come to mine and they almost take all the air out of me. I halt in my movements.

"I, um, left my bag in here." I say quickly scurrying past him to the couch to grab my bag.

I turn to leave but Rip is right there blocking me. He reaches out and tucks a strand of my hair behind my ear.

"You're building your walls up again, but I'm not going to fight them this time sweetheart, because you're right. It's not a safe world for you or Caden to be in. I'm not going to force you into my life, into my world." Rip rasps. His eyes show his pain when he says that. He cups my face and leans in, kissing me gently. My heart lurches, I grip onto his shirt tightly, because deep down I want him. I don't want to do this.

Rip breaks the kiss, still cupping my face in his hands.

"Go and find your happy, sweetheart." Rip rasps. He places a kiss on my forehead and then turns and leaves. My whole world feels like it has been tilted on its head. It's been turned upside down. I want to run after him and tell him I want him, but I don't. I just stand there. I let him let me go. Giving myself a mental slap, I grab my bag and force myself to leave. I ignore the pain in my chest, I ignore the urge to cry. Pushing my shoulders back and carrying on, I pretend I'm fine. I pretend that Rip hasn't just crushed my heart. Of course he couldn't have, because I don't let anyone near my heart.

CHAPTER SEVEN

I pretend over the next couple of days that it doesn't feel like there is a piece missing. I throw myself into organising things for my new job. I look at the local school for Caden and although it's currently shut for the summer, I know it's perfect for him. Daisy has kindly offered to help out with childcare. Everything is going perfectly. But if it's so perfect, why do I feel so unhappy?

I decide I better ring and check in with Mum and Dad as they had to head home pretty much straight after the wedding with Nan and Axel.

"Hello!" my mum says, waving into the camera. I smile. She's getting better at using the video call now, it used to be a nostril that greeted you.

"Hi Mum, how are you and Dad?" I ask.

"Oh all good, your dad is well. Although he's feeling a little off at the moment. It's his own fault, so don't go feeling sorry for him! I told him not to eat that vindaloo from the street vendor. But did he listen? Nope. Now he's complaining about his bad gut and saying that his arse is burning. I swear I've lost count how much bleach I've gone through cleaning that damn toilet." Mum sighs, pausing briefly. Before I can even comment or gag at the horrendous thought of Dad's stinky arse, she starts talking again.

"So what's new over there, Caden loving it? I bet he's having the best time. And what about you? Any of those hunky guys taken a fancy to you yet?" she beams.

I try to hide the sharp pain I get in my chest at her last question.

"Caden loves it here, and I've found myself a job at the hospital. I start tomorrow. It's only covering maternity, but Daisy has offered me a permanent job at her centre when it's up and running. So…surprise! Caden and I aren't planning on coming back." I say smiling. My mum's face falls.

"BEN! Get in here!" Mum yells.

"What is it woman? I swear to you, my arse is so sore it's like I shit a fireball." Dad grumbles, waddling slightly. I snort back a laugh.

"God damn woman! Can you please tell me when you're on one of these calls, so I don't go around running my mouth off."

"Oh shut up, it's only Rose. Listen, Rose has got a job at the hospital there and Daisy's offered her a job when the centre is up and running. Her and Caden aren't coming home. That's another child and now grandbaby we're losing to Mufftown. We have to sell up and move over there to be with them, I'm not missing out on both our grandbabies growing up. Ring the estate agents now and get them out." My mum orders. Dad sighs, pinching the bridge of his nose.

"Mum, you don't have to sell up and move over here." I say, rolling my eyes.

"It's okay baby girl, I got this. Penn, listen. We can't just sell up and move out there. It's not that simple, we've got my mum to think about, and visas. Plus maybe the girls want a bit of space from us, and maybe we can enjoy a bit of us time now they've all grown up and moved away." Dad tries to convince Mum.

"Of course we would take your mum, she'd love it, and we can sort all that out and start looking at properties over there. I want my family close. I can't have Axel close because of his job but I can have my girls close." She argues back.

"Christ, I hate it when you're right. Fine. We will look into it...but I'm not rushing things and settling for the first house that becomes available. If we are going to do this, we do it right. Now, if you'll excuse me the volcano is about to erupt again." Dad says, running off and holding his arse as he goes.

"Well that's exciting, looks like we're going to be moving over there with you all! Hopefully in the next few months! Oh I can't wait to tell your sisters." Mum squeals and claps her hands. I laugh. I'm not going to lie, as much as they are a little crazy, I'm glad they are coming to live over here. They are the most supportive parents I know, and lord knows I need that. Especially when I need a break from Caden every now and again, this could be good.

"This is great news Mum! Listen, I'm going to have to go. I've got to take Caden for a playdate." I say signing off. Mum for once is eager for me to go so she can start house searching.

I quickly change into an off the shoulder red summer dress that comes to just above the knees. I leave my hair and don't bother with any make-up. I grab my bag and head downstairs.

"Caden, let's go buddy!" I yell. Caden comes running towards me wrapped head to toe in toilet tissue.

"What on earth have you been doing?" I ask, shocked, looking at Caden who is currently covered from head to toe in what looks like milk.

"I thought I would make a smoothie for us to drink before we go. They're healthy and good for you. I did it all right Mum. I poured milk, fruit and a big dollop of honey. I even added that green leafy stuff people put in them. I pressed the button and whoosh! It went up like a volcano...I may have forgotten to put the lid on. Whoops." Caden shrugs. I look to the ceiling.

"For fucks sake. Count to ten Rose." I mutter under my breath.

"What did you say Mum?" Caden asks.

"I said go get yourself cleared up quickly while I clean up the mess you made in the kitchen." I say, smiling through gritted teeth.

"Sure thing Mum!" Caden says, running off upstairs. Taking a deep breath, I go to clean up the kitchen. There is fruit and milk everywhere, and there's even what looks like a splattered strawberry on the cupboard door. As I clean up it becomes evident that instead of putting spinach or kale in the smoothie, Caden had put lettuce leaves in. I let out a little giggle and shake my head. That kid means well but my god, he's like a bloody whirl wind. Just as I'm finishing up there is a knock at the door.

"I've got it Mum!" Caden yells. I sigh, chucking the mess of paper towels in the bin. I turn wiping my hands, and make my way to the door.

"Who is it buddy?" I ask. As I make it to the door, I see Caden looks a little uneasy, almost nervous. He is never nervous. Frowning, I pull him behind me.

I look up and standing there is a Mexican-looking guy in a suit, holding a clip board. He has a scar running from his ear to his jaw. I can see the very top of a tattoo poking up from his collar. The guy smiles and it makes my skin prickle. I quickly turn to Caden.

"Caden, do me a favour go call uncle Wes. Ask him what he wants for dinner tonight." I ask.

"But Mum, he said…"

"I know, but just ring him please." I interrupt Caden.

"Sorry, can I help you?" I ask the scary looking guy. He smiles.

"I'm in the area seeing if anyone has been involved in a crash lately. You may be entitled to compensation." He states, with a strong Mexican accent. I shake my head.

"No, sorry, I haven't. I really must go now." I go to shut the door, but the guy puts his hand up, halting me.

"What about those holes in your truck? They look like they're from an accident to me." He almost sneers, and point to the bullet hole from where the cartel shot at Rubble and I.

"I, err, um, hunting accident. Yup. My brother in law made the mistake of giving the gun to my son, who pulled the trigger and shot the car. Now if you don't mind, please remove yourself from the property." I say firmly. This time he smiles, sending more chills down my spine.

I don't give him a chance to say anything. I quickly shut the door and lock it. I take a deep breath to calm my racing heart. Caden comes running in with the phone.

"Mum, its uncle Wes, he wants to talk to you." Caden says and hands me the phone.

"What's going on?" Wes asks down the phone.

"Just some creepy, 'have you had an accident?' guy at the door. He freaked me out is all, no issues. I just wanted Caden to call you while he was here just in case." I lie down the phone.

"God you're a shit liar, just like your sister. Now tell me the truth." Wes demands.

"Fine, it was a 'have you had an accident guy', or so he says...but...you know Rubble had a run in with those cartel guys a few days ago? Well, I think he may have been one of them. Not the one I saw, but, he was Mexican, and wearing a suit just like the others. There was something about him that made my skin crawl. He asked about the bullet holes, that's when I got rid of him." I say to Wes. I hear him swear under his breath.

"Right, where are you right now?" He asks.

"Still at the house, I'm just about to take Caden on a play date with his friend." I say, nervously biting my thumb nail.

"Okay, go on the play date. Keep your eyes open for anyone following you. Text me when you get there." Wes orders.

"Okay, right. I'll text you when we get there." I say repeating his words.

"Darlin', you'll be fine, don't worry. Its a lot safer for you to be out there surrounded by people than in an empty house with no one around. Go on, go now. Text me when you're there." Wes says before he hangs up. I quickly get Caden into the truck, my heart beating fast. My eyes are looking everywhere.

I relax a little when we make it onto the main roads and there are people about.

We pull up to Owen's house and before I can even put the truck in park, Caden is jumping out and running towards the house. To my horror I watch as he doesn't knock or ring the bell. He just runs on in.

I make my way up to the house and Owen greets me at the door.

"Hey, I'm sorry for my rude son just barging

his way into your house." I apologise.

"It's fine! Zack's been looking out the window waiting anyway, he knew you guys were here." Owen says smiling. I watch as his eyes do a sweep of me. He leans in and kisses my cheek. I freeze, a little shocked by it.

"You look beautiful." He states. He turns and starts walking towards the kitchen.

"Come on through." He calls after me. I stand there like a complete plumb, a little stunned by his words and the kiss.

I walk on through. His house is nice, clean and welcoming, with warm woods and cream walls.

I watch as Owen moves around his kitchen, cooking and checking on things.

"Uh, Owen, I thought this was just a play date." I state, confused.

"It is, but I figured you guys might as well stay for dinner, it's not often we have guests over. Wine?" Owen asks, opening a bottle of white.

"I'm driving." I answer.

"Oh. We can call you a cab. Join me, won't you?" He asks smiling. I sigh and nod. Truth is, after the creepster earlier, I'm a little freaked and could do with something stronger than water. Owen hands me the glass of wine, and I take a large glug.

"See, looks like you needed it. Come on, let's sit out the back. Dinner won't be ready for another forty-five minutes yet." Owen says. He places his hand on my lower back and guides me to the back garden where we both sit.

"Owen, this is all very kind of you. You didn't have to go to all of this trouble." I say.

"I wanted too! You start your new job to-morrow, so you deserve to have dinner cooked for you." Owen says smiling.

I give him a small smile. We sit outside chatting, the wine making me relax a little more. Owen makes me laugh and he's easy to chat to. He excuses himself when he goes off to dish up dinner. I offer to help but he orders me to stay put and not lift a finger. I'm not going to argue with him. My phone goes off in my bag. I pull it out to see Wes's number.

"You got there okay then?!" Wes says sarcastically down the phone.

"Oh bugger, Wes, I completely forgot to text you. I'm so sorry." I apologise down the phone.

"It's okay, I know you're there safe. I had one of the Satans' do a drive by to make sure the truck was there." He replies.

"How did you know where I was going?" I ask shocked.

"Darlin', you mentioned Owen the other day and Caden playing with his kid. Mufftown is a small town, I know where Owen lives. It's not exactly hard to figure out. When you gonna be heading back? I will make sure the Satans' are on you."

"Um I'm not sure. We're having dinner and I've started on the wine." I answer.

"He cooked for you, huh? Damn, okay, well text when you're done. I will swing by and pick you guys up. No arguments. Laters darlin'." Wes disconnects.

I shrug and carry on drinking my wine, and a few minutes later Owen comes out with our food.

"The boys wanted to eat in there and watch a movie, so it's just us out here." He says placing the plate in front of me.

"It looks delicious, thank you." I say as Owen tops up my wine.

"It's my signature dish, lamb shanks. The other is lasagne." He says with a shrug. I tuck in and moan.

"Oh god, that is bloody lovely." I say smiling. Owen's eyes are on my mouth. He reaches forward and runs his thumb across my chin, wiping the sauce off. He then sucks the sauce off his thumb and smiles at me. I smile a small smile back.

"Sorry, I'm such a messy eater, I always manage to spill something." I say, continuing to eat.

Owen clearly wants more from me than just a friendship.

Why can't I like him instead of Rip? My life would be so simple and easy. But all I could think about when he wiped the sauce from my chin was Rip. It took me back to when Rip did it.

I shake my head, maybe I should just try with Owen. There's no harm in trying. I can give it a go. Some people say that you don't fall for each other straight away, it comes over time. Maybe that's what this is.

We talk and the conversation flows easily between us. We move to sit on the swing chair. The sun is starting to set and I'm starting to feel the wine.

"So, are you with Rip then?" Owen blurts out. I shake my head and smile a sad smile.

"No, that was never really a thing. It could never go anywhere." I answer, my voice barely a whisper. It still hurts to say that.

Owen leans forward, takes my wine from my hand and places it down. He moves closer, cupping my face in his hands, and kisses me. I freeze for a moment, a little stunned. I give in and kiss him back. Owen moans, kissing me harder and more passionately. His hands travel down, and he cups my breast. I try to push him off, to break the kiss. He's going a little too fast for me. But he doesn't let up. I push harder, and move my head.

"Owen, stop." I yell. He eventually stops and pulls back, panting. I get up and put some distance between us.

"I'm sorry Rose, I got carried away." He apologises. I cover my face with my hands. This is wrong, I'm not ever going to feel for Owen the way he does me. It's not fair to him or to myself to pretend.

"Look, Owen. I'm sorry. I thought maybe I could change my mind on how I feel about you, but I can't. God, I wish I could believe me, life would be so much simpler with you. I think I should just text Wes and get going." I grab my phone and quickly text Wes. Owen comes and stands next to me, his hands in his pockets.

"Don't apologise Rose, you can't help how you feel. Am I right in thinking a certain biker is the one who has your feelings?" He asks, smiling.

"Yeah, and I really don't want to like him either. I meant what I said earlier though, Rip and I aren't together. It's all just a messy situation." I sigh.

"Well I can't say I ain't disappointed, but I wouldn't want you pretending with me. Whatever you decide, be happy." Owen says, leans in and kisses my cheek.

"I'll go round up Caden for you." He turns and walks back in the house. I sniffle and wipe away a lone tear. God damn it! Why can't I want Owen. My heart is one twisted bitch that clearly likes messing with me.

Wes shows up around ten minutes later and Caden excitedly runs out to his truck.

"Thank you for having us and, well, being so understanding." I say, giving Owen a small smile. He returns my smile, and shrugs.

"Anytime." He replies.

I lean up and kiss his cheek, mindful that Zack is watching us. I make a quick move, grabbing Zack in a hug and giving him a kiss and raspberry on his cheek.

"Ewww, get off me! Girls have cooties!" He giggles. I let him go and he runs back inside.

"Well, I'll catch you around?" I ask.

"Always, I will try and catch you at work on your first day. I might even treat you to a canteen muffin." He teases.

"You better! See you tomorrow then." I wave over my shoulder and jump in the truck with Wes, he's grinning from ear to ear.

"What?" I ask. He just shakes his head.

"I see that's more kissing then Mum. Why

do the guys have to keep kissing you?" Caden moans, making gagging sounds from the back of the truck. Wes bursts out laughing. I laugh and thump Wes in the arm.

"Dude, you may not think it because she's your ma, but she's damn hot." Wes answers, laughing at Caden's reaction. Caden's face scrunches up like Wes has gone mad.

"I know Mum's pretty, but she's a mum." Caden argues back.

"Alright, that's enough thank you. Caden honey, I'm a lot more than just a mum, remember that. I am your mum and that's fine, but there is always more to a person than just one thing." I say.

"I have no idea what you're saying." Caden answers back. Wes snorts back his laughter.

"For example, you're not just a kid. You're a boy who likes playing, you like movies and you're very caring. See, you're a lot of things." I say smiling.

"You forgot handsome, funny, fast as lightning, Jedi master and a bad-ass." Caden points out seriously.

I fight the urge to giggle.

"Fine, and all those too. Now please stop saying bad-ass."

Caden lets out a yawn. I notice Wes keeps

checking his rearview mirrors. I instinctively turn round and see a motorbike trailing us.

"It's Rip, he's just following, making sure we're good." Wes states.

"Why didn't he send someone else to do it. He normally would, right?" I ask confused. I thought that was the whole point of being the president.

"Wanted to do it himself." is all Wes says.

"Huh." I answer, still looking back over my shoulder. We pull up at the house and I notice Rip stops further back, just watching. I jump down from the truck and turn to face him. We both just stare at each other. He's too far away for me to see his face properly.

Caden calls me inside. I turn and make my way into the house, Rip still there on his bike watching. I walk inside and close the front door, only then do I hear the rumbling of pipes in the distance. I see to Caden and get him to bed.

Bringing his washing down I load the washing machine up. Wes joins me and hands me a beer.

"Why you putting a wash on at near enough ten at night?" He asks, taking a long pull of his beer.

"Because, I start my new job tomorrow, and I'm back to fitting in housework as and when I can." I say, taking a sip of beer. I lean against the washing machine and rub my neck.

"What time you got to start?"

"Not until two, but I figured if I get the washing done tonight, I can dry it and put it away before work in the morning. Caden's sleeping over at Daisy's tomorrow as I won't be home until three AM." I say, not looking forward to the twelve hour shift. I yawn.

"You working that all week?" Wes asks.

"No, only three days of that shift, but Daisy is having Caden for the week. They've booked some cabin for a little holiday. So as much as I'm working, I also get a little break." I say smiling.

"That's good. So, you and Owen?" Wes asks wiggling his eyebrows.

"There is no me and Owen. We kissed, that's it. I don't feel anything for him in that way. We're just friends." I sigh.

"Rip?" Wes says questioning. I look up him and raise an eyebrow in question.

"Oh come on. You've got it bad for him and he has it damn bad for you. So come on then, why are you both being stupid?" Wes asks bluntly.

"I'm not being stupid. You know what's going down with the club, the cartel, you bloody well know more about it than me. I have a son to care for! I will not end up like Lily, or risk my son's life. As for Rip, I've got too much baggage for him anyway. Easier for him to cut me loose. I don't think he ever thought it through properly. Still, it's not like anything ever came of it all anyway. Can't miss what we didn't have. We can both just move on with our lives as normal." I say shrugging. Wes surprises me by throwing his head back and roaring with laughter.

"Oh fuckin' hell darlin'. Did you rehearse that little speech to convince me or yourself? Shit, you know as well as I do that you'd be protected. You could get hit by a bus tomorrow or be in a car crash."

"Err, thanks?" I say sarcastically.

"What I'm saying, if you just god damn listen, is anything can happen from one day to the next. You want to spend your entire life being careful? Playing it safe? Then by all means go on. But you do that, and you'll spend the rest of your life thinking 'what if' and feeling full of regret. Life is too damn short to screw it up by being scared to love. Because let's face it darlin', Rip makes you shit scared. This whole business with the Cartel was just the perfect excuse to keep him out." Wes states.

I'm taken aback by his harshness and the bluntness of his words. We both just stand in silence for a moment, staring each other down.

"Well fuck me, you've just called me out on

my shit." I sigh, my lips fighting back a smile. Wes roars with laughter and pulls me in for a hug and kisses the top of my head.

"Come on, let's get you to bed ready for your first day tomorrow. God knows you'll blame me if you don't get enough sleep." Wes says, pulling me towards the stairs. I stop and turn to him and kiss his cheek goodnight. Before I reach the top step, I spin round and shout to him.

"Oh, Wes?!"

"Yeah?"

"Can you take me to get the truck in the morning?"

"I will take you to work and drop you off, then bring the truck to your work ready for when you finish your shift. Now go to damn sleep!" He yells back.

"Alright, alright no need to get your balls in a twist." I snort.

"Night Wes, thank you!" I shout.

I don't hear his reply as I head to bed. It takes me a moment to fall asleep, all because of one beautiful biker. I wonder what he's doing right now, who he's doing. That thought makes my stomach roll. This whole thing is crazy. I mean, I've known him, what, two to three weeks? We've only had sex once and that was a quickie in the ladies toilets. It was a good quickie, but still. None of it screams relationship, I shouldn't be feeling the way I do. I should be excited and nervous for my first day at my new job tomorrow.

"God damn you Rip." I curse out loud to my dark bedroom. Eventually I manage to drift off, but of course I dream of him.

CHAPTER EIGHT

The next morning I wake feeling groggy, wishing I could just sleep that bit longer after having such a restless night.

After showering I check on Caden and see how he's getting on with packing for his holiday.

"Hey buddy, how's it going?" I ask as I walk into the room. He's sitting on the bed in his pants watching cartoons.

"All done Mum." He says, pointing to his little suitcase. I open it up to find a pair of pants and a toothbrush.

"Caden, you can't just take a pair of pants and a toothbrush for a holiday. Also, get your butt up and get dressed. Daisy and Carter will be here in less than an hour." I say switching the TV off. Caden huffs and gets up off of the bed, grabbing his clothes and walking out of the room to the bathroom.

"Alright woman, geez! Stop busting my balls!" He shouts over his shoulder. I freeze, feeling my eyes widen.

"Caden." I growl through my teeth. Caden realising he's way overstepped, shouts quickly back.

"Sorry Mum, didn't mean to. My bad." He slams the bathroom door quickly before I can chew him out for it. I sigh and let out a little giggle to myself.

I pack his clothes and bring his suitcase downstairs. Wes is leaning against the kitchen counter drinking a coffee. I watch him as he reads something off his phone. He's smiling. I don't think I've ever seen Wes smile like this before, his whole face has lit up.

"Who's the girl?" I ask. Wes makes quick work of putting his phone away.

"No one, just a joke text is all." He answers, drinking his coffee.

"Yeah, sure it was. If you want to keep it to yourself that's fine, I won't drill you. Yet." I tease, pouring myself a coffee.

Wes just grunts in response.

"So, all ready for your first day?" Wes asks.

"Yeah, is it weird that I'm not excited or

nervous? I'm just meh. Don't get me wrong, I'm chuffed to have got the job and to have new beginnings and all that jazz, but I think once you've worked in one hospital, you've worked in them all." I say shrugging. Before Wes can respond Caden comes barrelling in the kitchen.

"They're here! Oh yeah baby, holiday time!" He shouts then runs back out again to answer the door. Wes and I just look at each other and burst out laughing.

"God, there really is no mistaking that he's your son." Wes chuckles. I flip him off.

Daisy and Carter walk in and Daisy pulls me in for a hug.

"You've not slept, what's happened?" she whispers in my ear.

"Nothing major, I promise. Do I really look that bloody bad?" I reply. Not satisfied with my answer she takes my hand and drags me out back to talk. No one questions or asks where we are going.

Once outside Daisy crosses her arms and taps her foot.

"Spill." Daisy demands.

"Fine, but don't go all motherly on me." I say in warning. I tell her everything that went down with Rip but I slightly change up the part about the Cartel, just saying bad guys. By the end of it

Daisy is smiling ear to ear.

"He's getting through those walls, isn't he?" Daisy says happily.

"Daisy, I swear if you repeat this I will punch you right in the tit." I warn her. She giggles, knowing I'm full of shit. She crosses her heart in promise.

"God, I can't stop thinking about him. He's constantly on my mind. In bed when I'm trying to sleep, watching TV, now. God damn it! No matter what I do I can't stop thinking about him. He's like herpes, you know, never going away and always flares up when you don't want it too. God, I need to see a shrink." I wail. Daisy just laughs.

"Oh Rose, I don't think I've ever seen you this twisted over a guy before. Even dick, he never messed with your head like Rip is right now. I mean, yeah, he hurt you, but this is something completely different. I probably wouldn't tell him he's like herpes though, but that's just my opinion." Daisy snorts. I can't help but laugh.

"Oh this is just all bollocks. I hate feeling like this Daisy. I feel vulnerable. He has the ability to hurt me, you know? I didn't want to let him in, I really didn't. He's managed somehow to do it, the bastard. And what's really funny it didn't take much at all!" I say rubbing my temples, feeling a headache coming on.

"You need to tell him how you feel." Daisy

points out.

"Uh, no. Not happening. He has the power now, not knowing how I feel, imagine what how he could hurt me if he knew." I say, rubbing my chest over my heart.

"You know what, I used to think you were my big badass sister, not scared of anything. The truth is you're a coward, you have an actual chance of happiness and because you're too worried about what might happen if it goes wrong, you wont take that chance. Now I don't play the sympathy card ever but look what happened to me. I still, after all I went through, what I was married to...I still took the leap and trusted Carter. Now, for gods sake, grow a pair of bollocks and actually give Rip a chance. I promise if he ever hurts you I will be first in line to kick his arse." Daisy chastises me. I sigh. I know she's right.

"I hate it when you're right, do you know that?! Also, I'd pay good money to watch you try and kick Rip's arse." I giggle. Daisy thumps me in the arm.

"Just promise me you'll try with Rip. I really think you guys would be amazing together and it'd be nice to see you happy." Daisy says, hugging me.

"Whatever." I mumble.

I wave off Caden, after making him promise me not to be naughty for Daisy and Carter. I also made him promise not to moon people at the pool or pretend a snickers bar is a floater. He did that once at our local pool. It got evacuated.

I'm getting ready for work and putting on my new pink scrubs. I put my hair up in a messy bun, grab my bag and head downstairs.

"Oh hot nurse, you can check my temperature anytime." Wes says as I put on my comfy flats.

"Oh shut up. It's scrubs, there's nothing sexy about scrubs. Now come on chauffeur, I need to get to work." I say grabbing my bag.

Wes drops me right outside the hospital entrance. He says he will drop the keys in later and show me where he's parked the truck.

Everyone on the ward seems nice enough. It's busy and there isn't much time for a break.

"I can't believe you ditched me." I hear from behind me. I whirl around and see Owen smirking.

"Oh my god Owen. I am so sorry, it has been crazy busy. I haven't even stopped for a break yet. What time is it?" I ask.

"It's nearly seven. Don't worry, I guessed

that. Anyway, I'm finished for the day, I just thought I'd drop this to you as promised." Owen says handing me a brown paper bag.

I open it, look inside and smile.

"A canteen muffin. Thank you." I say.

"Rose, you're needed in bay three!" is shouted from across the ward.

"Sorry, I've got to run, will catch you next time though. Okay?" I say, running off to see the patient in bay three.

The rest of the shift carries on like that until I finish. Wes couldn't even show me where the truck was parked, I only had time for him to give me the keys.

Shelby, the nurse I will be replacing when she goes on maternity leave walks with me down to the car park to find the truck.

"Well, I don't think I've ever seen two good looking guys show up for someone before." She says winking at me.

"Oh, them. They are just friends, well, Wes is kind of my brother in law I guess. Your husband picking you up?" I ask. She nods and rub her belly.

"That was one crazy shift. Is it always like that?" I ask.

"No, unfortunately for you that kind of crazy only happens every so often. Just bad luck on your part that it was like that on your first day." she shrugs.

We walk around and I spot the truck. Her husband beeps, waiting for her, and we say our goodbyes. I walk to the truck and jump in. I pull out the muffin Owen got me earlier and shove the entire thing in my mouth. I'm so hungry.

I pull off and start my journey back, thinking about what I can make up quickly and quietly when I get back. It's 2;30am and I don't want to wake Wes. I yawn and turn up the air con to try and keep myself awake. I notice headlights behind me. My skin prickles. I shake it off, telling myself I'm being silly, it's just because it's late at night and I'm tired.

Biting my bottom lip anxiously I decide to see if I am just being silly. I take different turnings and they follow every time. My heart is beating fast. There's no one else on the roads. It's the dead of night. The problem is I've taken so many turnings I actually don't know where I am.

I am completely lost.

"Fuck!" I yell. I keep checking in my rear view mirror, it's only a matter of time before they realise I'm completely lost. Then what? They'll probably run me off the road. Shit. I grab my purse and my phone. I hit the call button, calling Wes. It rings and rings, no answer.

"Shit!" I hit the steering wheel. I don't have

anyone else's number apart from Daisy's, I only got the phone for the job. I decide to check the maps app on the phone. I do a quick glance and recognise the name of the road on the map. Satan's Outlaws clubhouse. Glancing in my rear view mirror again I realise I don't have much choice. I carry on driving towards the club-house.

The Cartel must realise where I'm going be-cause the next thing I know the truck is being rammed. I scream and grip the steering wheel to control the truck. I put my foot down, seeing the building up ahead. The car makes chase and drives alongside me. My foot is flat down on the gas, I am praying I make it to those gates. I no-tice their window goes down and the next thing I know I'm being shot at.

The window shatters, there's glass all over me. I scream and try and duck down as low as I can as they fire off another round. I beep the horn, holding it down constantly in the hope that who ever is at the clubhouse will hear the noise and come out. I quickly turn into the club-house and I drive straight through the metal gates. All I can hear is the sound of metal on metal and the window screen cracking. I pull up and slam the breaks on, screeching to a halt. I look behind me to see the car drive off. I sigh and release my iron tight grip on the steering wheel. I scream as my door is wrenched open. Khan is stood there with a gun aimed at me.

"Fuck." He yells. He puts his gun away. I literally jump to him and wrap my arms tightly around him.

"Whoa, shit. You're trembling darlin'. It's okay, you're safe." Khan says soothing me. I don't loosen my grip. Khan doesn't say anything else, he picks me up and carries me towards the clubhouse. I hear a few of the guys come out. They curse.

"Secure the gate, the best you can. Take shifts in patrolling it until we can get it completely secure again...and for fucks sake, one of you find Pres!" He orders. I don't look up, I'm still clinging to Khan, burying my face in his chest. My whole body is shaking uncontrollably.

"It's alright darlin', I got you." I hear loud music coming from the distance. Khan takes me into a room and sits on a sofa with me, gently rubbing my back still holding me not letting go.

"It's okay. We're in Rips office. You're safe, I'm just going to put you down and pour you a drink, okay? It help with the shock." Khan says gently. He moves and pours me a drink. I knock it back, coughing, it burns. I shake the glass for another and Khan refills it. I down that too, feeling it warm my body. I'm still shaking but I feel a little better.

There's a loud commotion from just outside

the door. Rip barges in wearing just his jeans. His perfect tattooed body is on display. He rushes towards me and crouches in front of me, pulling me into his arms. I let a few tears fall as he comforts me. I am nuzzled close into Rip's chest.

It is then I smell it. Perfume. My whole body locks tight and I go completely rigid. I push back and jump up to move away from him. Rip stands and comes towards me.

"It's okay sweetheart, I've got you." He says approaching me. I keep stepping back and holding my hand up in front of me, trying to keep him away from me. I keep going until I hit my back against the wall.

"Get away from me." I whisper, wrapping my arms around myself. Rip stops. A confused look on his face.

"Sweetheart. I got you. Ain't no one gonna fuckin' hurt you." He says gently, thinking I'm freaking out from the car chase and being shot at.

"Too late, you already have." I say with a whisper as I let a tear fall.

"Perfume." is all I say.

I watch as realisation hits him. He sighs and rubs his face.

"Shit, sweetheart it's nothing...fuck! I..." I put my hand up, stopping him. I shake my head.

"It's fine, it's not like we were together, right? You don't need to apologise." I say trying my hardest to keep the pain out of my voice, but by the look on Rip's face I'm not doing a very good job. He looks as though I've slapped him. We both just stand and stare at each other.

"Rip, baby, come back to bed. I'm getting lonely." A beautiful tall blonde says, walking in wearing nothing but a bed sheet that she's wrapped around her. I blanch. I curl into myself further. I watch as Rip grips his hair and looks to the ceiling.

"Get the fuck out Darcy!" Rip barks, not even looking at her. His eyes never leave mine. I watch as she jumps, clearly confused. Her eyes flicker back and forth between Rip and me. Her face hardens and her eyes narrow.

"Rip, baby. Come on, I'll do that thing that you like. I need you." she whines.

I feel the bile rise up, and this time I blanch like I've been slapped. Rips watching me, his face turns to stone cold anger.

"Someone get the fucking bitch out of here now!" Rip roars, he spins round, pinning Darcy with a glare.

"Never fucking come back to the clubhouse again! You hear me?" Rip growls. Darcy pales in fear for a second before she straightens her back and pins me with an evil glare.

"I can't believe you're kicking me out for that ugly skank!" she yells and points to me.

"He will get bored of you, he will come back to me. He always fucking comes back to me. I can give him exactly what he wants, you bitch!" she screams as Khan fireman lifts her out of the room.

Rip turns back to me. He walks towards me and tucks my hair behind my ear. He leans in to kiss me and I turn my head.

"I can smell her on you." I rasp. Rip freezes and steps back. He picks up a glass and throws it across the room.

"Fuck!" He roars. I jump as the glass smashes against the wall. I can't be here any longer, I need out. I need air. I rush past him to leave, but he turns and grabs me, holding my back to his front.

"Please, I just want to go home." I whisper.

"It's not safe. You're staying here." Rip says in my ear.

"Just let me go Rip, please. I won't go home but I need out of here. I have to get away from you." I rasp, fighting back the emotion.

"Fuck, I got through didn't I? I already broke through and now I've gone and fucked it up." He states. He lets me go and I stop in the doorway and turn to face him.

"I'm not just rebuilding them Rip, I'm mak-

ing sure I never let you close to my heart again."
I say and walk away, not looking back. I make it
outside to the back of the clubhouse. I go around
the corner where no one can see me, and I break.
The tears fall and my body racks with sobs. I'm
not sure how long I'm there for, but I hear someone approach. I look up and see Trudy. She offers
me a sympathetic smile. She walks towards me
and pulls me into her arms, offering me comfort.
This just makes me cry more.

"Oh my poor girl, shh now, it's okay. Come
on, let's take you inside." she soothes.

She takes me to a small bedroom. It has a
double bed, side table and a bathroom attached.
It's very basic. She flicks on the lamp on the side
table and pulls the curtains.

"It's only basic but it will do for you. This
will be your room for as long as you're here.
We will sort out getting your stuff across, don't
worry about a thing. I will have the boys bring
you in some draws so you can at least put some
things away." She says smiling.

"Um, what?" I ask confused.

"It's not safe for you, being out there. So you
are to stay here until things calm down. Don't
worry, you're safe here." she answers.

"I can't, I have my new job. I have to go to
work tomorrow. I have Caden, I can't just stay
here and hide away." I state.

"It's taken care of sweetie, Carter has been informed about what's going on. They are going to extend their holiday for a few more days, to keep Caden safe. As for your job, you or I can ring them in the morning." Trudy answers.

"Okay." is all I say. I don't have it in me to fight. I will stay hidden in here and avoid Rip.

Trudy gives me a t-shirt to wear to bed and goes to leave. She stops in the doorway and turns to me.

"I'm not making excuses for my son, but I hope you find it in your heart to forgive him." Trudy says with a small smile, and leaves, closing the door behind her. I sit for a moment staring at the wall, before deciding to shower and get into bed.

I lie awake and sob quietly into my pillow, my emotions are all over the place. I feel hurt and betrayed, but I also feel angry at myself for letting Rip in. Even if it was just a little bit. I'm not even that upset by the nights events. Don't get me wrong, I've never been so scared in my life, but seeing her, and smelling her on Rip. Well, that hurt more than it should have considering we aren't even together. I rub my chest. I eventually drift off to sleep, and again my dreams are plagued by Rip.

CHAPTER NINE

I wake the next morning and I can hear people walking about and talking. I don't get up, I just lay there, staring at the wall. Eventually nature calls and I have to use the bathroom.

Once I've take care of business, I check my phone for any messages from Daisy. She's sent me a picture of Caden dive bombing into the pool. I smile and sigh, putting my phone down. I stare out of the window, there's nothing there, just a wire fence and fields. I grab my scrubs to put on. I have nothing else here. I take off the t-shirt and throw it on the bed for now. I bend over, just putting one leg in my trouser when the door swings open. I quickly look over my shoulder and see

Rip, freshly showered in jeans and a black fitted t-shirt. Taken by surprise I stumble and fall to the floor.

"Ow, shit! That hurt." I groan, rolling to my side. I put the other leg in and stand up.

"What's the matter? Haven't you heard of knocking before?" I yell, placing my hands on my hips.

Rips eyes are bright and his lips twitch, fighting a smile.

"You always wear that?" He asks.

"What, my scrubs? It's because I have nothing else to wear." I say in defence.

"No, do you always wear underwear like that? Even when you're working?" Rip asks.

Crap. I forgot. I'm standing here in my scrubs trousers and my navy lace bra. Deciding I'm going to pretend I'm not at all fazed by his presence, I shrug nonchalantly.

"I always like to wear pretty matching underwear. Do you know how many people I've seen in A&E with mismatched underwear on? Or tatty underwear with holes in? I like to make sure that will never be me." I say, screwing up my face. Although if you get hit by a bus, what underwear you are wearing is the least of your worries.

"Is that right sweetheart?" Rip grins, and god

I have to do everything in my power not to swoon. Last nights events hit me and I immediately remember why I'm hurt and pissed off at him.

"So is there something you want?" I ask, reaching for my scrub top.

"Yeah, Wes is dropping your stuff off in a bit. Came to see if you wanted some breakfast." He asks.

"Sure." I answer. Rip smiles. I look away.

He's herpes, he's herpes. I repeat in my head over and over. Rip places his hand on the small of my back, guiding me. I tense at his touch and move slightly, making him drop his hand.

"Just through here. He holds a door open to a large kitchen area. Trudy is at the stove frying up bacon, she turns and smiles.

"Hey honey, how did you sleep?" she asks, pulling me in for a hug.

"I've slept better, but not too bad considering." I answer honestly.

"Oh honey. Well, today you can just rest and put your feet up. Now there's fresh coffee in the pot and the food will be ready in a minute, but be quick now because once the guys descend, you won't get a look in, they're like animals." she says with a wink.

I turn around and Rip hands me a coffee, I

take it and mumble my thanks. I take a seat and Rip sits right next to me, his arm and leg brushing mine. I let out a shuddering breath. I slowly look up to Rip, his eyes are watching me intently. He leans forward and gently strokes and tucks my hair behind my ear. I lick my suddenly dry lips, his eyes flick to my mouth. He leans in and pauses just millimetres from my mouth, I can feel his breath brush across my lips.

"Say it." He whispers across my lips.

"Huh?" I say confused.

"I'm not going to kiss you unless you ask me to." He says quietly.

" I don't, I..." I mumble.

"I've gotta hear you say you want it sweetheart. Tell me you want my mouth on yours. Tell me." He rumbles.

I lean in closer, my lips grazing his. My body wants him. I want him to kiss me. Then the memories of last night hit me.

"I can't, I just can't Rip, last night...you...it killed...." suddenly the door bursts open and in come Khan, Mammoth and Rubble, followed by Wes. I jump back away from Rip. I cover my face with my hands and shake my head. What was I thinking, he was fucking another girl last night. Christ, he's kryptonite, and not just any kryptonite, herpes infected kryptonite. He makes you weak and then he takes over you, never really going away, even when you're not with him. He is dormant in your mind and heart, never letting you forget or ignore him. Being locked up in here is going to be the hardest week of my life.

"Hey Flo, how you doin' darlin'?" I lift my face from my hands and look into Mammoth's kind face, I smile.

"I'm okay Mammoth, really. Just a little tired I guess."

"Why you calling her Flo?" Wes asks, taking a seat on the other side of me.

"She fixed me up from the other day, a proper little Florence nightingale." Rubble winks. I smile and roll my eyes.

Wes puts his arm around me, pulling me in close and kisses the top of my head.

"She looks pretty hot in nurses' scrubs too." Wes says teasingly. I jab him in his side, he just grunts and laughs.

"Did you bring my clothes?" I ask.

"Yeah darlin' they're in your room ready for you. Gotta say, you wear some sexy as fuck underwear." Wes winks at me as he pours his coffee.

"Oh my god Wes you're such a pervert, looking at my underwear. You'll start flashing women in parks next." I laugh. The guys around the table all laugh.

"Wes." Rip says pissed off. The whole table stops laughing. I turn to look at Rip who looks really pissed off, he's staring down Wes. I look to Wes who has a shit eating grin across his face.

"So darlin', you seeing that Owen guy again? It was only your first kiss, I think you should give him another chance." Wes says smiling, not taking his eyes off Rip. He's clearly goading him.

"What?" I ask.

Before I can do anything Rip has jumped from his seat and pulled Wes out of his chair. He has him pushed up against the wall. The guys all jump out of their seats, ready to intervene if they need to.

"You shut your fucking mouth." Rip growls at Wes. All Wes does is smile and shake his head.

"You're a fucking idiot, cous'. You know how you feel now hearing about that little kiss. Imagine if she fucked him. Now tell me how you're fucking feeling? After everything! You giving Blake shit about Lily, and here you are! Not just taking what she has to give, which is a fucking lot, but you should be on your damn knees thanking fucking god she even gave you a shot. So what you gonna do about it, hit me? Go on then, if it will make you feel better fucking hit me. I tell you now, you are putting far too much effort into being pissed at me. You should be fucking grovelling and giving her the damn world. Fucking coward." Wes says angrily.

Wes barely finishes his sentence when Rip's fist connects with his jaw. I jump out of my seat and go and stand in front of Wes.

"Enough! For fuck's sake!" I shout with both of my hands on their chests, separating them.

"Wes. Are you okay? Does it hurt?" I ask.

"A little." He says holding his nose.

"Good, because you fucking deserved it." I say. The guys all snicker and I even hear Trudy giggle. I turn to Rip who's smiling.

"I don't know what you're smiling for, Wes may have been out of line in getting involved and saying what he said, but he's right. You just proved me right. I know exactly what you are now." I say. I watch the smile fall from Rip's face. I move out of their way and turn to Trudy.

"I've suddenly lost my appetite, sorry Trudy." I turn and walk out of the room, leaving them all staring after me. Once in my room I grab some clothes out of my bag and go straight into the shower. I sob. I curl up into a ball on the floor, letting the water cascade over me. I cry, letting out everything I've kept in. I'm not a crier. I'm normally the strong one of the family. But for once Caden isn't here and I don't have to cover it up to protect him.

I hate that I'm feeling this way. I hate that I've let Rip make me feel this way. God I'm so bloody stupid. The first guy I start to fall for happens to be a player, president of an MC and I've been shot at because of him. Well, I've gone from having a very normal boring life filled with routine and no social life to being in what feels like my own bloody television drama.

"Nice one Rose." I say to myself as I wipe my eyes.

I stand and wash my hair, feeling a little better for letting it all out. I'm not looking forward to staying here one bit. I couldn't even make it through breakfast. I dry myself off, brush my teeth and put on clean underwear. I walk into my room to change into what clothes I had picked out, not looking up until I reach my bed. I jump back and let out a scream. Led on my bed with his arms behind his head, smiling, is Rip.

"What the fuck?" I yell.

His ice blue eyes travel hungrily over my near naked body. I'm wearing my black lace French knickers and matching black lace balconette bra with a towel wrapped round my head. I click my fingers, getting his attention.

"Eyes are up here. I will repeat, what the fuck?!" I say with my hands on my hips, tapping my foot.

"I brought you some breakfast, didn't want

you getting hungry." He points to the plate of food on the side.

"I said I lost my appetite. Now if you would bugger off so I can get dressed in peace that would be great." I state. I watch as his lips twitch and his beautiful ice blue eyes sparkle in amusement. He is herpes, he is herpes, I repeat in my head over and over.

Rip moves so he's standing in front of me. He is so close our bodies are just touching. I have to tilt my head back to look at him. His eyes roam over my face, he slowly leans in. He cups my face with one hand. I think he's going to kiss me and my eyes flutter closed. I suck in a breath.

"I'm sorry sweetheart, so fuckin' sorry." He whispers in my ear, then just walks out of the room and leaves me standing here. My eyes fly open and I feel heat in my veins. I storm over to the door and follow him out to the corridor.

"Enough!" I yell after him. He stops in his tracks and turns to face me.

"Just stop, okay? Just fucking stop whatever game you're playing with me! I can't take it anymore! I just…" I sigh, pinching my nose.

"Just leave me the hell alone." I say exasperated. I go to stomp back into the room when Rip calls me.

"Not a fuckin' chance!" He yells.

I stop and storm towards him. There is amusement in his eyes.

"Stop finding this so fucking amusing. I am not laughing. You're really starting to piss me off! So just back the fuck off!" I yell poking his chest.

Rip leans forward so his face is just an inch from mine.

"No." Rip says, smiling.

"Arggh! My god you're so annoying! I really want to punch you in the dick right now. You're so arrogant! Do you know what, when we shagged I didn't even come! You were the worst lay I've ever had. So Mr Arrogant, stick that in your pipe and smoke it!" I fume. Rip is still smiling, his arms crossed over his broad chest. God he looks so sexy right now. Herpes! He's herpes! I repeat in my head.

"Nice try sweetheart, I know you fuckin' loved it, I felt your pussy squeeze tight around my cock as you came hard." Rip says brazenly.

I gasp and also feel myself clench at the memory. Of course he's right but I'd be damned if I'm going to let him know that.

"And sweetheart, you might want to go back to your room now, because I think you've given my brothers enough of a show." Rip says with a wink.

I freeze and look around/ Rip and I are stood in the entrance to the bar area, where all the guys are sat smiling, and admiring my near naked state. I gasp, remembering I'm only wearing underwear and quickly cover myself. I run off back to my room with hoots and whistles from the guys.

"Alright that's enough. Don't look at my fuckin' woman again!" Rip yells.

"I AM NOT YOUR FUCKING WOMAN!" I shout before I slam the door behind me and lean against it.

My heart is beating wildly in my chest, I've never been so pissed off and turned on all at the same time. I wanted to punch him so hard then jump on him and shag his brains out. Talk about a complete head fuck.

The rest of the day I don't leave my room. Thankful that Wes has brought my kindle too, I lay down and read one of my favourite books. Meghan Quinn's The Virgin Romance Novelist to try and distract and cheer myself up. It works. I am full on belly laughing when someone knocks on the door.

"Come in." I yell, still chuckling from a particular funny scene in the book.

Raven sticks her head around the door and smiles.

"Hey, I heard all about what went down and figured you'd be hiding in here so I came to cheer you up, but it looks like I don't need too." She says, nodding to the kindle on my bed.

"It's a funny book." I say smiling.

Raven walks in and sits next to me on my bed. She nudges me with her shoulder.

"So you and Rip huh?" she asks, wiggling her eyebrows.

"There is no me and Rip. Why does everyone think there is?!" I moan.

"Oh I don't know, maybe because you two have it so bad for each other! The sexual tension around here is so strong I think I'm pregnant! I heard about the little spat you guys had this morning. Big Papa told me it was so heated that you were creating sparks. So yeah, you and Rip." Raven says laughing like I'm crazy.

"Yeah well, he slept with what's-her-name and that was immediately after he said he was a patient man who would wait for me to realise that I wanted him. So yeah, there may be sparks but I was starting to trust him and he let me down. I'm not ready for there to be a 'me and Rip'." I answer truthfully.

"Yeah, I heard about that too. That was a real prick move. Darcy is a prize bitch. I mean I've had to chuck that bitch out of the bar a few times for trying her luck with Big papa. Which is extra disgusting because she used to play with Patty when they were kids. She just wants the old lady title. She ain't the only one either, I've seen women throw themselves not only at Rip but the others for the chance to be an old lady." Raven states.

"Okay, don't take this the wrong way, but why? I mean it's nice and all that, but they are just men, it's not like they're all millionaires." I say confused. I mean I'm currently sat in a concrete room, there's no luxury about it.

"It's for the lifelong protection, for the security of family. You may not see it, but every single one of those guys would lay down their life for you now. You're family even without the cut and the old lady label. But because you don't have that cut or title, the biker whores like Darcy don't have to respect you. It means you wouldn't get the same respect out on the street as you would if you were a Satan's Outlaw. You are lucky to have a supportive, loving family, most of the people that came to join Satans' didn't." Raven says with a small smile.

"Okay, I get it. I guess I should feel bad for Darcy then?" I ask.

"Oh hell no! That bitch is evil. You can have a shitty home life and still be a nice person. She decided to be a bitch."

Raven sits with me for a while and talks me into going to the kitchen for some food. I'm relieved to see no one in there. We make ourselves a sandwich and take it to eat outside as it's so nice. While out there I make a quick call to the hospital to apologise. They inform me that they've already been contacted by the Satan's Outlaws and are, effective immediately, terminating my contract. They will not have anyone who is gang affiliated. Hanging up I walk back over to Raven and sit down.

"I really, really need to get drunk." I say slamming my head down on the picnic table. Raven laughs and rubs my back.

"Oh honey, I'm guessing the work call didn't go so well?" she asks.

"Nope, because I'm gang affiliated, they've fired me effective immediately."

"Shit. That's not right, this isn't a gang." Raven comments.

"Yup, pretty much. Now I'm out of a job. I now have to try and find another one soon before they deport Caden and I. Oh and my mum and dad were going to move over here because I got that job. Fuckety, fuck, fuck!" I yell.

"It'll work out I'm sure. Now, as for getting drunk it just so happens it's party night tonight in the clubhouse. Things can get a little crazy, but if you're up for it you better go and get yourself ready girl." Raven winks.

"Damn right! I'm on it. What time?" I ask.

"I will come get you in about an hour or so. Just remember to have an open mind, okay?" She states.

"Open mind, got it. I will see you in a bit." I say skipping off excitedly, leaving Raven laughing. I'm laughing when I turn the corner to go to my room.

I run into a hard chest. Arms come around me to stop me falling back. I look up into those ice blue eyes.

"Why are you so happy?" He asks. My eyes drop to his mouth. God he's so good looking, it's really not fair.

"Sweetheart?" He says chuckling.

"Huh? Oh, umm, just got fired. But Raven said there's a party tonight, so I'm looking forward to that." I say smiling. Rip's smile falls.

"You ain't coming to no party sweetheart." He states.

"What? Yes I am." I argue back.

"No fuckin' way, it ain't for you. It will get wild. You wouldn't like it." He argues back.

I push back out of his arms and move off past him.

"Fuck you Rip, I'm going. You cannot tell me

what to do." I yell over my shoulder and flip him off. I slam my door before he has a chance to respond.

CHAPTER TEN

I shower and change my outfit about ten times. I finally decide on a basic dress. It has black capped sleeves, a square neckline and it is form fitting to the knee. It's a bit reserved for a biker party but I don't have any sexy biker party type clothes.

I spend time on my hair, adding to my loose natural curls and putting product in to keep the shape. I apply soft make-up. I never really wear much, so I just stick with what I know.

There's a knock at the door and Raven walks in wearing a pair of skinny jeans, killer spiked heeled ankle boots and a black glittered cami top, with her property of Big Papa cut. She has smoky eyes and blood red lipstick. With her long Black hair, she really does look like a biker babe. You'd never know she's a grandma.

"Wow!" I say whistling.

"Thanks babe, good to know I've still got it after all these years." She says with a wink.

"How old are you?! I know it's rude to ask but, well, you look late thirties, early forties at a push." I ask.

"I'm turning fifty next year honey." Raven smiles. I stand with my mouth wide open.

"Oh wow! You're going to have to tell me your beauty routine. You look unbelievable." I say in awe.

"So, what you planning on wearing?" she asks, sitting on my bed. I gesture with my hands up down pointing to my outfit.

"Oh sweetie. I'm sorry, it's just it looks like you're off to work at the office. You got nothing else?" She asks. I shake my head.

"Right, hold on, I'm calling Trudy." Raven says pulling out her phone.

"Trudy, we have an emergency. Yup, Flo has nothing to wear for tonight. Can you grab what you can and head on over to her room? Yup. Oh, and Trudy, bring make-up too. Yeah we're gonna really mess with your boy." Raven laughs into the phone.

"Mess with her boy?" I ask raising my brow.

"Just leave it to us, we will have you looking like hot biker babe." Raven winks. I shake my head because there's no point in arguing with her.

We hear the music vibrate through the walls as the party gets underway. Trudy come barrelling through the door a moment later with a big holdall. She dumps it on the bed and starts pulling out various clothes.

"Here, try these." Raven hands me a pair black skinny jeans with revealing rips in them. I nod and take off my dress.

"On second thoughts, maybe she should just walk out like that. That would drive him nuts." Raven says, pointing to me standing here in my red lace push up bra, a matching red lace thong, and high heels. I snort back a laugh and roll my eyes.

"Honey you have a hot body! You should definitely flaunt it more." Raven says.

I take off my heels and put the jeans on. They are like a second skin. Raven hands me a metal looped belt to put around my hips while she rummages through the bag for a top.

"Ha! Got it." Raven says pulling out a black lace cami top. She holds it out to me.

"But it's see-through." I say holding it up.

"Trust me, with your red bra underneath you will look hot. You're not a mom tonight honey. You're a woman and you're going to have a damn good night and look fuckin' hot while doing it." Trudy states smiling.

I put on the cami top and tuck it into the jeans. Raven pushes me to sit on the bed and starts pulling out make-up.

A little while later she stands back and smiles at her work.

"Done. Now put your heels on and go look in the mirror." Raven orders.

I do just that and stand in front of the mirror in the bathroom. I barely recognise the woman looking back at me. My eye make-up is a light shimmer with winged eyeliner and what look like fake lashes. She has put blood red lipstick on me, which makes my lips look amazing. My outfit, although a little revealing, is really sexy. I turn slightly and look at my behind and see there's a rip right along the bottom.

"Oh my god you can see my arse!" I cry out.

"Yeah honey, that's kind of the point! Anyway it's only the bottom part. And you do have a fantastic ass. It's all that running around you do as a nurse. Now come on, tequila is waiting! We all need a drink!" Raven says, walking back into the room and bagging everything up.

"You look stunning sweetie." Trudy says grinning like a cheshire cat.

"Thanks." I say feeling a little awkward.

Just as we walk down the hall to the party, Raven and Trudy pull me to one side and warn me.

"Now remember, this is a biker party. You ain't seen nothing like this before. There will be some naked whores and some whores working, if you get what I mean." Trudy says. I nod, understanding. Raven and Trudy exchange a look and then we continue to the party.

They were right. It is nothing like I've ever seen. There are women prancing around in thongs. Some of the guys are slapping their asses as they pass. I swear one of the bikers is getting sucked off in the corner while drinking his whisky. The music is heavy rock and it is loud. I can smell weed, but there's no sign of any other drugs use.

We make our way to the bar. Bikers whistle as we walk in the whores give us filthy looks. Raven orders our drinks and a bottle of tequila. We make our way to the table. The whole time my eyes are scanning the room, looking for Rip.

Once we sit down, Raven pours us some shots and we knock back a couple. I welcome the buzz and feel myself relax a little more.

Mammoth and Rubble come and say hi to us and chat for a minute until a whore starts dancing around them, distracting them.

It has been at least an hour, and I've lost count how many tequila shots we've had now. I notice Trudy had stopped a little while ago as she's the designated driver, who comes over with Big Papa and joins us.

"Hey Big Papa, Max. Oh, sorry, do I call you wheels here? What's the protocol?" I ask giggling.

"You can call me whatever you like darlin'. My son pulled his head outta his ass yet?!" He asks. I shake my head.

"Nope, he shagged that Darcy. I let him in, and he shagged her." I say drunkenly.

"Sorry darlin, I'll kick his ass for you." Max says smiling, and god, Rip looks so much like him. He has his mum's eyes but he's just like his dad.

"You blabber the truth when you're drunk or what?" Raven shouts over the music.

"Yup, it's how you know I'm drunk. I speak only the truth." I laugh. Raven smiles at me.

More drinks flow and there's more laughter. Raven and I have got up and started dancing around to some older classic rock music. I spin around laughing and when I come to a stop, sitting just in front of me is Rip. His eyes aren't on me. They are focused on Darcy who is currently in nothing but a thong, giving him a lap dance. I feel like I've been slapped. Coming up behind me Raven sees why I've stopped.

"That son of a bitch! I'm going to kick his ass." she roars. She goes to storm over to him, but I grab her arm, halting her. She turns to me and I shake my head.

I look back to Rip and our eyes meet. It takes him a moment in the dark room to realise it's me. When he does his jaw sets hard and his eyes sweep my body. I pull Raven away and walk back to our table, purposefully putting more of a swing in my step than usual.

We reach the table and I see Raven tell Big Papa and Max what Rip is up to. I down another shot, then I make my way back on the dance floor as Nine Inch Nails' 'Closer' blares over the speakers. I smile to myself, Rip wants to play. It's fucking game on.

I start dancing right in the centre of everyone. I sway my hips seductively, my hands caressing my body. I drop low and rise slowly, swaying my hips. As I do that, the guys are hooting and cheering. I smile, feeling powerful. I don't look at Rip. I lift my top slowly, eventually taking it off completely. I smile when the guys cheer and throw it away. I move to Rubble who is sat down and I turn just in front of him. I keep my legs straight but I bend down and slap my arse, winking at him. He whistles and roars with laughter. I walk away and grab a chair, I straddle the chair and on the lines in the song 'I want to fuck you like an animal' I move my hips suggestively. My eyes land on Rip and I blow him a kiss. His body is rigid, and he looks like he's about ready to either throw me on the table and fuck me or kill me. Either way the look has me turned on.

I sit down and straddle the chair. I lean back, holding one hand on the back of the chair and I run the other slowly from my throat down over the curve of my breast, down to between my legs. Before my hand even reaches my stomach I'm being lifted over a shoulder. I let out a scream in surprise. The whole room erupts with laughter and cheers.

I lean up and realise it's Rip carrying me out of the room and down the hall.

"Put me the fuck down! " I yell.

Rip walks into a room and slams the door behind us.

"With fuckin' pleasure sweetheart." He puts me down so quickly that I wobble on my feet. He moves, standing toe to toe with me.

"What the fuck do you think you were doing?" He roars angrily.

"Having a good time. I don't see how me dancing in jeans and bra is an issue when there are naked women walking around. You seemed to be having a fuckin' good time with Darcy. Equal rights sweetheart!" I yell back at him, panting in anger.

"She came over and started dancing in front of me. I didn't ask her to and if you bothered to look back before you start fuckin' stripping for my club I told her to fuck off." He growls back at me.

I pause for a minute, not sure what to shout back.

"You're drunk aren't you sweetheart." He states.

"Yeah, and so what?! I was having fun." I bite back crossing my arms.

"So you do this thing don't you when you're drunk, you speak the god's honest truth. Don't you?" He says smiling. My heart rate picks up, and I look away.

"Was that dance in there for my benefit sweetheart?" He asks, tucking a strand of hair behind my ear. I huff, ignoring him.

He leans in close and speaks softly in my ear.

"You want me to put you on my desk and fuck you until you're screaming my name?" My whole body shivers and I clench my legs tighter at the thought.

Shaking myself out my daze I push him out of the way and storm past him. I stop at the door and turn and face him.

"Yeah Rip, I do want you to fuck me on your table, but there's no damn way I would let you after what you've done to me. So you'll have to go fuck one of your whores, I'm sure they'd be more than happy to help." I go to open the door but don't get the chance as I am being pulled away and pinned up against the wall. Rip has hold of my hands above my head. I don't get a chance to ask him what he's doing. His mouth comes crashing down on mine. The kiss is hungry, passionate. I kiss him back with everything I've got. I moan into his mouth, as his other hand moves around my behind, lifting my leg and wrapping it around his waist, pushing his hard erection into that perfect spot. I move my hips for friction and he growls into my mouth.

He trails kisses down my neck, nipping and biting. I moan.

He lets go of my hands and grabs my other leg, lifting me off the ground. I wrap my legs around his waist.

"Hold on sweetheart." He says as he carries me and perches me on his desk. I start frantically undoing his belt and jeans, while Rip takes off his t-shirt. I stare at his hard, muscled, tattooed body. I run my tongue along my bottom lip. Rip lets out a throaty growl and leans forward, taking my mouth, pushing me to lie back across his desk. He makes quick work removing my bra. His mouth is on my nipple. I let out a moan.

"God you are so fuckin' beautiful." Rips says kissing and nipping at my breast.

He takes off my heels and throws them then undoes my jeans and pulls them off with one tug.

"Fuck sweetheart." is all he says before he tears away my thong and takes me in his mouth. I throw my head back and cry out at the feel of his mouth and tongue on my clit.

"Oh fuck Rip!" I shout. He stops and smiles at me as he frees his long thick cock from his jeans. He just stands there for a second stroking himself, looking at me. Watching him has me desperate for him.

"Rip please." I beg. He reaches into his jean pocket and pulls out a condom. He rips it open with his teeth and I watch as he slowly slides it down his shaft.

Positioning himself at my entrance he leans forward, kissing me. With one quick thrust he fills me. We both let out a moan. His hips start moving and I wrap my legs around his waist. He leans back watching himself fill me over and over.

"Fuck you're the most beautiful thing I've ever fuckin' seen." Rip pants. He quickens his pace, hitting that perfect spot harder and faster.

"Yes! Rip don't fucking stop!" I cry out as I feel my orgasm descend.

"Fuck, I can feel you milking my cock sweetheart. Fuck. Come on my cock!" He growls. I throw my head back and my whole body tenses as I reach my orgasm. It comes hard and fast and I cry out his name. Rip picks up his pace, slamming into me and releasing his orgasm. He throws his head back and lets out a throaty groan.

We are both panting. Rip's eyes meet mine. He leans over me and kisses me tenderly, the kiss makes my heart swell.

Rip breaks the kiss and slowly pulls out of me.

"Let me just take care of this sweetheart." He says pulling his jeans up and walking into a connected bathroom which I never knew was there. I get up and find my underwear, putting it back on, as well as my jeans as quick as I can. I can't believe I gave in, I am so angry at myself. I leave my heels and creep to the door.

"Where the fuck do you think you're going?" Rip asks walking up behind me. He spins me around so my back is pressed up against the door. He leans in kissing along my shoulder and up my neck.

"You're mine now sweetheart, I ain't letting you go." Rip says in between kisses and nips at neck.

"But Rip..." I try to protest.

Rip's ice blue eyes come to mine, and he cups my face in his hands.

"But nothing. I gave you space, it didn't work. I fucked up, nearly pushing you further away. I'm done playing games sweetheart, I'm not going anywhere and neither are you. I know you feel it too, I promise this between us will be un-fucking-believable, if you just accept it." He says stroking his thumb across my bottom lip.

My heart is about ready to burst, I want nothing more than to say yes and to hell with it but something is stopping me. I just can't bring myself to let go.

"I see you've rebuilt what I broke down, and I tell you what, we will take it slow. Let me prove to you that I can give you what you deserve, that you can trust me." He states. I close my eyes, take a deep breath, and nod.

"Okay, I can do that." I say. I am rewarded with Rip's smile. He leans in and kisses me, his mouth caresses mine, his tongue teasing me. I moan into his mouth, he responds by pinning me with his whole body. I can feel every hard solid inch of him. He breaks the kiss, resting his forehead on mine.

"I promise I wont fuck this up. I swear to you. You have no fuckin' idea how sorry I am to be the one to cause you that pain." He says sincerely.

I swallow my emotions and give him a brief nod.

"Okay, well, I should get to bed." I whisper unsure of what else to say.

"You go on sweetheart, I will be there in a minute. Let me tell the guys to turn it down." Rip says, grabbing his t-shirt and putting it on.

"Wait what?" I ask confused.

"I will be there in a minute." Rip repeats.

"But you just said we're taking it slow." I point out.

"I am, if I was going at the speed I want you'd be at my house in my bed with all of your stuff, and you wouldn't be leaving either." He says smiling.

I'm not smiling. I open and close my mouth shocked at his words.

"You can't be serious? I mean we hardly know each other, that's just crazy talk." I say in disbelief.

"Sweetheart, when you know, you know. You don't waste time on petty shit, you go for it. I've wasted enough time, and that's my own stupid fault, but I'm not wasting anymore. So yes, this is taking it slow for now, I'll let you get used to it. Now go on, I will be there in a sec." He orders, then kisses me and sends me on my way.

I walk back to my room in a confused daze. I

get changed into the big t-shirt that was given to me and wash my face, removing all the make-up and false eyelashes. I brush my teeth and look at myself in the mirror. I'm sure Rip will soon walk away when he sees me like this.

I walk back into the room and climb into bed. I curl up and stare blankly at the wall. I'm not even sure I know what just happened. One minute I wanted to kill him, the next minute I coming so hard I'm screaming his name, and now I'm led here waiting for him to come to bed. I make a mental note to ring Lily or Daisy tomorrow, because my head feels like it's going to explode.

The door opens and in walks Rip. I watch as he kicks of his boots, takes off his t-shirt and jeans and walks towards the bed in just a pair of black fitted boxers. My mouth waters, taking in every inch of his body.

He climbs in and pulls me to him, leaning over me. His hand glides up my thigh and continues up under my t-shirt. It stops just under the swell of my breast, his thumb lazily stroking back and forth, making me shudder.

"I like you in my shirt sweetheart." He says softly. He leans in and kisses me.

"But I like you a whole lot more without it." He states. Using both of his hands he lifts the t-shirt over my head and throws it on the floor. I am now led in front of him completely naked. His eyes take in every last inch of my body. I instinctively move my hand, covering my few stretch marks that I got from having Caden. Rip notices straight away and moves my hand.

"Don't. You're fuckin' beautiful and your body is incredible." He says trailing his hand over my stretch marks, moving them lower to my centre. His eyes are on mine the whole time. He gently moves his finger inside me and I let out a gasp, moving it teasingly slow in and out and circling my g-spot. He's driving me wild. His eyes watch me. He places his thumb over my clit and starts moving it in slow circles. My hips buck, and I push against his hand and the sweet torture he is giving me. I close my eyes and move my hips against his hand, needing more.

"Open your eyes sweetheart, keep your eyes on me." He orders, his voice low. I open my eyes and watch as he leans down and takes my nipple in his mouth. I arch my back as he ever so slowly circles his tongue around my nipple.

"Oh god, please Rip." I beg, needing that bit more to bring me over the edge. His slow sweet relentless torture brings me so close.

Rip smiles as he sits up on his legs, stopping everything he was doing.

"Ahh Rip!" I yell, feeling beyond frustrated.

Rip just smiles as I watch him suck myself off

his finger.

"Hhhmm, fucking heaven." He moans.

He gets up and stands. I give him a look like I'm going to kill him.

"What the fuck Rip! You can't just stop there." I pant angrily.

"Oh I'm not fuckin' stopping sweetheart. I'm just getting started." Rip growls. He takes off his boxers and frees his cock. The sight of it has me licking my lips. Before I know what's happening Rip has grabbed my ankles and pulled me towards the end of the bed, kneeled down, and his mouth is on me. I cry out, his tongue swirling around my clit. It's all too much. My orgasm hits me so hard I nearly buck off the bed.

"Holy fuck Rip!" I scream.

Rip just carries on. I'm panting and my legs are shaking. He slowly stops and stands, reaching for his jeans.

"Move back up the bed sweetheart." he growls.

He grabs a condom from his jeans, tears it open and makes quick work putting it on. He crawls over me, positioning himself at my entrance. He grabs my thigh, lifting my leg around his hip as he very slowly fills me inch by inch. We both let out a throaty moan. He stops when he's filled me to the hilt.

"Open your eyes sweetheart. Keep your eyes on me." Rip orders as he slowly starts to move. His pace is slow, taking his time with each thrust and hitting that delicious spot. He takes my nipple in my mouth and I moan. His pace starts to quicken and I feel myself building for another orgasm.

"Shit...fuck...Rip...I think I'm going to come again." I pant.

"Oh you fucking will. God you're so fucking tight I can feel you sweetheart. Fucking come for me, let me feel your pussy tighten around my cock." he growls. He starts pounding into me, our skin slapping, I scratch my nails down his back as I feel my legs tighten around his waist. I arch my back and scream, calling out his name.

"Fuck, I feel that. Fuck you're beautiful." Rip growls low in his throat. I watch as his muscles tense and he throws his head back, letting out a low groan finding his own release.

We're both panting, our bodies covered with a sheen of sweat.

Rip leans over me, stroking my face. He gently kisses me before pulling out to dispose of the condom.

I watch as he struts to the bathroom, watching his perfect naked arse. I smile and bite my lip. I have just had the most mind blowing sex of my life.

Rip walks back into the room and climbs into bed, I turn into him, resting my head on his chest.

"You good?" he asks tilting my chin up so he can look me in the eyes.

I nod and smile.

"Yeah I'm alright." I shrug.

Rip, quick to move, flips me on my back tickling me. I burst out laughing and beg him to stop.

"Fuckin' full of shit alright! Sweetheart I've just given you two orgasms, that's three tonight so far. I know you're more than alright." He says, his eyes alight.

"So far?" I ask.

"Oh yeah sweetheart, we ain't done yet. There are so many things I want to do to you." Rip promises, his voice low and husky. I feel my nipples harden at the promise. Rip looks down and smiles.

"My woman likes the sound of that." He growls and crashes his mouth down on mine.

Rip did a lot more mind blowing things to me that night. I fell asleep blissfully exhausted and thoroughly pleasured.

CHAPTER ELEVEN

I wake up the next morning to my body aching in places I didn't even know it could ache. I roll over to see an empty bed, rubbing my sleepy eyes I sit up and listen for the shower, nothing. I frown. Confused I look again around the bed to see if he has left a note. Again, nothing. I lie back down and sigh. Maybe he has been called away for something, he is the president of an MC after all.

I get up and go to the toilet, wash my face and brush my teeth, hoping to wake myself up a little bit. After that I decide to go and search for him, starting to feel a little peed off. I try his office but no luck, so I keep on searching. I can hear voices coming from another room further down. I'm about to knock but stop myself when I hear Rip talking.

"We are to fuckin' kill whoever the fuck is on our turf, I don't want them thinking they can just do what the fuck they want and get away with it." Rip orders. There's a few grunts in agreement.

"You know this could start a war." I hear Mammoth say.

"I know brother, but we can't have the Cartel pushing drugs and trafficking women through our town. We are all in for a fucking shit time, but we are the damn Satan's Outlaws. We will tear anyone that should try to takeover what is ours apart, we've worked to damn hard to keep this town clean. We've all got families, people we care about. We do it for them, we fight for them." Rip states.

"Yeah now you've got your old lady to fight for too Pres! Fuck, we could hear her wild cries all damn night. Surprised your damn dick ain't fallen off the amount of action you got last night." A voice I think is Khan says laughing. All the brothers join in and laugh with him.

I feel my face heat with embarrassment, I

can't believe they heard me. Shit.

"Yeah alright, just shut the fuck up the lot of you. Now speaking of Rose, I don't want none of this shit getting back to her, do you hear me? I've just got her to start letting me in again. I don't want anything scaring her off. I will call Blake and Carter and brief them. Rubble, you call Wes bring him up to date on the plans. I mean it though, one more strike from the Cartel we go on full lock down. I won't risk anyone getting hurt." Rip orders. There are a few murmurs.

"Right, anything else we need to go over?" Rip asks.

Feeling a mixture of emotions, from fear to anger that Rip is trying to keep this information from me, I walk into the room. All eyes come to me. I see a few of the guys smile, others try hiding their smiles. I cross my arms over my chest.

"You want to fill me in on what's going on or do you want to continue to bullshit me?" I ask angrily.

Rip sighs and bangs the gavel.

"Church is over. Now all of you fuck off." Rip orders.

One by one the guys get up laughing and snickering.

"Good luck Pres, maybe if your dick ain't falling off from last night's action you could give her another round, she might not want to kill you so much then." Khan says laughing out the door.

"Fuck off Khan!" I yell over my shoulder. He just roars with laughter in response.

"Shut the door sweetheart." Rip orders. He stands up and walks towards me.

Before I can say anything I'm in his arms and he's kissing me. Of course my body just melts into his and my brain turns to mush. He slows the kiss and pulls back slightly.

"Morning sweetheart."

"Huh," I answer feeling wonderfully dazed from his kiss.

Rip smiles and again my brain and body respond, I quickly close my eyes.

"Herpes, he is herpes. Kryptonite covered herpes." I repeat.

Rip burst out laughing, my eyes fling open. Shit.

"Who's herpes? Sorry, I mean kryptonite covered herpes." Rip asks teasingly.

I let my head fall to his chest. Bugger me, this is not a good day. First I find out all of the guys could hear me last night and now I've just told Rip he's herpes.

"You, you are the herpes covered Kryptonite, okay?! I say it in my head when you use your magical powers on me. It helps to keep me focused." I admit.

Rip throws his head back laughing. I watch as this perfect creation of a man laughs and looks beyond sexy doing it. I smile.

"My magical powers?" He asks smiling, raising his eyebrow in question.

I roll my eyes.

"Yeah, like you don't know the effect you have on women." I point out.

Rip sits back perching on the end of the table and pulls me to him so I'm stood between his legs.

"Nope, you're going to have to tell me what effect I have on you. Not other women, because I don't give a shit about them. I only give a shit about you." Rip says.

"Good answer. Also, that's one of them, smooth talker. You are incredibly handsome, you have the most amazing eyes. Then there's your smile, the way you laugh, the way you talk, move, hell I reckon you could scratch your crotch, pick your nose and fart and you'd still make it incredibly sexy. It's your super-power." I say. Rip laughs, shaking his head.

"I can't help those things sweetheart." He answers.

"I know, and...Wait a minute you've made my brain go all fuzzy. I was mad at you for keeping stuff from me. You were supposed to be telling me what's going on. Bloody super-powers!" I say, getting exasperated.

Rip laughs, he pulls me even closer to him, so my body is pressed up against his. He cups my face and kisses me slowly and softly. I've read about kisses like this. They feel like they're floating, their whole body is consumed by that very kiss. I honestly thought what a load of horse shite when I read it in romance novels. But right now I take it back because the way Rip is kissing me, I am feeling all of those things and more. Rip stops kissing me and leans his forehead on mine.

"Shit sweetheart, I knew that when I found it, it would be good, but I never thought it could be like this. You say about me and my magical powers, but you forget you have the power to bring me to my knees sweetheart. You hold it all. No one, and I mean fuckin' no one, has ever been more fuckin' perfect for me than you. One night with you and I'm already screwed." Rip says softly.

"Herpes, herpes covered kryptonite." I mumble under my breath. Rip chuckles.

"You can keep saying that sweetheart. I know it's just you trying to keep me out, but I will keep telling you things like that every damn day until I can break through your fortress." Rips states.

"Shut up now please." I whisper, gripping his shirt.

My chest fills with his words. I don't know how to handle them. Rip has already making me feel things I've never felt, and I am absolutely terrified.

"Tell me what's going on." I say moving back a little, putting a little distance between us so I can think clearly. Rip smiles like he knows exactly what I'm doing.

"Okay sweetheart, I can't tell you everything because that's club business and that's just how it is. The Cartel have been trying to move in on our town for a long time. As you know, with what went down with Lily. Anyway they are getting more and more restless and are trying to push us out. That's why they went after Rubble and then you. By doing this they are asking for trouble. They are asking for war. Now listen to me, the club has you protected, and Caden. Do not let any of this shit twist in your head into something that you will use to run off from me again because woman, I will hunt you down and bring your ass back to me where it belongs." He threatens.

"Okay, I get it, you're a badass. I'm yours

blah, blah, blah. Now get to the point tell me what I need to expect." I say rolling my eyes.

"Don't test me sweetheart, I know it makes you feel better to play down how you feel, but next time you mock me I will put you over my damn knee." Rip threatens.

I gasp and bite my lip. Rip takes in my reaction and growls low in his throat.

"Christ, I've met my fuckin' match with you." He says leaning forward and nipping at my neck.

I laugh and push him back.

"Now come on, tell me." I ask.

Rip tucks a piece of my hair behind my ear.

"I want to lie to you to tell you it will be fine and not scare you. I want to protect you." He sighs.

"The truth is sweetheart, it could get ugly. It could become war and that's never a good thing. You have to trust us." He says.

"You mean full on guns and stuff? People shooting each other?" I ask.

"Yeah, but we are good. We're not stupid and we are not to be messed with. We are all fully trained one way or the other. I promise you our family is always protected." He finishes. His eyes search mine looking for my reaction.

"I don't like the thought of war at all, I don't like the thought of you or any of the other guys putting yourselves in danger. But I know why you're doing it. That part I overheard" I state. Rip looks as though he's bracing, ready to stop me from running. I take a long breath.

"I hate it, I hate letting Axel go off to fight and do whatever it is he does. But I know he's doing it for good. So if there is a war, you're going to need your own Florence Nightingale to look after any injured men." I say smiling.

I watch as what I'm saying hits Rip, his face splits into a shit eating grin. He jumps up lifting me, his hands cup my behind and I wrap my legs around his waist. I laugh as he storms out of the room.

"Where are we going." I giggle.

"We're going back to bed." He states.

I laugh into his neck. The guys see us and hoot and wolf whistle, all laughing.

Rip got the prospects to bring us some lunch in bed. I offered to get up and get something for us, but he shut down that idea. I am cuddled into Rip lazily tracing the outlines of his tattoos. My phone rings and I reach to get it, I see it's Daisy video calling me, and I move so Rip isn't in view.

"Hey, how is your holiday going? Is Caden

being good?" I ask

"Hiya, yeah, all good. I've got Caden here to speak to you." Daisy says and hands Caden the phone.

"Hi baby! How are you? Are you having the best time?" I ask. Seeing his little face I realise how much I miss him.

"Hi Mum, yay, it's totally cool. I went on this water slide, it went like super-fast, like faster than a rocket. I swallowed so much water it was coming out of my nose. So cool! I'm going on it again." Caden says excitedly. I smile and shake my head.

"That sounds fun, but just remember, don't try and stay under water too long okay? Don't go scaring auntie Daisy and uncle Carter." I tell him.

"Okay Mum, who's that?" Caden asks squinting at the screen. My eyes go wide, and I try smiling and shrugging.

"Is that Rip? Hi Rip! Wait Mum, are you still in bed?!" Caden yells.

I cover my face with my other hand and pinch the bridge of my nose. Apparently he doesn't notice three week old stinking yogurt left in his bedroom, but he damn well notices this. Rip chuckles behind me, he wraps his arm around my waist, pulling me back and rests his chin on my shoulder.

"Hey dude, how's it going? Got any girl-friends yet?" Rip asks.

"Ewww no way! This one boy was pushing a girl around, so I punched him in the peanuts, and now this girl won't stop following me around. It's so annoying!" Caden says rolling his eyes.

"Oh they're about to turn the wave machine on! Got to go Mum! Bye. Love you!" Caden yells practically chucking the phone at Daisy.

"Don't you dare say a word." I warn her.

"What would I say? Other than I knew it! I knew you too were hot for each other. Now just don't mess it up. I'm going to, um, leave you to it, because well I feel a little uncomfortable with you both being naked." Daisy says smiling.

"Wait, how do you know we're both naked?" I ask.

"Because when I said it you both looked down to check nothing was popping out. Oh my god, Mum is going to lose her shit over this! Mum was ready to sign you up to the nunnery." Daisy says laughing.

"Alright sis, love you, byeeeee!" I disconnect leaving her laughing.

"Nunnery?" Rip asks smiling.

"Um, it has been a little while since I've been with anyone." I say shrugging.

Rip moves us so we're led down and he's leaning over me.

"How long?" He asks.

"Um, Caden's father was the last person I slept with." I answer.

"How long ago sweetheart?" He ask.

"Okay fine, Caden was a baby. So like six and a half years maybe." I shrug like it's no big deal.

"Christ sweetheart, no wonder your ma thought you were going to end up in a nunnery."

"Yeah well, I had Caden to look after. He is my number one priority."

"I get that sweetheart. Now let me make up for all those years." Rip says trailing kisses down my neck. I moan.

We are soon interrupted by my phone ringing. Rip reaches forward and hands me my phone.

"Hello?" I answer while Rip is still trailing kisses down my neck.

"Rose?"

I jolt up.

"Richard?" I ask, even though I know it's him.

"Why are you calling?" I ask. He knew we were on holiday. I haven't approached the conversation about Caden and I moving here yet. Although I don't think he will have much of an issue with it.

"I saw your mum. She told me all about your new job and the plans for you and Caden to live over there. Is this true?" He asks.

I pause for a moment, because, well, I don't want to mention the losing my job, and the whole MC thing. He just won't get it, and he'd probably take Caden off me if I told him.

"Uh yeah, um, well it's all up in the air a little at the moment but it's looking that way. Obviously I was going to call you and discuss it before I was fully decided." I lie.

"Well, here's the thing, I actually think this is a good thing you see. I was trying to find the right way to tell you...well...I got a job and I'm moving away too. In two weeks actually." He says hesitantly.

"Well, um, congratulations, so why didn't you just tell me this before?" I ask confused.

"Because the job is in Australia." He replies. I put my head in my hands, dreading having to tell Caden that his dad is moving to the other side of the world. God only knows when he will see him.

"Right, what's going to be the plan for Caden then? I know I was thinking of moving out here, but I would have made arrangements with you to still see him. But with you the other side of the world makes it a lot harder. What am I supposed to tell Caden?" I ask

As much as he is a dick, he is still Caden's father and this will have an effect on him.

"Just tell him that he can come for holidays over to mine, he will still see me. But instead of every other weekend it'll be holidays instead." He replies. I sigh and pinch the bridge of my nose.

"How exactly do you plan on him coming to yours?" I ask.

"By plane of course, I will cover his tickets." He replies like I'm an idiot.

"On his own? Are you insane? He is seven! There is no way he is flying to the other side of the world on his bloody own. For Christ's sake!" I point out, frustrated.

"I knew you'd be like this, this is a great opportunity for my career. You could at least be happy for me. You were planning on staying in Texas with him and you don't see me kicking off about it." He bites back.

"That's because you know damn well I would have flown back to England a few times a year so you could see him! And you'd be welcome over here anytime. I know what's going to happen, you're going to move over there and the contact with Caden will dwindle away and you will give up and not make the effort. For once this isn't about you, this is about our son!" I yell angrily.

"Whatever. I will send you my new address once we're settled." He responds before he hangs up on me.

Rip comes behind me, pulling me into his arms.

"Problem?" He asks.

"Caden's dad is moving to Australia and, while I couldn't give a shit where he lives, I know contact will slowly disappear. It's Caden that's going to be hurt by it. Dick can't see what the problem is with sending him on his own on a plane across the world." I complain.

"Sweetheart, he will be okay, whether his father bothers or not. He has enough love around him to see him through that. It will all work out I'm sure. It's his father who's being a cunt, he is going to miss out. Caden's a great kid." Rip says trying to reassure me.

"Yeah I suppose."

"Now where were we? Oh yeah, I do believe I was about to make my woman scream my name again." Rip says trailing kisses.

"Hhmm, Rip?" I moan.

"Yeah sweetheart?" He answers.

"One question, what's your real name? You know, in case I feel like screaming that instead." I say smiling.

Rip stops, resting his chin on my stomach.

"Okay sweetheart, but you have to know that Rip is also my real name. Well, it's actually Ripley Noah King." He says with a wink.

"So your road name is just your nick name?" I ask.

I watch as his eyes change shade slightly. He tenses his jaw and pauses for a moment, looking past me.

"Rip, what is it? You can tell me." I state stroking his face, his eyes come to mine, and he places a kiss on my palm.

"Okay sweetheart, what I am about to tell you may freak you out, but you have to know I would never ever hurt you or Caden in any way." Rip promises. He pauses, waiting for my acknowledgement. I nod my head and he continues.

"Right, well I've been with the club my whole life. My upbringing would have been very different to yours, but we still have the same morals, just a different way of life. So I learnt from a very young age how to defend myself, how to shoot, and how to kill." he says, watching my reaction.

I don't react. I just wait for him to continue.

"I was never a big fan of guns, I liked knifes and blades. I started collecting them. When I got older and started prospecting for the club, my skills with a blade were valuable. I know exactly where to put a knife in a man to kill him instantly. I know where to put the knife to make it slow and painful. I know how to cut someone so quickly they don't feel it until its too late." he says.

Rip's eyes come to mine and I can see the love and enjoyment he gets from talking about it. Rip has a dark side, he is putting everything on the line by telling me all of this. I again don't react and nod for him to continue.

"I've killed men, sweetheart. I've stood over them and watch them die. I've watched them take their last breath, I've had them beg for their lives. The thing you need to know is that I wouldn't change any of it. I don't regret taking their lives, I don't feel remorse for doing it. I'm not justifying it but sometimes in my world there have been moments where it's kill or be killed. The men I've killed deserved to die at my hands. The Satans', well, we protect, we will kill or even die to protect our family. So now you know all there is to know about me. You why my road name is Rip. It's because I am known to rip the flash off of men with my blades." Rip finishes.

I lay there, processing everything he just said. I think of Daisy and Tony. I think that any of us could be capable of murdering someone if pushed to do so. I know Axel is trained to do it.

But taking enjoyment from it is a different matter.

"Sweetheart, say something, you're killing me here." Rip says bringing me out of my thoughts.

"Come here." I say.

Rip crawls up my body and leans over me.

"That's a lot to take in." I sigh.

I watch as Rip tenses, waiting for me to continue.

"But, you're not a cold blooded killer. Your way of life is very different to mine. I'd never even seen a gun until I came over here. I know you wouldn't hurt me or Caden, I don't know how I know that, I just do. I know you'd lay down your life for your family and protect them at any cost. The fact that you've killed men before, well, my brother has killed, and you know Daisy has. I believe anyone can kill, it's just a matter of whether we are pushed to our limits or trained to do it. You telling me this hasn't changed what I think of you at all, if anything, you've made a little bit of the fortress crumble by trusting me with it." I say. I cup his face.

"You are not an evil man, Rip. You are a good man who fights for what he loves, for the people he loves. The only thing you're guilty of is loving your family and your club so fiercely that you'd risk your own life fighting and killing for them." I say meaning every word.

He isn't a monster, he's a trained soldier born into this world. He is a protector.

"I'd fight for you, I'd kill for you." Rip rasps, his voice rough with emotion.

I jolt at his words, my heart feels like it's about to leap from my chest. Rip watches me, the look in his eyes tells me he knows exactly what his words have done to me. He smiles down at me.

"Think I just saw a bit more of your fortress fall away sweetheart." Rip says as he wraps my legs around his waist, he presses against my entrance and fills me to the hilt with one thrust. He stops. I gasp and Rip groans.

"I'm going to fuck you now sweetheart, I'm going to take my time and you're going to scream my name over and over again." Rip promises.

Rip always keeps his promises.

CHAPTER TWELVE

Spending the next few days at the club compound was fine. Well, it was better than fine because eighty percent of it was spent in bed with Rip. But as it got past day three I was getting cabin fever. I needed to go out, I needed a change in scenery.

"For god's sake, please! I'm going to go crazy if I spend another minute in this place. No one else has to stay here and as much as I think the guys are great, there's only so many tits and arse jokes I can take. There's been no sign of the Cartel for days. I mean, can't I just stay at yours instead? I lost my job because of this and will probably be deported when my visiting visa ends so could I at least enjoy the rest of my time here?!" I plead with Rip. I really am fed up of looking at the same concrete walls. I need a long soak in the bath, even to lay on a couch and watch a movie would be heaven.

"Okay sweetheart, but it will come with protection. Someone on you twenty-four-seven. They will be in a truck so not to alert the Cartel. You won me over with the thought of having you in my home and in my bed." Rip says pulling me onto his lap. I smile and kiss him.

"Go pack your stuff up sweetheart and go see Ma, she's making us lunch. Ask her to wrap it up for us to take." Rip states kissing me one more time.

I hesitate and Rip notices.

"What is it?" He asks.

"Umm well, I haven't seen your mum or dad since the night of the party." I state.

"And your point is?" Rip asks confused.

"Let me think, I stripped! I did a strip tease in front of your parents!" I remind him.

"Firstly, you only took your top off. Secondly, Ma knows it isn't something you normally do. I caused it, my folks know that. You seem to forget my parents are bikers, it would take a hell of a lot to offend them." Rip reassures.

"Fine, I will go see her and pack my stuff. One more quick question." I state, Rip smiles and nods for me to continue.

"How are we going to fit my suitcase on your bike?" I ask.

"I will get one of the guys to follow us in the truck with your bags." He replies.

"So we're going on your bike?" I ask excitedly.

"Yeah sweetheart."

I jump off of his lap and do a little dance on my way out of his office.

"I'm so excited I might pee my pants!" I shout over my shoulder. I hear Rip's laughter and I can't wipe the huge grin off my face. After packing up my stuff I go in search for Trudy.

I walk into the kitchen, where I find her making up loads of sandwiches.

"Hey." I say walking in.

Trudy's head comes up and she smiles.

"Hey honey, you come to take some lunch with you back to Rip's place?" she asks.

"How did you..." I stumble over my words.

"These bikers may be big scary men, but they gossip like old women." She winks.

I smile and take a seat on the stool.

"Listen Trudy, about the other night, I'm so sorry I behaved like that. I'm no angel but I don't usually strip either. I made such a fool of myself, I'm just sorry you and Max had to see that." I apologise.

Trudy stops what she's doing and places her hand over mine.

"Honey, we are bikers. I've seen a hell of a lot worse than that before. I'm also well aware that the tension between you and Rip helped tip you to make that drunken decision. My son is no saint. Anyway, it worked, you two are happy. It's good to see." she says smiling.

I smile in return and let out a relieved breath.

"Um, I do have one thing to confess to you, though." she says sheepishly.

"What?" I ask curiously.

"Well I may have told your mom. She rang me yesterday to catch up and was telling me all about the move over here. She asked how you were doing because she hadn't spoke to you since before you started your job, so I filled her in on what's happening. Well, not about the Cartel because I knew that would worry her. Are you mad at me?" she asks.

I laugh and shake my head.

"Are you kidding? Of course not! I know for a fact my mum would have probably screamed down the phone excitedly, then maybe gone on about weddings and babies, am I right?" I ask.

Trudy laughs and nods her head.

"See, so you actually did me a favour." I reply.

Trudy hands me our lunch. I give her a hug and she promises to come and see me soon.

I am walking looking for Rip and eventually find him outside leaning against his bike, waiting for me.

I stop for a moment just to stare at him and admire how unbelievably hot he is.

Stood in faded jeans, a fitted black t-shirt stretching over his toned muscled body, with his leather cut over the top. His muscled arms are covered in tattoos. His jet black hair is messy from where he's constantly running his fingers through it. His stubbled jaw and perfect lips, oh god. Then there are his piercing ice blue eyes, eyes that can melt you on the spot. Since when did I get so bloody lucky?

Rip turns his attention my way and spots me staring. He smiles and walks towards me.

"You enjoying the view sweetheart?" He asks, pulling me to him.

"Meh, I've seen better." I say teasingly.

Rip doesn't say anything, he bends down and lifts me over his shoulder. I scream and laugh as he smacks my arse, walking to his bike.

He places me down, leans in and kisses me, his lips and tongue caressing mine. He slows the kiss and nips my lip playfully.

"You ready to ride sweetheart?" He asks with a playful smile on his lips.

"Oh I am so ready." I say grinning.

Rip leans over his bike and holds open a leather jacket for me to put on. My eyes alight with excitement as he helps me.

"Did you get this for me?" I ask doing a little twirl.

"Yeah, with help from my ma on the sizing." Rip says smiling.

I strike a pose and wiggle my eyebrows.

"What do ya reckon? Do I look like a hot biker babe now?" I ask laughing.

Rip pulls me to him, not answering he crashes his mouth down on mine, giving me a hungry passionate kiss that leaves me feeling lightheaded and breathless.

"I take that as a yes then?" I breathe.

"Sweetheart, in them skinny ass jeans that hug your skin, with them high heeled boots and that jacket, you're a walking wet dream." Rip states.

I may have got changed when Rip said we were going on his bike, I dressed in the hope I would look sexy. But also because being a nurse in A&E, I know what happens to your skin when you come off a bike in inappropriate clothes.

Rip climbs on and starts up his bike.

"What about a helmet?" I ask.

"We're not going to be going fast sweetheart and the roads we are taking are dead, you'll be fine. Plus Rubble is driving the truck right behind us." he says. I spin around and Rubble gives me a chin lift from the truck.

I climb on and listen to the directions Rip gives me. He takes my hands and wraps them around him. I splay my hand across his hard stomach.

"Easy sweetheart, I still need to concentrate. I can't concentrate if you give me a hard on." he growls.

"Sorry." I smile.

He kicks back the stand and slowly moves the bike to the gate. The prospect opens it up and smiles when I wave at them. Rip pulls out and I let out a scream and giggle. I feel Rip's laughter vibrating through my hands.

As we ride the cool breeze blows through my hair, there is no one on the road except us. I get confident and let go of Rip, lifting my arms up in the air.

"This is fucking amazing!" I shout.

I wrap my arms back around Rip feeling his rumble of laughter. I rest my chin on his shoulder. In this very moment, I feel alive. There's nothing between us and the open road. Feeling the wind against my face, I close my eyes and just feel it. The freedom. I feel some more of my fortress crumble away. At this very moment I feel like I belong, like I am meant to be here with Rip on his bike.

We ride for around twenty minutes before Rip pulls up to a large house and turns off the bike. I climb off and stare up at his house.

"You have a beautiful home." I say smiling.

Rip comes to me and takes my hand in his and drags me up to the house.

"What about my stuff?" I ask as he opens the front door and slams it shut behind us.

"Rubble will sit in the truck and wait."

"Wait for what?" I ask, confused as Rip pulls me down on his lap on the sofa.

"Sweetheart I've just rode all the way here with the biggest raging hard on, the feel of your hands across my stomach, your soft tits pressed up against my back and the sound of pure fucking joy coming from you at being on the back of my bike. I need to fuck you now." Rip states, undoing my jeans.

After more amazing sex on Rip's sofa, we are both panting, trying to get our breathing under control. I have never felt this way about anyone before. The spark between us is electric. He can give me just one look and I'm ready to strip off and shag all day and night. I'm worse than a horny teenager.

I lift my head up and look into Rip's eyes, both of us not saying anything to each other. Rip cups my face and runs his thumb across my bottom lip.

I feel that the mood is getting too intense. I'm feeling things I'm really not ready to admit yet. Feeling like a horny teen is one thing, but I'm not ready for all the deep and meaningful stuff. I pull back and stand up.

"You better go and help Rubble." I say grabbing my clothes off of the floor.

"Where's the bathroom?" I ask.

Rip points to the stairs, I nod and smile and go to walk past him. He reaches out and grabs my arm.

"I know you're scared about what you're feeling sweetheart, but I'm not. In your own time it'll hit you and when it does, I will already be there waiting." he says leaning forward. He places a kiss on my forehead. I give him a little smile and scurry off to the bathroom.

Cleaning up in the bathroom I splash cold water over my face. Why is it I have such an issue letting myself fall? Sure, I've been hurt, but hasn't everybody? I shake my head, this isn't the time to delve into the issues I seem to have, this isn't an episode of Dr Phil. I towel off my face and head back downstairs.

Rip is talking to Rubble in the doorway. I walk over and Rip puts his arm around me, pulling me in close.

"Right if that's all Pres, I'm gonna shoot. I think Fury will be doing a drive by in about twenty minutes to scope the area. See you around Flo." Rubble says winking. I blush and roll my eyes.

Rip shows me to his room where my suitcase is. His house is beautiful, you can see he's been fixing it up. I offer to cook dinner, but Rip won't have any of it. Instead he cooks for me.

"Bon appetite, steak and mashed potatoes." Rip says placing down my plate.

"Looks delicious, but can I ask one thing?"

Rip nods, tucking into his steak.

"No veg or salad?" I ask

Rip scrunches his nose up.

"You sound like my ma, no sweetheart. I can only cook meat and potatoes. Well, and mac n cheese." he shrugs, taking another bite of steak.

I smile and tuck in, I moan when I taste the steak.

"God, you really do know what to do with meat." I compliment.

Rip chokes on his food.

"That's not the first time I've heard that." Rip says winking while having a drink of his beer.

"Oh shut up, eat your dinner." I say smiling.

"So your mum has told my mum err, um… about us." I say watching for Rip's reaction.

Rip just nods and continues eating his dinner.

"So you're good with that? You know what my mum can be like, right?" I point out.

"Yeah. She was trying to set me up with you before I'd even met you, I know what to expect." Rip shrugs.

We carry on eating when my phone goes off, I see it's Lily calling.

"Hi Lil', I've got you on speaker, I'm just eating my dinner at the moment. What's up? Blake's knob fallen off? Have you overused the poor boy?" I snort.

"You're dating Rip?!" she shouts in a high pitched screech down the phone.

"Err Lil' you might w…"

Lily carries on completely ignoring me.

"I can't believe you finally went there with him, I mean I love Blake, it will always be Blake, but Rip is H.O.T. That guy could melt the polar ice caps! He is a walking talking ball of hotness. So come on, dish the dirt, is the sex off the charts? Has he given you multiples? Ooo what's his cock like? Is it big? Tell me everything." Lily says excitedly over the phone.

I just slam my head onto the table. Rip laughs. He picks up my phone.

"Hey Lily. To answer your questions, yes the sex is off the charts, yes she has had multiples, and as for my cock your sister seems to like it. Oh, and thanks, your sister thinks I'm hot too." Rip answers chuckling.

"Oh for goodness sake, do you know what? I'm not even embarrassed. Laugh it up but she will crack and tell me all. Rose if you can hear me I'm back from my honeymoon in two days. We are getting the girls together then I shall get you drunk and get you singing like a canary. Love you skin and blister, bye!"

Lily hangs up. Rip, still chuckling, squeezes my neck.

"Sweetheart, there is never a dull moment when your family is concerned." he says, still chuckling.

Completely changing the subject because it's something that's been sat at the back of my mind and for some unknown reason I just have to get it off my chest.

"Did you want to get with Lily?" I ask sitting up and looking at Rip. His laughter stops, and the smile falls from his face. The whole atmosphere around us changes instantly. It doesn't give me a good feeling.

"Sweetheart, now either way I put this it isn't going to come across great, but I know you will want honesty and that's what you'll get." Rip pauses and runs his fingers through his hair.

Lily told me everything that went down between her and Rip, I know how she feels, obviously she married Blake, but I need to know how he feels. I need to know that he's not just settling for second best.

"There's no other way of putting this, but yeah, I thought Lily was hot, I was attracted to her. She was a breath of fresh air around here. I sound like a dick but being president of the Satan's I had women throw themselves at me regularly. So your sister was different, and she caught my eye. She's a good woman too, but I saw it, I saw how she looked at Blake and I saw him with her. I knew then that she wasn't meant for me, them two were made for each other. Now don't go telling folk, because I have a rep to think about. But my pa, always told me, Blake, and Wes that when you find the right woman you'll know, because they will consume your thoughts whether you want them to or not. They will be the first thing you think about when you wake up and the last thought before you sleep. They will invade your dreams, you won't be able to go a single minute without thinking of them." Rip pauses, cupping my face in his hands.

I'm holding my breath, trying to calm down my erratic heart. I bite my lip nervously. Rip's eyes drop to my mouth and he smiles.

"You know exactly what I'm saying don't you sweetheart? It's okay, you don't have to admit it to me or yourself yet. You don't have to say shit, because I feel it." Rip says, leaning and kissing me softly.

"Bollocks." I murmur.

Rip smiles and lets out a throaty chuckle.

"Come on sweetheart, I think we need an early night." Rip says standing and pulling me with him.

I look at the clock.

"Um Rip, it's only nine." I say.

"I said we're having an early night, I didn't say anything about sleeping." Rip answers, leading the way upstairs.

Smiling I happily follow, now very much

looking forward to the early night. I figure with the amount of sex we are having I may never walk normally again. Oh well, walking normally is overrated, just call me John Wayne.

CHAPTER THIRTEEN

Over the next few days I kept myself busy by cleaning Rip's house, not that it was dirty, but just for something to do. Also when Rip was home he found many fun ways to keep me entertained.

I'm mopping the floor when there's a knock at the door, I quickly go to answer it, being careful not to slip over the wet floor.

When I reach the door, the person starts pounding on the door again. I check the peephole before opening it. That's something I promised Rip I would do, and I sneer when I see who's stood on the other side.

Darcy, the slut whore from the club. I swing open the door and clearly catch her by surprise. She wasn't expecting me to answer.

"He's not here, what do you want?" I ask crossing my arms over my chest. I really can't be doing with this girl's bullshit right now.

"Well I need to see him, it's important. I will just come in and wait until he comes home." Darcy replies. She flicks her hair over her shoulder and moves to walk in. I put my arm across the doorway, stopping her from coming in.

"I don't think so skank, Rip said not to let anyone in. That includes your whoreish self. Now if you don't mind you can piss off, I've got things I'd like to be getting on with." I say. As I go to slam the door in her face she puts up her hand, blocking it.

"Ring Rip. It's important, he will want to know what I have to tell him." she says smiling. Her hand goes to her stomach and she gently rubs it. I freeze, realising what she's getting at. I quickly gather myself hoping she didn't see that she got to me, but it's too late. Judging by the smirk across her face she knows she already has.

"Wait out here, you're not coming in. I will ring him." I say and quickly shut the door.

I grab the phone and call him.

"Hey sweetheart, I can't really talk right now I'm in church, what's up?" He asks .

"Um, slutty McSlut Face is here, aka Darcy." I say.

"Why the fuck is she there? She causing shit?" Rip asks.

"Uh well I think maybe you should just come talk to her, she has...well...something she needs to talk to you about." I reply. It is not my place to tell him why she is here.

"Fuck sake. Ok sweetheart, I'm on my way, just don't let her talk shit to you." He says and I hear him mumble to the guys.

"Oh don't worry, I won't. I haven't let her in, I shut her out on the front porch. I've just cleaned I'm not having her skanky arse touch anything in here." I say smiling when I hear Rip burst into laughter.

I disconnect and sit and wait. My mind going ninety miles per hour. What if she's telling the truth and she is pregnant with his kid? I'm not sure if it's something I could be ok with.

I hear the rumbling of motorcycle pipes approach the house. I get up and head out the front, I'm surprised to see Khan and Mammoth with Rip. They pull up Rip gets off his bike. Darcy is posing against her car like some model on a car advert. She smiles and flicks her hair flirtatiously as Rip walks towards her. He doesn't even glance her way, his eyes are on me and he walks straight past her. My lips twitch, fighting a smile. Rip notices and graces me with his own smile, right before he pulls me into his arms and kisses me.

"Hey sweetheart." He says softly across my lips.

I smile.

"Hey." I reply

"What the fuck Rip? I'm here to see you, it's important. I can't believe you'd walk past this for that ugly bitch." Darcy seethes behind Rip.

Moment broken. I watch as Rip's eyes almost turn dark, his jaw sets and his body tenses. Now looking at him I know he's a scary biker outlaw.

He spins round so quickly I don't have time to react. He grabs Darcy and pins her by her throat against the wall. I suck in a breath, Darcy's eyes go wide in fear.

"Rip! No!" I shout at him. He turns to me, his eyes slightly softening.

"Sweetheart I'm not hurting her, see." He replies, showing me he has only has his hand placed there. It's a warning to Darcy, he's showing her what he is capable of. What's actually pinning her there is his murderous gaze.

"Why have you come to my fucking house? And why do you think you have the right to bad mouth my fucking woman?!" He barks at her. I watch as she flinches. She soon tries to turn on her charm, fluttering her eyelashes at him and pouting.

"Rip, baby, you know I go crazy for you. You know what you do to me, what your hands, mouth and co..." I've had enough at this point. I can't hold it back anymore.

"Oh for the love of god woman have some god damn respect for yourself! He doesn't want you! You were just a shag, an easy lay. You knew that, it was just sex. Now it's over. He told you it's done. Now have some bloody dignity and accept that. Just be thankful you ever had a lay as good as him, although the thought physically sickens me. Now why don't you take your rotten beef curtains and go find yourself a guy that actually wants you and stop opening your damn legs. Christ, at least keep them closed while you're pregnant." I rant.

"WHAT?" Rip barks loudly. I jump.

"Sorry, didn't mean for it to slip out. Darcy, tell him why you're here." I apologise.

Darcy smiles, well it's more of a sneer at me.

"I'm pregnant with your baby." She coos. I watch as Rip looks stunned and swallows. He removes his hand and runs it through his hair. I put my hand out to the side to support myself, I honestly thought it couldn't be true. I thought deep down that he would call her out on it. But watching this now is like a huge kick in the gut.

"Khan, Mammoth, go to the store and get me every different type of pregnancy test they have. NOW!" He shouts across to them. They both nod, glance a look at each other then ride off.

"I used condoms, every damn time." Rip points out.

"Accidents happen baby, one must have split." she says walking towards him, she places her hand on his arm and comforts him affectionately. He doesn't stop her, his hand on the railing and his head hung low. She moves in closer.

"It's okay, we can work it all out." she says taking his hand and placing it on her stomach.

I can't watch this for a second longer. I take off into the house and run straight out to the back garden, needing air but to be as far away from him as possible.

I hear Rip come after me. He pulls me into his arms, but I push him away.

"Don't, please, I can't right now ok." I whisper fighting back the tears.

"Sweetheart, I didn't mean to, fuck! I was careful, I just have to make sure...and if she is...

I will be there for my kid, nothing has to change with us. I still want nothing to do with her." Rip says his eyes pleading with me.

"Doesn't it? Rip come on, we've literally just started out and you could already be expecting a baby with another woman. It's not like a woman has turned up with a kid and said it's yours. You slept with her like four weeks ago." I point out.

"Fuck!" He roars, gripping his hair.

"I knew I shouldn't have fuckin' gone there with her." He sighs.

A few minutes later we hear Mammoth and Khan return with a brown bag full of pregnancy tests. Mammoth shoves the bag at Darcy, she frowns and looks inside it, her eyes go wide. Frowning I watch her reaction.

"Why have you brought these? I have a picture of the test I can show you as proof." She whines and pouts.

"I want to be fuckin' sure, now go pee on them." Rip turns to me.

"Can you go watch her please? I don't trust the bitch, she is probably carrying some pregnant woman's piss in a pot knowing her." He asks. I scrunch up my nose in disgust.

"I'm not having her come in with me." Darcy complains.

"It's either her or you pee with the door

open and we all fucking watch you." Rip threatens.

"Fine, where is your bathroom?" she asks.

I'm taken aback that she doesn't know where the bathroom is, I would have thought she'd been here a lot of times. I shake my head at that thought.

"This way." I show her to the bathroom. I hand her a plastic pot to pee into so we can use all the tests. She does this then hands me the pot smirking. She obviously doesn't know I'm a nurse and that I've touched much worse liquids than a little bit of pee on a pot. I open the door and shout for Rip as I set the pot on the side and wash my hands. I open the bag and take out the first test. Opening it I dip it in and hold it there a few seconds and place it down. I do the same with three more and set them on the side.

Rip followed by the guys comes into the doorway. I point to the tests on the side. I step back. I look to Darcy, she's biting her lip. I can't read whether she's anxious to prove us all wrong or nervous because she's lying. I hope it's the latter.

"It's time to check." I state.

Rip walks towards the tests, he turns to me.

"What am I looking for?" He asks.

"Two blue lines is positive, meaning she's

pregnant, same for the other. It'll be a cross in-stead on that one, and the other is digital and will say pregnant." I answer.

Rip nods picking up each test one by one. His back is to me so I can't see his expression to know what the outcome is. The room is tense, Rip places the last test on the side and lets out a long sigh.

"Get out of my damn house." Rip growls low and threatening.

I look to Darcy who has paled, she scurries past me.

I walk over to Rip and look down at the re-sults. All negative. I feel elated for a second then pure anger descends. I run after Darcy as quick as I can.

"Stop her, she'll fucking kill her." Rip yells at Mammoth and Khan.

"Whoops sorry Pres, she's just too quick." I hear them chuckle. I run out the front door and manage to lunge and grab Darcy, pushing her to the ground. I straddle her, pinning her.

"Are you fucking crazy? What? Did you think he wouldn't notice there was no baby in nine months time? Or were you planning on fak-ing a miscarriage too?" I fume.

She avoids eye contact. That's it, that's what she was planning to do.

"You mother fucking whore! You disgust me. You know there are women that can't have children and there are women that try and try but have so many miscarriages it near destroys them. And here you are faking it all just so you can have Rip! Do you know how insane that is?! You nearly destroyed my happiness! You nearly took the man I love away from me!" I shout, completely losing it now. I slap her hard across the face.

"I fucking love that man and you nearly tore us apart!" I yell in her face. I feel myself being pulled off her.

"Mammoth, Khan, get this piece of fuckin' scum off my property. If I ever see you near me, my club, or my woman again, you'll have more than just a slap from Rose to worry about. Now fuck off." Rip barks.

Mammoth and Khan get her in her car and they follow her on their bikes.

I'm panting, my anger slowly evaporating.

"Sweetheart, look at me." Rip orders, he lifts my chin and I look into his beautiful eyes.

"You love me." Rip states softly.

I suck in a breath, my heart beating wildly in my chest. I realise that I said that and he heard me. I close my eyes, wishing this moment wasn't happening.

"Sweetheart, look at me." Rip says softly stroking my cheek.

I open my eyes and reluctantly look into his.

"I fuckin' love you too..." is all Rip has a chance to say because I jump up and wrap my arms and legs around him. I kiss him, he quickly put his hands under my behind to carry me. I kiss him with everything I have, pouring all that I feel for him into the kiss.

"Hold on sweetheart." Rip breathes in my ear as he walks us back into the house and upstairs to his bedroom.

He lays me down on the bed, I make quick work taking my clothes off as does Rip.

Rip is quick, before I know it he's back on top of me, kissing me and nipping my neck.

"Look at me sweetheart." Rip says huskily. I open my eyes.

"I fuckin' love you." Rip says, his eyes on mine and thrusts himself inside me, filling me. I gasp and Rip moans.

He starts to move slowly, his eyes never leaving mine.

"I fuckin' love you sweetheart, you're made for me." Rip growls out as he thrusts.

Rip grabs my hands pinning them above my head, his whole body cocooning me. I wrap my legs around him, holding him close.

"I can feel it sweetheart, I can feel your damn fortress crashing down. I can feel your love. You fuckin' consume me sweetheart, every damn part of me. Fuck. You feel perfect. I love you." Rip whispers in my ear, while circling his hips, hitting that spot.

"Oh god Rip" I moan.

"Say it sweetheart. I can feel your body saying it to me. Let me hear your mouth say it." Rip says thrusting hard.

My head rolls back and I moan.

"I love you." I whisper.

Rip stops moving and I moan in protest. My eyes fly open.

"Say it louder. I want to hear you scream it when I make you come." He demands.

"I love you." I say louder. Rip thrusts hard, I gasp

"Keep those eyes on me sweetheart." Rip pants and he continues to thrust harder and harder.

I can feel it building within me.

"Oh fuck." I moan.

"Say you love me, scream it sweetheart." He orders, never slowing up his relentless pace.

My orgasm hits hard.

"Rip I fucking love you!" I cry out, my back arching as pleasure takes hold of my body.

Rip lets out a low throaty growl, reaching his climax.

We're both panting. Rip still has hold of my hands and his face is buried in the crook of my neck. I feel in this moment, with our bodies pressed together and connected, completely and utterly consumed by Rip. My heart feels full again. It's a feeling I haven't felt in a really long time. I sniffle back my tears, struggling to handle this wave of emotion. Rip pulls back, his eyes soft. He cups my face wiping away my tears.

"Sweetheart?" He questions.

"God damn it. I'm not a crier. You see what you've made me into? I just can't handle all these emotions I'm feeling right now. I can't even remember the last time I felt this way, my heart being this full. It's been just me and Caden for such a long time and that's been fine, because he's my world, but I guess I forgot what this feels like. I think I forgot how it feels to be in love and to have someone love me." I say honestly.

I look up to Rip and see him smiling down at me.

"Why the hell are you smiling at me like that?" I ask irritated.

"You've gone all sweet and mushy on me."

Rip answers still smiling.

Annoyed I shove at his chest, trying to get him off me. Rip laughs and manages to roll us so I'm on top. I sit up and pinch and slap his chest playfully.

"I am not mushy! I was telling you how I feel, and you're laughing at me!" I giggle as Rip takes my hands in his and sits holding my hands behind my back.

"I love that I make you that way sweetheart, it means that your mushy side is all for me. No one else gets that. You're all mine." Rip says before kissing me. I start moving my hips slowly and Rip moans deep in his throat.

"You don't have to go back to the club do you?" I ask softly.

"No, you've got me for the rest of the day sweetheart. I'm all yours." He answers, kissing along my neck.

Rip and I spent the entire day in bed, we ate in bed, we watched tv and we made love a lot. For a day that started off so shitty, it actually turned into an amazing one.

I'm sitting in bed next to Rip, looking up things to do with Caden when he gets back, when a notification comes through that my mum is video calling me.

Without thinking I answer.

"Sweetie, hello, I just thought..." Mum pauses because Rip has come up behind me, swept my hair aside and kissed my neck, completely unaware that my mum is on video call.

"Oh my!" Mum swoons.

Rip freezes and smiles. I watch my mum swoon again. I roll my eyes.

"Hey Mrs Rocke." Rip winks.

"Oh my, I'd almost forgotten how handsome you are Rip. You must work out a lot." Mum states, her eyes pinned on Rip.

"For god's sake Mum, control yourself. You can be such a pervert." I say giggling.

"I am not a pervert!" Mum screeches.

Dad walks in, newspaper in hand.

"Who's a pervert?" Dad asks.

"Mum is." I say laughing, watching mum get all flustered and pissed off.

"I am not!" she denies.

"Penn, were you perving over the young lads again? Honestly, talk about give a guy a complex." Dad grumbles.

I snort back my laughter as does Rip.

"Oh Ben, you know you still do it for me. It was only last night I couldn't get enough of you, only you do that to me…My Big Ben" Mum whispers.

"Oh god. Seriously you two! I think I'm going to be sick." I gag.

Mum spins round and smiles.

"That's for calling me a pervert." she winks.

Rip bursts out laughing. I sit here, a little stunned that Mum just played me.

"Well played Mother, well played." I commend.

"So my darling daughter, it's true then, you are together. From the lack of clothing and the smile on your face, you're happy, too." Mum says smiling from ear to ear.

"God damn it woman, I don't need to hear that." Dad grumbles.

Rip puts his arm around me and pulls me to him so I am leaning against his chest. I can't wipe the stupid grin from my face.

"Yeah Mum, I'm happy." I reply.

"I am so pleased for you honey." Mum sniffles.

"How is Caden? How is he about this?" Mum asks.

"He doesn't know yet, he's still away with Daisy and Carter. He will be back in a couple of days so we will see how that goes." I answer.

I am anxious for Caden to be happy about this. I'm praying that it will all go smoothly but I know it can't always.

"He will be over the moon I'm sure. Maybe take him out somewhere together. Hold hands, kiss and drop hints subtly. Then speak to him. That way he gets to see how happy you are and gets to know Rip a little better." Mum suggests.

I nod in agreement.

"There's a safari park with some rides not too far from here, we could go out for the day." Rip suggests.

"Yeah, Caden would love that." I agree.

"So anyway, I don't want to keep you love birds any longer than I need to, but I'm just calling to say our house has had an offer and we've accepted. They are first time buyers, so there's no chain behind them. If it all goes smoothly we will be with you all in the next twelve weeks. Your nan is beside herself with excitement. You may want to warn the young men!" Mum says laughing.

"I don't think I will, it will be far more funny watching them feel awkward." I laugh.

"You're right, it would be kind of funny watching them deal with your nan flirting. Now I have to go, I promised Wendy across the road we would go to Zumba together. You should try it honey, I've learnt lots of new ways I can move my hips. Adds a little surprise in the bedroom department. Anywho! Love you honey, see you soon. Bye." Mum blows a kiss and disconnects.

I sigh and close down my laptop and cuddle into Rip more, letting out a yawn.

"Well that went easier than expected. I was half waiting for her to ask if I'm having regular orgasms, or something just as embarrassing." I mumble.

Rip chuckles.

"Well maybe she's saving that for the next time you speak to her." Rip says, soothingly stroking his hand up and down my back.

I feel my eyes becoming heavy, and I'm struggling to keep them open. I start to drift off to sleep.

"Love you Rip." I mumble. I don't hear his reply because I am out like a light.

CHAPTER FOURTEEN

Over the next couple of days Rip and I spend as much time together as possible. I still haven't gone out yet, but he hasn't said anymore about the Cartel. To be honest, I haven't wanted to ask and burst the happy little bubble we're in.

Lily and Blake arrived back from their honeymoon yesterday, and Daisy, Carter and Caden are due back any minute. As soon as Lily got back she called around and arranged for all the girls to be here for lunch. I didn't get a say in the matter. I'm chopping up food for a salad. I decided to do kind of a tapas-style lunch for us all, that way everyone can help themselves. I look at the clock. It's nearly eleven am.

I am dying to see Caden. As much as the break has been, well, amazing, I've missed my boy. I need his cuddles. I hear a beeping and smile and run to the door to see Carter pull up. Before the car is even in park Caden jumps from the truck and sprints towards me, jumping into my arms.

I catch him and hold him tight, showering him with kisses. I feel Rip come up behind me and gently give me a sweet kiss on the head, before going to help Carter unload the truck.

Caden pulls back slightly.

"I had the best time Mum, but I did miss you. Just don't tell the tough guys okay? Or they won't think I'm a badass." he whispers.

"Don't worry buddy, I won't tell them. I missed you so much." I shower him with kisses.

Caden pushes and squirms out of my arms and wipes his face.

"Ewww Mum. Stop. Oh, I brought you a present." Caden says excitedly. He runs off, taking his backpack from Carter.

Once we are all inside. Caden pulls out his gift for me. I unwrap it and smile.

"It's a dream catcher Mum, I got one too. It catches your bad dreams. So we will have no more nightmares ever again. You always say how much you love sleeping, well now you can do it without a bad dream waking you up." Caden beams.

Placing the dream catcher down I smile and pull him in for a hug and a kiss.

"Mum, what did I say! I'm a badass. Stop kissing me." he whispers under his breath, trying to act cool in front of Carter and Rip.

"Sorry bud. Thank you for my gift, I love it." I say pinching his cheek.

We stand around chatting for a little while while Daisy and I prep some of the food for lunch.

"So I'm guessing you want me to make myself scarce this afternoon and I ain't getting any of this food?" Rip states pinching a piece of serrano ham.

"No, sorry, but if there's anything left I will wrap it up for you to have when you come home. Only if you're a good boy and leave us be." I tease.

Rip growls playfully, standing behind me. He wraps his arms around me and nips my neck. I giggle. He cups my face and guides my mouth to his and kisses me.

"Are you and Rip boyfriend and girlfriend Mum?" Caden asks.

I freeze. I thought he was in the other room

watching tv. How could I forget that he can creep up on you like a little stealth ninja?

"Uhhh..." is all I say because Rip turns round and pulls me with him, his arm still around my waist.

"Yeah little man, we are, but only if you're cool with it. Our main focus is that you're happy. If you're not, you can talk to us we can try and sort it. What do you think? You cool with me and your ma being together?" Rip asks. I am tense waiting for his answer.

I watch as his eyes flick back and forth between me and Rip, then his little smile spreads across his face.

"Yeah I am cool with it. Does this mean I'm a Satan's Outlaw now?" Caden asks. I sigh with relief and roll my eyes. I should have known that would be his main source of excitement.

"Yeah little man, it does." Rip answers smiling.

"That's so cool, when I start my new school no one will ever pick on me because I'm a proper badass now! I'm part of Satan's Outlaws. The other kids are going to be so jealous." Caden says excitedly before turning and running back into the lounge.

I feel my body sag, relieved that it went so smoothly. The next hurdle will be telling him about his father.

Rip and Carter leave and Daisy helps me lay out the food and drinks. The doorbell goes not just once but continuously. I look to Daisy and we both shake our heads, knowing exactly who is at the door.

I open the door and I am greeted by Lily, looking like a kid at Christmas, full of excitement. With her are Evelynn, Suellen and Louisa.

"First, I have to pee, then food and while I eat you spill all the details. Don't miss anything out, we all want to know." Lily states giving me a quick hug and running past me to the toilet. I turn back around and Evelynn and Suellen both stand there smiling brightly and nod.

"What she said minus the peeing." Evelynn states walking in with Suellen.

We sit out back, all eating and laughing.

"So that's enough of the niceties, yeah I had a lovely honeymoon with lots of sex. Rocked my world. Now tell us about how Rip rocked your world." Lily sits back with a plate resting on her now very big bump, eating.

"You really want to hear it all?" I ask.

The whole table nod in agreement.

"Fine, what do you want to know?" I ask.

Suellen sits forward pulling her notepad out of her bag, she puts on her glasses and flips a few pages until she finds the one she is looking for.

"Here we go, right. Is he good with his mouth? Hands? Is he into kinky stuff? What's his cock like? Is it pierced? Does he talk dirty? Has he said he loves you yet? And lastly, what would you rate his performance out of ten?" Suellen finishes, removing her glasses and placing her pad and pen down. All of them stare at me, waiting for my response.

"Just saying, Raven is bringing Trudy over in a minute, so unless you want to talk about this with her present then I suggest you spill. Plus Raven said she doesn't want to know as she remembers him in nappies and it would gross her out. Now stop withholding, you have bagged the infamous Rip president of the Satan's Outlaws. Just be thankful the whole town isn't lined up to hear this too." Lily states, taking a big bite of her bread.

"Alright fine, he's very good with his mouth, hands and cock. If by kinky you mean butt plugs and anal beads then no, and no he is not pierced, he says things yes but nothing too creepy, I can't give him a score out of 10 because 10 is too low a number for him and lastly, yes he has said he loves me, and I have told him too. Anything else?" I ask, and take a long sip of my wine.

They all exchange looks then Lily jumps from her chair, startling me, as does Daisy and they both swamp me with hugs. Well, Lily tries but her bump gets in the way a bit.

"We are so bloody happy for you. We knew there was something between you two." Daisy says elated.

"Well who would have thought, you girls so far haven't had much joy in the love department, just a few months in this place you're all in love and have found your happiness. You girls are riding the gravy train with biscuit wheels! Maybe I should move to your hometown and find myself an English gentleman." Suellen states.

"If you're going, I'm going too, the English accent is hot. Maybe I could meet a rich banker or a lord. It's that damn Downton Abbey! We all want to be in the big beautiful dresses and shit with all the grandeur." Evelynn snorts.

I burst out laughing, as do Daisy and Lily.

"Is it not like that then? You know, like all Hugh Grants and Colin Firths?" Louisa asks.

I take a bite of my sandwich and lean forward.

"Okay, there are men that think they are the Colin Firths of the world, but they are not. Generally they have little dicks and cry to mummy. Now there are the Tom Hardy's, Idris Elba's and boy they are rough ready and will show you a bloody good time. To actually find a guy like that in London that's decent, honest, and not already taken is hard. I can't speak for anywhere else because, well, I haven't looked. I'm speaking from watching my friends date men like them. And well, my ex-husband is like a cross between Benedict Cumberbatch and Henry Cavill and while he is good looking, charming, and intelligent, he was a dishonest cheater and a liar." I state.

"Wow, way to kill that little fantasy. Thanks for that." Suellen grumbles.

I chuckle as do the others.

"Sorry, but I'm sure it's the same over here, although every guy I've met in this town seems to be either lovely, hot badasses, funny, and again, hot!" I point out.

"This is true, your little town damn right has a magnificent selection of incredibly hot guys. Most of the guys back home do not look like them, believe us." Daisy points out.

We sit chatting for a while. Trudy and Raven arrive and join in with the chat and the laughter.

"How's your daughter Patty?" Daisy asks Raven.

Raven's smile drops from her face and she shakes her head.

"I'm not sure. We haven't seen her since the wedding. We've tried calling her, but we keep getting no answer. I am worried about little

Maddie, I miss her. We don't like the guy she's with, he's bad news." Raven states.

"Have you told her he's not a good guy? Maybe he's playing her and she doesn't know the real him?" Lily asks.

"She knows he has a record for domestic violence, stealing, and grand theft auto. We showed her, she just said that it was over five years ago and that he's changed. She threw the club in our faces saying we have no grounds for judging him. There's a difference between being an outlaw and being scum that steals off of old ladies and hits their women. The club may break laws, but they are honourable, honest and do good for their family and community." Raven sighs, clearly frustrated and worried about it all.

"You know if my parents told me they didn't like a guy I was with, I would have carried on regardless just to prove them wrong. If she's anything like me she'll be clinging on to the fact that she can change him, live in denial and of course feel like this is the best she can get. Give her time she will come around." I reassure her.

Raven gives me a small shrug.

I clear some of the table and take the dishes into the kitchen. Trudy comes in to help me.

"Honey, I just want to say I heard what happened with Darcy." Trudy states, loading the dishwasher.

"Oh shit." I blurt. Trudy snorts back her laughter.

"Oh honey, I'm not upset by it, in fact I wanted to thank you. Many of us have wanted to take that girl down a peg or two over the years. Well you took care of that and also defended my son. So thanks for that. If I see her believe me I will be giving her a piece of my mind. Trying to trap my son like that, faking pregnancy. Her mama was the same, a user, flittered from man to man taking what she could. I suppose she didn't have much hope being brought up like that." Trudy states carrying on filling the dishwasher.

"Nope, don't make excuses for her. Some people have the shittiest upbringings, that doesn't excuse them being an utter dick in life. People still know what's right and wrong." I say tying up the trash bag.

"I'm just going to take this out, be back in a sec." I say over my shoulder.

I head out the front and to the trash cans at the side of the house. As I lift the lid and put in the bag, the hairs on the back of my neck stand on end.

I look around as I feel like I'm being watched, but I don't notice anyone. I clock a blacked our car at the end of the drive, as soon as I start walking towards it, it speeds off, tyres screeching and leaving a cloud of dust in its wake.

I stop and frown in confusion. Maybe it was just someone looking for a house and realising it was the wrong address once they saw me? Something tells me there is more to it, but I can't go on what my gut is telling me. I shake my head, I'm just getting carried away. I can't go worrying about a car parked up at the end of the drive.

Walking back out to the girls I can hear them all cackling with laughter.

"What's got you all cackling like a coven of witches?" I ask.

"Oh you have to tell Rose, Evelynn." Lily snorts.

I look to Evelynn who is wiping tears from her eyes.

"Okay, well there was this guy and I was young, he was a cute Texan boy. He asked me out and we went on a couple of dates. He was nice, I liked him. So I thought, yeah, I'm going to sleep with him. Anyway the night came, and we were making out, things were getting steamy. He pulled out the condom and I thought I'd be all sexy and I said I can put that on with my mouth. Now I'd never done something like that before, but I figured, what the hell? It can't be that hard, can it?" Evelynn pauses, taking a sip of her drink.

"So he wiggled out of his jeans, I should

point out we were in the back of his parent's truck. Anyway, I tear the condom wrapper with my teeth, being all sexy. I place the condom between my lips ready to put it on. I bend over and nearly choke on the damn thing. Now I'm not one to belittle any man, and size isn't normally an issue. Well, this was an issue. His pecker was smaller than my pinkie finger. In fact probably around the same size." Evelynn says waving her pinkie finger about.

"Oh what a let-down! What did you do? Run away with your knickers around your ankles?" I asks giggling.

"No, we were at least two miles from town in the middle of nowhere. I had to give it the best performance of my life. So that is what I did. I swear when I put the condom on, it just hung off it loosely. Looked like I'd put a damn trash bag on it. I almost wanted to pet it, I felt sorry for the little guy." Evelynn chuckles.

I laugh at Evelynn, still wiggling her little finger about.

"So I hopped on, didn't even know if it was in, honestly my tampons are bigger. I got moves, bless him he was having a great ol' time. Thankfully he was like a two pump chump, so I didn't have to put up with it long." Evelynn shrugs.

I'm laughing so hard my belly hurts.

"Tell her the rest, don't leave it there hanging." Suellen snickers.

"Alright, now don't you go thinking I got a big ol' pussy, because I do my exercises. I look after my little lady. He just had a tiny dick. So he drops me off home, I get in and go to get showered and changed. Well, as I'm getting changed, I lift my leg up to pull my sock off, and I feel something in my area. Before I can think any more of it, I hear something land on the floor, and there's the damn condom! The guys pecker was that small, it nearly got the god damn thing lost up in there!" She shrieks.

"You're full of shit! No way did your pussy suck up a condom?!" I roar with laughter.

"God's honest truth! I dumped his ass the next day. Found out through a few girls over the years I wasn't the only one this happened to. Even the smallest condoms on the market were too big for him. You know he's married now with three kids. Poor wife always looks miserable. I don't think he's even found the clit!" Evelynn giggles.

We are all laughing so hard we don't hear the guys the come in.

"What's got you girls laughing so much?" Blake asks, walking to Lily and kissing her on the head.

"Oh nothing. It's nothing big." Lily snorts and we all carry on giggling. The guys just smirk, looking back and forth at each other shrugging.

I wipe my tears. Rip walks to me smiling. He just picks me up and sits down with me on his lap. He takes my chin and brings my mouth to his.

"Hey sweetheart." He whispers across my lips, I smile.

"Hey." I reply

"Oh now that's hotter than a preacher's knee." Suellen states, fanning her face with her hand.

I hear everyone snicker and giggle at her comment. I just smile, looking at Rip. He returns my smile and kisses me before turning his attention to everyone around us.

I look to see Carter has Daisy on his lap, but Blake is sitting next to Lily with her feet across his lap. He's rubbing her feet.

"Why haven't you lifted me and put me on your lap?" Lily huffs, crossing her arms over her round pregnant belly.

"Blake, answer carefully, because what you say she will use against you everyday for the next ten years." I warn.

"Thanks Rose." Blake says rolling his eyes, before turning his attention to Lily.

"Darlin', if you want to come sit on my lap, you come sit on my lap. I didn't want to lift you incorrectly and hurt you or the baby. Plus I thought you'd enjoy the foot massage instead." Blake states, all the while still massaging her feet.

"You're sweet, even if you are full of shit. It's one of the reasons I love you." Lily smiles.

Blake just smiles and gives Lily a wink.

"Where's Wes?" I ask.

"Had some other business to see to." Rip says cryptically. I look to the other guys who all have a tense look on their face. They're clearly keeping information from us.

Everyone heads out and we promise to catch up soon. Daisy is off to look at the site tomorrow for her new victims of domestic abuse centre. Construction is under way and she is very excited, she is going to take us on a tour soon.

Shutting the door I head to the kitchen to clear up. Thankfully with Trudy helping me earlier there isn't much mess left. Rip walks in and pulls the cloth from my hands and lifts me over his shoulder, carrying me upstairs.

"Rip, Caden! I whisper hiss at him.

Rip just smacks my ass and continues on up the stairs.

"He's fine, he's in his room. He's fallen asleep, it's all good. Just remember not to scream too loud." Rip states as he kicks the bedroom door closed behind us.

He was right, Caden was fast asleep, meaning the rest of our night was blissfully uninterrupted.

CHAPTER
FIFTEEN

"For god's sake Caden! Will you hurry up and get your arse down here now?! We will be late and not make it to the bloody safari park." I yell from the bottom of the stairs.

"Damn you're sexy when you shout orders!" Rip teases, coming behind me wrapping his arms around my waist.

"Piss off." I mumble.

"Eww, do you guys always have to be hugging, kissing or holding hands? It's gross." Caden whines, coming down the stairs.

I chuckle and pause when I see what he's wearing.

"Honey, what are you wearing?" I ask.

"Mum, we are going on safari. I have to dress so I don't spook the animals and I still look bad-ass." Caden shrugs jumps down from the bottom step and starts walking out the front door to the car.

Caden is wearing full desert camouflage. Shorts and t-shirt. He even has green and brown face paint on his face. Let's not forget the binoculars around his neck.

Today is going to be an interesting day. I turn to Rip who is holding back his laughter.

"Laugh it up, he's with both of us today. He will embarrass you too, just give it time. It's what he does, it's his super-power. Never fails." I say patting Rip's face and walking out to the truck. The poor guy is in for such a shock.

We drive for over an hour to get to the safari park. The whole way Caden has not stopped informing us of all of the animal facts.

"Did you know Capuchin Monkeys pee on their hands to wash their feet?...Did you know male ring-tailed lemurs will stink fight by wafting scent at each other, also the wombat poop is cube-shaped...and.."

"Okay buddy we get it, please stop talking.

We're here now." I interrupt, pinching the bridge of my nose. I feel a headache coming on.

Rip reaches over, takes my hand in his and brings it to his mouth, kissing it.

"Ewww, please stop being all gooey. It's gross." Caden complains.

Rip turns round to Caden.

"Here's the deal little man, I love your ma. I love holding her hand, I love holding her and I love kissing her. I know it grosses you out and I will try to be considerate of that, but little man, I ain't gonna stop. So you're going to have to be a big man and suck it up, because it'll be happening a lot. Is that good with you?" Rip suggests.

I'm absolutely taken aback by Rip's statement but loving how warm my heart feels. I turn to Caden to gage his reaction. He looks from me to Rip and back to me again, clearly having a deep thought about what Rip just said. His face then splits into a massive grin.

"You love my mum?" Caden giggles.

"Yeah, I love her." Rip confirms.

"That's good cause mum needs someone to love her, apart from me. She's happy so I suppose I can't moan too much. Can I roll my eyes instead? Like this?" Caden rolls his eyes and shakes his head in disapproval.

"Yeah, that's cool." Rip answers, chuckling.

I'm giggling to myself. God I love that kid so much.

Rip pays for our tickets and comes back to the truck. As we start to drive slowly through the park looking at the animals, Caden has his little face pressed up to the window in excitement. I lean forward and kiss Rip.

"Thank you." I whisper across his lips.

"Shut up and kiss me." Rip says before he brings my mouth to his. He quickly pulls away, kisses me briefly on the forehead, and starts slowly driving through the park. I watch as he adjusts his jeans, noticing his arousal. I can't help but laugh.

"Keep laughing sweetheart, because as soon as we're alone I'm fucking you." Rip says with a low growl. I bite my lip smiling. Rip looks at me and groans in his throat.

"Fucking torture." He mumbles under his breath.

I lean forward and peck him on his cheek, still laughing. I turn and look at Caden who hasn't paid the slightest bit of attention to us.

"Mum! Look! There's the buffalo's! They're huge!" He shouts in excitement.

"Wait until we get through to the next enclosure, there are giraffes." I say looking at the map.

"Oh I like giraffes." Caden replies, his little face still pressed up against the window.

As we continue to drive through the park, Caden's excitement doesn't die down. If anything it builds. The thought of seeing the monkey enclosure and lions is making him bounce in his seat. I smile warmly, watching his little face light up.

"You know this is the last place I'd picture a badass MC president coming. Does this not destroy your reputation?" I ask laughing.

"Ain't nothing I could do to destroy my reputation sweetheart. All this shows people is that I have people I love and will do anything for. Now for a man like me, that's dangerous for anyone that upsets, messes or even attempts to take away the people I love...because they know I would damn well kill to protect what's mine." Rip answers, kissing the back of my hand.

His words hit my heart like a freight train. To have someone say they would fight to the death for you, fight your battles for you and do whatever it takes to protect you, it's completely soul consuming. Apart from my parents I don't think I've ever had anyone love me like Rip does. He loves so fiercely, so passionately. It is all or nothing with him and I love that.

We pull to a stop in the monkey enclosure, and Caden is giggling away in the back as the monkey's run and chase each other over the truck.

"Climb over here little man, you'll be able to see better and you can help me drive the truck." Rip says to Caden over his shoulder.

Before Rip can even finish his sentence Caden is climbing over and sitting in his lap.

"Oh look!" Caden points to the monkey sat on the hood of the truck. soon there are two more sat with him. Caden is fascinated and smiling from ear to ear. I'm not paying any attention to the monkeys, I'm fixated watching my son and Rip sat together. My heart swells. I sneakingly get my phone out and snap a picture of them. I put my phone down and look to Rip who's eyes have gone wide.

"Err, sweetheart." Rip murmurs, nodding his head towards the monkeys on the hood.

I gasp and snort back my laughter. The only way to describe what I am looking at is a monkey threesome. Two are going at while the other appears to be jacking off.

"Mum, why is that monkey doing that?" Caden asks.

I watch as Rip's shoulders move up and down in silent laughter. I sit here with my mouth opening and closing, wondering what on earth to say.

"He's err, um, got an itch. Yup he has got an itch. Rip lets go see what other animals they have, won't that be fun?" I say, my voice going a little high pitched.

"Sure sweetheart." Rip coughs, still trying to hide his laughter.

"Okay Mum, we should tell the ranger. That monkey should see the vet. He was itching it like crazy." Caden states.

Rip laughs, no longer being able to hold it in.

I don't know if I should be thankful for the fact he didn't know the other two monkeys were shagging. I just know this will be the one thing he'll tell everyone at school on Monday when he starts.

We drive through the lions and they come up close to the truck. Even I can't help but be amazed by these beautiful animals.

Once we've driven through, Rip parks up at the park shop so we can get an ice cream and Caden goes to play on the play area.

Rip pulls me on to his lap and I can feel a few of the other parents stare at us.

"People are staring." I whisper.

Rip looks around. I notice a few parents giving us a few disapproving and disgusted looks.

"Ignore it sweetheart, it's the cut. It's the

stuck up assholes that judge because I'm a biker and part of an MC. They will look and stare, but they will never have the guts to say anything because they are a bunch of bitches." Rip states.

"I thought with it being 2019 there wasn't really any prejudice or judgement towards people. I mean, I knew there would be a little, but you're a biker, so what? They don't know you, god those pricks make me so mad." I seethe.

Rip takes my face in his hands and crashes his mouth to mine, hungrily kissing me and leaving me breathless.

"I fuckin' love you." Rip growls low across my lips.

"And I fucking love you too biker boy." I smile.

"I really fuckin' wish we weren't in a fuckin' play area right now." Rip grumbles.

I laugh and kiss him briefly.

"Calm down biker boy, you can get some later." I say standing to look for Caden. He's on the top of the monkey bars hanging upside down, looking through his binoculars. I shake my head and smile.

Just as I'm about to turn around and sit back down a boy, maybe around a year older than Caden, comes along and tugs on Caden so hard that he falls to the floor. The evil shit throws his head back and laughs. I go to march straight over there, but Rip grabs my arm, holding me back.

"Wait a second, let's see what Caden does. Give him a chance to stand up for himself sweetheart." Rip holds my hand, holding me back.

The evil kid stands there still laughing, watching Caden get to his feet. It's taking everything in my power not to give that kid a peace of my mind. Caden looks up at the kid, his little face is angry. His hands are clenched into fists at his side.

"I've got to go over there, he's going to thump that kid." I say.

Rip still holds me back.

"Let him, he needs to know he can stick up for himself. It doesn't work if he knows you have his back." Rip points out.

I nod, my eyes never leaving Caden.

I watch as my boy throws sand in the kid's eyes, making him cover his face. Then Caden kicks him straight in the nuts. The evil rat bag kid drops to his knees, holding his crutch, and rolls in the sand.

"See, he's got this." Rip whispers in my ear.

I smile, feeling proud of my boy for sticking up for himself. I watch as the other boy's mum rushes over and starts yelling at Caden.

"Oh I don't fucking think so!" I stomp across,

ready to chew the bitch out. I stand in front of Caden and face the woman.

"Don't ever speak to my son like that." I warn.

"Your brat of a son just kicked my son. Maybe if you taught your child some manners and how to behave he wouldn't be going around assaulting innocent children." She spits angrily.

"Oh so you saw that, did you? I suppose you just happened to miss the fact your fugly son here pulled mine off the monkey bars then proceeded to laugh his arse off about it? I will talk to my son about kicking yours, but he was only retaliating, defending himself from sloth here." I say, pointing to her son. The woman's mouth hangs open in shock.

"Did you just call my son sloth?" She asks, outraged.

"Yup." I say crossing my arms over my chest.

"Hell, no one calls my baby boy sloth and gets away with it. You've messed with the wrong mama." The woman pushes her son out of the way and starts pushing up her sleeves. She's a big woman she's got at least a foot in height on me, and probably an extra 30lbs too. Still, I've never been one to back down. So I smile at her.

"Caden honey, go play with Rip, okay?" I say sweetly, but my eyes never leave the woman.

"Punch her hard Mum!" Caden shouts as he runs to Rip.

I pause and realise I'm not setting a very good example to my son. So I try to reason with the she-beast.

"Look, let's be mature about this. We are both mothers, we have to show our children how to resolve conflict without violence." I state.

"You chicken shit? Getting all scared because I will kick your ass. You Brits are just a bunch of pussy's." The woman drawls.

My back straightens and I feel myself becoming even more pissed off.

"Now I'm pissed off. You're ruining our day out and clearly you're a thick bitch who doesn't know when to back off." I seethe.

The woman almost lets out a growl and charges forward, taking a swing at me. I move to the side and stick my foot out, making her fall face first in the sand. She gets up, growling at me like a rabid dog. She charges again, this time I'm not quick enough and she punches me right across the cheek. I grab her hair and yank her back and slam her head into the climbing frame. The woman falls flat on her back, I go to jump on her and give her more but two strong arms circle around my waist, pulling me back.

"God damn it Rip! Let me at her!" I screech.

"Easy there Rocky, Caden's watching you." He whispers calmly in my ear. I relax instantly and look to Caden, who has a huge grin on his face.

"You stay away from me and my kid, and learn to control your kid and your mouth or you'll find this sort of thing will happen a lot." I warn her before leaving her and walking to Caden.

"Mum! That was totally amazing! You totally kicked her arse! So cool! Wait till I tell everyone when I start school, no one will pick on me." Caden says, happily skipping ahead to the truck.

Rip pulls me into his arms and I tilt my head back to look at him.

"Damn badass woman, I knew you were perfect for me. Perfect biker bitch, perfect old lady material." Rip smiles down at me.

I suck in a sharp intake of breath. I know what an old lady is. It means I am his property, and I'll be wearing his cut. It's a declaration to the club members and others, like a wedding band.

"Sweetheart, don't start that shit." Rip warns.

I furrow my brow in confusion.

"What shit?" I ask.

"Building up that damn fortress, just so you know in advance. You will be my old lady and I will be putting a ring on your finger. We will get married and I definitely plan on getting you pregnant. I am not going anywhere. You and Caden are not going anywhere. You are it for me. I don't want anyone else, I don't need anyone else, the sooner you get that into your head the better." Rip states. He gives me a brief kiss on top of my head and walks off to the truck, leaving me stood there, my heart beating hard through my chest.

It takes me a moment to process what he has just said, the normal panic I've felt before from him declaring his feeling doesn't come, instead I feel warmth and excitement spread through me. The thought of spending the rest of my life with Rip feels right. I don't want to be anywhere else, or with anyone else. This is it for Caden and I. Our life starts now.

I'm led in bed with Caden giving him cuddles after reading his bedtime story. I've been putting it off, but I know I need to tell him about his father.

"Caden, honey, I need to talk to you for a second about your dad." I say gently.

Caden looks up at me, waiting.

"Well you know we will be moving here, and this will be our new home. And well, your dad is also moving, but not closer. He will be moving further away. He is moving to Australia, which is really, really far away. Now I promise we will sort something out that means you can still visit with your father...but instead of it being at the weekends it will be when you have summer holidays, and maybe other holidays. I promise I will make sure you still get to see him honey. I will make it work." I say, running my fingers through his hair.

"Mum, Dad won't come and see me. I'm sad, but I know he won't. He will forget about me, like he has now. I sent him a postcard from my holiday with aunty Daisy. He hasn't rang me and it's been forever since I've seen him. He's already forgetting me so when he moves further away, I know I'll be forgotten." Caden says sadly.

My heart breaks for my little boy. I wrap him tightly in my arms and kiss the top of his head.

"Honey your dad will never forget you. You are far too special and brilliant. He loves you too much, you are unforgettable. Your dad is just silly and gets too busy and forgets to do things. But that doesn't mean he's forgotten you, okay?" I try to soothe him. Inside I am raging and want nothing more than to ring my stupid twat of an ex husband and scream at him. I won't. All I can do is be here for Caden and hopefully my ex won't let him down.

"I'm alright Mum. I have you, and I really like being here." Caden says yawning.

I give him a kiss, get up, and tuck him tightly in bed.

"Goodnight honey, you'll always have me. I love you." I whisper and kiss his cheek.

"Night Mum, love you." Caden mumbles sleepily into his pillow.

CHAPTER
SIXTEEN

The next few days run smoothly, Caden doesn't mention anything about his father. Things have been amazing with Rip. We even managed to have sneaky sex in the laundry room while Caden was busy playing on the Xbox. I've started calling it Charlie Chaplin sex, because we had to be silent. It's how I imagine it would have been in a silent movie. I may have giggled to myself for a good five minutes after. Who am I kidding?! I still giggle to myself about it now. Even a quickie with Rip is off the charts amazing. I can honestly say I've never felt chemistry like this before, all he does is give me a look, or even just a smile, and I want to pounce. It's like my body is trying to make up for the six and half years of nothing.

It's not just the sex, he makes me feel like I'm the only woman in the world, like no one else matters. I never thought I would end up as one of those annoying dopy love-sick type people, that are constantly smiling and happy, but I am. Well, an R rated version of that, anyway.

The day has finally come for Caden's first day at his new school. I can see he's nervous. He's trying to play it down, but I can see the nerves behind his eyes.

"Alright buddy, you got everything ready to go?" I ask.

"Yeah, I'm ready." he answers, biting his bottom lip anxiously.

"Come on then, let's go." I hold out my hand and he takes it as we walk down to the truck. Just before we open the door the sound of motorcycles approaching the house stops us in our tracks. I look up to see Rip, followed by Khan, Mammoth, Rubble, Wheels, Big Papa, even Wes, Blake and Carter, all of them on bikes. The sight of all of these beautifully hot guys on Harleys literally takes my breath away. Rip gets off his bike and walks towards us. He kisses me briefly, before crouching down to Caden.

"So it's your first day at your new school, me and the guys thought we'd escort you and I figured because you're badass, you'd want to arrive like a badass on the back of a Harley. Does that sound cool to you?" Rip asks.

"Hell yeah!" Caden shouts with excitement.

I smile and sniffle back my tears. Rip tells Caden to go see Khan for his helmet.

I pull Rip to me by his cut.

"I fucking love you biker boy." I say before kissing him. "You're so getting laid for this." I whisper across his lips.

Rip smiles.

"I was fuckin' planning on it." Rip states smacking my behind.

I climb on the back of Rip's bike and Caden is on the back of Khan's, he is grinning from ear to ear the whole way there. I didn't think it was possible to love this man more, but he just keeps surprising me.

When we arrive at his school, everyone stops and stares as we pull up. I get off of Rip's bike and go to Caden. He goes along fist bumping the guys and thanking them. I can see all of the women, mums and teachers, looking with a lot of appreciation at the guys. Khan, never one to miss an opportunity to get his leg over, smiles, turning on the charm and giving them a wink. To my surprise Rip comes alongside me and takes my hand in his. I smile up at him and he kisses the back of my hand.

Once we meet Caden's teacher and settle him in we leave. Just before I get on the back of Rip's bike, I walk along all the guys, giving them a kiss on the cheek and thanking them for doing this for Caden.

"You're family, it's what we do." Mammoth shrugs.

I make it back to Rip's bike.

"You want to keep kissing my men or are you done?" Rip asks sarcastically.

I slap his chest.

"Shut up, what you and your men did means the world to Caden and I. You get your own thank you when we get home, so stop your bitching and get me home biker boy." I say climbing on the back of his bike.

"Hold tight sweetheart." Rip says over his shoulder before pulling off quickly, making me hold on tightly and scream with laughter.

I am sat astride Rip on the sofa, we didn't make it to the bedroom. I am riding him hard and fast, my orgasm building.

"Oh fuck Rip, I'm going to come!" I cry out.

Throwing my head back my orgasm hits. I don't stop, I ride it out as wave after wave of pleasure consumes my body.

"Fuck I love you." Rip growls out.

He grips my hips and buries himself deep inside me as he comes.

I lean forward and kiss Rip, both of us panting and trying to get our breath back.

"I love you Ripley." I say smiling.

Rip groans and nips my neck, I giggle.

"You keep that up I'm going to flip you over and spank that ass of yours." Rip warns.

I purposely clench around him and bite my lip.

"Promises, promises." I say wiggling my hips, trying to tease him.

Before I can do anything else, Rip has picked me up and flipped me on my back, pinning me to the sofa.

"I hope you're ready for this sweetheart, I'm gonna spank that ass then fuck you hard." Rip threatens. It's a threat I like very much.

"Do your worst biker boy." I goad.

Just as Rip is about to turn me over his knee someone knocks on the front door. Rip groans in frustration.

"Stay there, stay naked." He orders as he gets up, pulling on his jeans and walking to the door topless. I watch his tattooed muscled back walk to the door. Perfection.

I'm in such a sex induced daze admiring Rip's hot body I don't notice his whole body tense.

"Who the fuck are you?" Rip asks firmly.

"Ah, well, this is the address Lily gave me. I was wondering if Rose is there? I'm her ex-husband, Richard." I hear snootily said to Rip.

My whole body tenses and my eyes near pop out from how wide they are. I quickly jump up and grab Rip's cut and run to the door.

"What the fuck are you doing here?!" I yell.

Richard is taken back by my outburst. He looks down over my body, his eyes go appreciative briefly, before his face turns to disgust.

"Sweetheart, go get some clothes on." Rip orders.

"I'm fine," I snap. "So why are you here? You said you were going to Australia, and that you'd call, and we'd sort out an arrangement with visiting. Now you show up here uninvited and completely unexpected. As you can probably tell I was kind of in the middle of something, so forgive me if I am a little pissed off and not rolling out the damn red carpet for you!" I rant.

Rip pulls me to him, his arm circling my waist. Richard doesn't miss it either.

"I emailed you Rose. I am stopping over, just for today, I fly out tomorrow to Australia. I took a brief detour to see Caden. Now where is my son?!" He barks, getting irritated. I go to shout back but Rip gets there first.

"Now listen to me and listen fuckin' good. You do not raise your damn voice on my property, you do not raise your voice to my woman. Now you're going to calm the fuck down. Sit on my steps and wait until Rose is decent. I swear to fuckin' Christ if you so much as raise your voice at her one more time I'm getting my fuckin' gun and I'll show you how good my fuckin' aim is. Clear?" Rip threatens.

Richard grits his teeth, clearly pissed off, but I can see the fear behind his eyes. He nods and walks to the steps and sits down.

Rip pulls me inside and slams the door closed. He pins me against the door.

"Do you have any idea what you are doing to me? Standing there naked in my cut? What I wouldn't give to fuck you right now against this door. To let that prick of an ex hear you scream my name as I make you come. Letting him know you are mine." Rip rasps low in his throat.

"Fuck! I hate my ex even more right now. Kiss me biker boy." I order.

Rip smiles.

"With fuckin' pleasure sweetheart."

He crashes his mouth to mine, his lips and tongue possessing me. I moan, kissing him with everything I have. Rip breaks the kiss and lightly bites my neck. I gasp.

"Did you just give me a hickey?" I ask.

"Just making it know to your ex that you're mine sweetheart. I don't want him getting any ideas. Go get dressed." Rip kisses me swiftly before walking to the kitchen.

I shake my head, dumbfounded that he can be so cave mannish, like I'd even give my ex a second look. I think me pretty much being near naked stood with Rip was enough of a sign that I'm not interested in my ex.

I make quick work putting my clothes back on. Rip hasn't put a shirt on, he has just put his cut on with his jeans. He looks unbelievably hot.

I open the door and gesture for Richard to come in. He walks in, looking around, almost sizing up the place.

"Coffee?" I ask.

"Please." I show him to the kitchen and make us all a coffee. Rip is leaning against the counter, his arms crossed over his broad chest, his eyes never leaving Richard.

"So you with him now?" Richard asks nodding his head in Rip's direction.

"Yes." I answer, not elaborating.

"You're a biker? What do you do? Meet up with your buddies on a Sunday and go for bike rides?" Richard asks, mocking Rip.

I cover my face with my hand and shake my head, secretly praying Rip doesn't tear him to pieces.

"I am the president of Satan's Outlaw MC. This is our town. We run it. In fact, we own it." Rip answers taking a drink of his coffee.

"You're in an MC? As in Sons of Anarchy and Easy Rider?" Richard swallows nervously. I can't help the smirk on my face and enjoyment it brings me to watch him shit his pants.

"Err, yeah, but we're fuckin' real." Rip states, crossing his arms across his broad chest. The look on his face is almost daring Richard to mock him, just so he can knock him out.

Richard is still standing here stunned like someone's shoved a sharp stick up his arse. His eyes are flickering back and forth between me and Rip.

"Richard." I call, breaking him from his stunned statue like state.

"You can't be with him." Richard rushes out.

It's my turn to look stunned. I feel Rip's body tense beside me.

"I'm sorry, what?" I ask dumbfounded.

"You cannot be in a relationship with him, he's a convict. He's probably sex trafficking girls, selling drugs and whatever else it is that they do." Richard says in disgust, like Rip's a piece of shit on his shoe.

I feel my blood boil and I can't contain my anger. I surge forward. Rip tries to put his arm out to stop me, but I brush him off. I don't stop until I am toe to toe with Richard.

"Don't you dare tell me who I can and cannot be in a relationship with. You have no right to that part of my life, and how dare you accuse and insult the man that I love! God! What on earth did I ever see in you? You're a pompous weasel with no backbone. You have no integrity and no loyalty. You think you're above everybody and considering you're a doctor, you have bugger all empathy. You care for yourself and what people in your yuppy circle think. You don't seem to care about what Caden wants or worry about what he thinks. That man you forbid me from having a relationship with is everything you are not. His family come first in everything he does, the people he loves are his number one priority. What he does for this town and the community is all good. To sum it up Richard, you can fuck off." I say angrily.

"What?" Richard asks, shocked by my outburst. Before I would have maybe made a snide comment, afraid that if I pissed him off he would take me to court for Caden. I'm not afraid anymore, I know that I have Rip and the Satan's behind me. I know that in Richard would never stand a chance of taking Caden from me.

"I said fuck off." I repeat. I take the mug of coffee from his hand and place it on the counter.

"But I came all this way to see Caden." He says over his shoulder as I shove him towards the front door.

"You will see him, when he has finished school. We will meet you at Jeanie's diner at four o'clock. You can have dinner with him, but I will not have you in Rip's house when you're being such a rude prick." I say as I give him one last shove out of the front door. He turns to say something, but I get in there before he has a chance.

"See you at four at Jeanie's." I slam the front door in his face.

I sigh and turn to face Rip.

"I am so so sorr…" I start to apologise, but stop when Rip just bursts out laughing. He's bent over holding his stomach. I stop and watch him, I've never really seen him laugh like this before. Even now, his laugh is hot and sexy.

He stops laughing and walks towards me, pinning me against the cupboard.

"Sweetheart, you kill me. How the fuck were you ever married to that? But not just that, I don't think I've ever had a woman apart from my Ma defend me or my club like that. You are completely fuckin' made for me, made to be mine." Rip says trailing kisses up my neck.

I hum in agreement, too distracted by Rip's lips to actually form an answer.

Rip's cell interrupts us and Rip groans in frustration.

"What?" He growls into his phone.

I smile and roll my eyes at his brashness. Rip smirks back at me but his smile soon falls from his face when whoever is on the phone starts talking. My smile falls too, sensing whatever he is being told is not good.

"Get the men to church now, I'll be there in twenty minutes." Rip orders and disconnects.

"What is it?" I ask concerned.

"I can't say sweetheart, club business." He answers.

I huff and cross my arms over my chest. I hate this rule of club business being kept between the men.

"Don't sulk with me woman. It's how we do things to protect our old ladies, now I will tell you some things but not everything. You're just gonna have to accept that. So stop pouting and kiss me." Rip demands.

I huff, lean up, and kiss him.

"I will be back later. We will go and pick up

Caden and then meet your ex. Now tell me you love me." Rip says, tucking my hair behind my ear.

"I love you." I say smiling, Rip kisses me goodbye and leaves. I stand for a few moments just sighing in a lovesick daze. I shake my head to snap myself out of it and decide to go shower.

Once showered I go into Caden's room and grab his dirty laundry. Walking downstairs I notice the front door is wide open. I pause briefly before I stick my head outside to see if anyone is there. No one. I shrug and shut the door, guessing that Rip hadn't shut the door properly when he left. I load the washing into the machine and make myself some lunch.

I lean against the kitchen counter eating my sandwich and sigh. It has only been an hour since Rip left and I'm already bored. I can't spend everyday doing nothing. I have months yet until Daisy's centre is open, I'll need to find something to occupy myself with. I'm not used to this. I've worked as a nurse doing crazy shifts and long hours for as long as I can remember. The only time I had off was when Caden was off school.

I decide to ring Lily and ask why she gave Rich the dick Rip's address.

She answers on the second ring.

"Hey skin and blister." Lily answers.

"Why did you give Dick Rip's address?" I cut

straight to the point.

"He showed up didn't he! Tell me did he shit his pants seeing Rip?" Lily says with amusement in his voice.

"It isn't funny Lily, we were kind of in the middle of having sex when he knocked on the door." I inform her.

"Oh my god that is brilliant! I wish I was a fly on the wall to see his face. Tell me more." Lily says and it sounds like she's opening a bag of crisps.

"Seriously? You're enjoying this aren't you? Are you eating crisps?" I ask.

"Yes and yes. Look I gave the address because I thought it would be good for you to be able to rub his face in it, okay? For him to see that you're finally happy and living your life, and for once make him feel uncomfortable. I didn't actually think you'd be shagging, although that is the icing on the cake. Did Rip answer the door? Oh my, was Rip near naked when he did? God I bet it made Dick feel as small as his little one inch penis." Lily chuckles.

I snort back my laughter.

"No, not completely naked. He pulled up his jeans, I put on his leather cut. I had nothing else on, so yeah, I think even dick would have guessed what we were up too. He insulted Rip by implying he was just in a little motorcycle group, but Rip enlightened him on the truth. Then the dick decided he could tell me what to do and somehow not allow me to have a relationship with Rip. I gave him a piece of my mind, threw him out the house and told him to meet us at Jeanie's at four to see Caden after school." I relay to Lily.

"Holy shit, I really wish I was a fly on the wall. We will be there at Jeanie's with you." Lily informs me.

"Lily, you don't need to, Rip will be there to support me." I reply.

"Skin and blister, as much as I would be there to support you, I know Rip would be there for you. I'm merely coming for the show, and it will be a blast to see Dick's face if we're all sat there too. That'll shit him right up, I will call Daisy tell her to meet us there. See you later." Lily says before she disconnects.

I sigh and pinch the bridge of my nose. God it's going to end up being a bloody circus later. I hope is that Dick behaves himself, because one word out of turn in any way and these guys will be on him, kicking his arse into next week.

I spend the next few hours cleaning even though the house is pretty clean, just for something to do. Soon it's nearing pick up time for Caden. I decide to sit outside on the porch steps in the sun and wait for Rip to arrive. I sit down and close my eyes, leaning my head back and enjoying the feeling of the sun on my face. I hear a car approach. I open my eyes and see a smart black car pull up. A built guy in a suit with tattoos on his neck gets out of the front passenger side and walks around to the back and opens the door. An older guy maybe late forties, early fifties gets out. His jet black hair is gelled back. He is in a suit, a very expensive looking suit. He has a thick gold chain around his neck and dark olive skin. He's good looking in a dangerous way and his eyes are near black. There's something about the way he is looking at me that make my hairs stand on end and my stomach recoil.

"Hola Rose." He says in a thick accent.

I stand up, a little taken aback that he knows my name.

"Are you a friend of Rip's? He's not here at the moment." I say wearily.

The guy stops right in front of me and takes my hand in his and kisses the back of it.

"You're un angel bello, Rip is a lucky man." He states smoothly, his eyes never leaving mine.

I give him a tight smile, not liking this guy one bit. I go to take my hand back, but his hold just tightens.

He sneers and leans in close to my ear.

"Let me go." I grit through my teeth.

"Now bella dama, listen carefully. You tell Rip that he is to back down and let us do our business or I will start a war he cannot win. I will take away every last one of his Familia, his hermano's, his loved ones. All of them will suffer." He whispers in my ear and runs his nose along my neck. My whole body is completely rigid and frozen still.

"Hhhmm, I see why Rip has taken a liking to you." He says moving back slightly, a smile spreading across his face. He lets go of my hand and clicks his fingers. The big guy in the suit opens the car door for him. Before he gets into the car he turns to me smiling.

"I hope Caden enjoyed his first day at school." He winks before getting into the car and shutting the door. The car speeds off, kicking up the dust in its path.

I feel my knees go weak and I grip hold of the railing before I fall. It was them. It was the Mexican Cartel. They have been watching us, they know about Caden and I. I'm so consumed with panic and worry I don't here Rip and the guys show up. The next thing I know Rip is crouched in front of me, concern across his face.

"Sweetheart? What is it? Is it Caden? Is he alright?" He asks, cupping my face.

"They've been watching us. They know everything. They know Caden is at school. There will be a war Rip, if you don't back down there will be a war. You need to stop whatever it is you and the club are doing." I ramble in a panic.

I watch Rip's face turn from concern to a pure murderous expression.

"Luis was here?" Rip questions.

I shrug.

"He didn't give his name."

"A guy, early fifties, Mexican, in a suit? Probably called you bella el angel." Rip questions.

I nod.

Rips stands, runs his hands through his hair, and yells.

"Fuck!"

He turns on his feet and yells orders at the guys.

"Luis was fuckin' here at my damn house. I want you all to escort us to get Caden, then you will stay with us until we are back at the clubhouse. Call your family and everyone else. The club is under full fuckin' lockdown. No excuses. I want everyone safe."

Rip turns to me and pulls me into his arms.

"Sweetheart I promise tonight I will sit down with you and we will go over this, but right now we need to pick Caden up and put on an act for him and for your dickhead of an ex too.

I want to know everything he said to you, we just need to get through this first. Are you okay?" Rip asks cupping my face.

I take a deep breath and nod. Rip kisses my head and takes me to his bike.

I climb on and we ride to pick up Caden. The whole way there I replay what Luis said. I know I need to focus on Caden right now and act like we are all okay. Even more so, because if Dick was to catch wind of this there is a chance that he would take Caden away from me. There is not a chance in hell I would let that happen.

CHAPTER SEVENTEEN

We pick up Caden from school and I do the mum thing of putting a smile on my face and pretending that everything is completely fine. I can't help but look over my shoulder constantly on the ride to Jeanie's.

We are all sat on the other tables away from Caden and his father to give them some time together. Rip, Blake, Wes and Carter have all stepped outside for a quick chat. The rest of the guys from Satans' are spread about Jeanie's, inside and outside the diner. To anyone walking past they are all just hanging around grabbing a bite to eat and chatting, but I know their eyes are everywhere scanning, constantly on the lookout. Every single one of them is on alert.

"You know they will sort it, they will get him, and you won't need to worry." Lily states, drinking her milkshake.

I turn to her and lean forward and whisper.

"The head of the Mexican Cartel threatened me personally, no, not just me, Caden too. That's not to mention the whole of Rip's family. That means you too. I'm thinking this isn't going to be so simple so excuse me if I'm not about to kick back relax and think this is all just a little misunderstanding. I can feel it and so can you. Every one of the guys is tense and on high alert. This shit is big, if it wasn't, why are pretty much the whole of the fucking Satans' here?!" I hiss angrily.

Lily frowns and leans forward.

"Do not speak to me like I'm stupid. You forget what I've been through. I get that you're shook up, I get that this shit going down is seriously scary shit. That doesn't give you the right to speak to me like a raving PMT bitch. What I was trying to say is these guys know what they are doing, you have to trust them. Also it doesn't do anyone any good to be sat here stressing and worrying. So try and chill out." Lily fires back.

"Enough you two, there's no need to start taking chunks out of each other. You're both right. Yes, we need to be on alert and concerned, but we also need to try and relax and let them handle it. From what I've overheard we're all going to be staying at the clubhouse together so we could turn this into a fun time!" Daisy interjects.

I look to Lily and she looks at me. We both roll our eyes at each other.

"Always the peace maker, hey Daisy?" I say nudging her.

"Piss off." Daisy replies smiling.

We talk for a little while when Richard comes over with Caden.

"Was it really necessary having the entire club here?" Richard asks.

"I didn't ask them here, they all came to pick Caden up from school and wanted a bite to eat. They aren't here for you."

"Sure, well I have to go. I have to leave for the airport. I've been allocated an earlier flight. So I have to go." Richard states looking at his watch.

I lean down to speak with Caden.

"Honey, why don't you go and ask Jeanie for one of her chocolate brownies to go for your dad to take on his long journey." I say handing him the money.

"Good idea Mum! Dad you will love them,

they're the best." Caden says running off the counter.

"You've been moved to an earlier flight? I thought you were in town for the day and flying out tomorrow?" I question.

"Yeah well things have changed." Richard mumbles in return.

"You changed your flight, didn't you? I cannot believe you! You've spent exactly two hours with him, that's it! And when the hell will you see him again?" I ask, feeling my temper rising.

"I'm not sure, I've got to settle into the house first. We have to ship our belongings across and I can't just take time off when I've started a new job." Richard shrugs, checking his phone again.

"God damn it! You're his father! For once in your life put him first. Do you know what, just say your goodbyes and I will deal with our sad and upset son. I'm fed up of forcing you to have a relationship with him." I say frustrated. I would love nothing more than to throttle him right now.

Caden comes running over, giving his dad the brownie.

"Thanks Caden, listen, I've got to go. I will be in contact when I'm settled into my new house, okay? Be good for your mum." Richard says scuffing his hair and leaving. No hug, no 'I will miss you' or 'love you'. That's it. I watch Caden's shoulders sag in disappointment. I pull him into my arms and hug him tight. Lily and Daisy come over with a huge ice cream sundae with sparklers and four spoons.

"Hey Caden, there's no way we can eat this all by ourselves, reckon you could help us?" Lily asks. Caden's sad little face changes into a smile and he nods enthusiastically. I mouth 'thank you' to my sisters. I'm so thankful that I have them here to help show Caden that he is surrounded by people that do love and care about him.

We arrive at the clubhouse and Caden is beyond excited. Just as we enter little Maddie comes running up, her little legs moving as fast as she can make them.

"Pwincess Lily! Pwincess Daisy!" She screams excitedly. She jumps straight into Daisy's arms. Her little face splits into a full smile. God! She's such a cutie.

"We're having a big slumber party! I'm so excited! All us pwincesses together! You are a pwincess too Rose! It's the pwincess club." She giggles throwing her hands in the air, cheering. We all laugh apart from Caden who grumbles beside me.

"Hi Caden." Maddie waves shyly.

"Hi Maddie."

We walk into the clubhouse which is packed with families from the club. There are children running around and women bringing out dishes of food. There's no sign of the guys, they must be in a meeting. I spot Raven and go to speak with her. I give her a hug, she looks tired and stressed out.

"Hey, you okay?" I ask concerned.

"Yeah, I'm fine. It's Patty, Maddie's mum. She refused to come in for lockdown. Or should I say, her boyfriend refused. She handed me Maddie to bring in for safety. You should have seen her, she looked worn out, exhausted, and I swear I saw bruises on her arms. I have Maddie safe with us, but I don't have her." Raven states with worry in her voice.

"Oh god, I can't imagine how worried you are, but she will come crawling back, I'm sure. She will eventually see what this guy is and get rid. She's a smart girl, soon she'll realise she's missing out on her daughter and a real chance of happiness." I answer, hoping that I'm right.

I make a sneaky exit to Rip's office. The door is open, so I just walk in, shutting it behind me. I sit on the little sofa and curl my legs up. I use the peace to let what has happened sink in. To let the threat, well, the promise, that was made sink in.

The door opens and I look up, seeing Rip enter. He closes the door behind him and walks toward me, sitting next to me and pulling me onto his lap. I bury my face in his neck and just inhale his scent, it soothes me. Rip caresses my back, stroking it in soothing movements.

"Tell me sweetheart." Rip says softly.

I nod and relay everything Luis told me. I feel his body tense and his hand pauses in places, but he soon controls himself. When I've finished I sit up and cup Rip's face in my hands.

"Please don't go to war with him, there's something about him that is pure evil. I felt it. I saw it. It radiated off of him. I don't get scared easy, but he scared me Rip. He meant every word. He will destroy you and everyone around you." I plead.

Rip takes my palm and kisses it.

"Sweetheart, we're already at war with him. The moment he decided to sell drugs and traffic women through our town was when he declared his intentions. The day Ven took Lily and did what he did, he declared war against us. By having Ven and his pa plus other police force members on his books he declared war, not just on us but on our town. This has been a long time coming sweetheart. I'm sorry but there is no other way to shut him down than by fighting against him and killing him."

I sigh and rest my forehead against his.

"I can't lose you. I can't bare the thought of anything happening to you. I wouldn't survive it. I know I wouldn't." I say softly.

"Sweetheart, look at me." Rip orders, stroking my cheek.

I open my eyes and look directly into his piercing ice blue eyes.

"I can't promise that nothing will happen to me, but I can promise I will fight for you, for Caden, for us. I'm not willing to give up on us. I will fight for you until my very last fuckin' breath." Rip states firmly.

Hearing that doesn't ease my worry or fear, but I know Rip will fight to the end for the people he loves, and I have to take solace in that. He's right, if the satan's backed down Mufftown wouldn't be the same, this beautiful town would crumble.

"Okay, well then, if you're fighting and going to war then I will be right by your side, supporting you and the club. Like the guys have said, I am the club's very own Florence Nightingale." I say running my hands through his hair.

"I'd give anything to lay you on my desk and fuck you right now." Rip replies. I smirk.

"I can't because the club is full of family but fuck me what did I do to deserve you? Sweetheart, I'm not a religious man, I run with the devil...But I thank the fuckin' lord every damn that day I found you." Rip states softly kissing me.

We're interrupted by a knock on the door. Rip groans deep in his throat.

"What!" He barks.

The door opens and Khan sticks his head through the door, his eyes land on us and he smiles.

"Sorry Pres, but it's important. Two of Luis men are out front, demanding to talk to you." Before Khan can even finish Rip is moving me off his lap and walking out of the office.

I quickly jump up and follow.

"Stay inside." Rip orders me.

Of course I completely ignore him and follow him. Rip and Khan walk through the door and to the front gate. I follow, keeping low so that no one will notice I'm there.

I see two of Luis' men stood on the other side of the gate, both dressed in suits. They both have gold chains around their necks and their hair is immaculately gelled. One of the them places a hand on his hip purposefully, to show he's carrying a gun. I swallow back my nerves. It's like watching a movie, the air is tense, and I'm scared for the guys. The Cartel could pull their guns and shoot Rip and the others at any moment. I hear clicks to the side of me and see Rubble, Wes, Wheels and Blake all with guns in their hands, aimed directly at the Cartel. This eases my worry just a little, although the look in the Cartel's faces show that they are not appreciative of the guns aimed at their heads.

"You appreciate I have to protect myself and my club. Now what do I owe the pleasure of Luis sending his two goons for a visit?" Rip says sharply.

There's almost a completely different tone to his voice that I've never heard. It's a menacing tone, a tone that means he will not stand for any bullshit.

"Luis sent us to offer you one last offering, a deal. He will cut you in, twenty percent. If you reject him, mi amigo, there will be muerte. I am sure you wouldn't want that mi amigo. What will it be?" One of the Cartel says, sneering at Rip.

I know what muerte means...death. My heartbeat picks up speed and my body tenses in fear.

Rip smiles like the guy just commented on the weather and didn't threaten to kill everyone.

"Don't be mistaken, I ain't no friend of yours or Luis's. I promise there will be death but it won't be my men or any of my family. It'll be you. You should fear death because I promise it's coming for you, and me and my men will be the one fuckin' delivering it. So how about you be good little messengers and tell Luis he can shove his offer right up his ass. I'm coming for him." Rip threatens.

I watch as one of the guys goes to pull his gun from his holster. Without even thinking I run out from where I'm hiding.

"No!" I shout as I run in front of Rip. All of the Satans' and the Cartel look surprised to see me.

"Ah bella el angel, it is good to see you." The bigger guy says, his accent thick. He places his hand on the other guy, stopping him from pulling his gun, and shakes his head.

Rip wraps an arm around my waist and pulls me behind him.

"What the fuck are you doing out here?" He growls angrily in my ear.

I don't get to answer because the big guy speaks again.

"It seems you need to control your woman, I'm sure I'd be able to control her." He goads, smiling at Rip.

Before anyone can stop him Rip pulls a gun and aims it straight at the big guy's head.

"You ever speak about my woman like that

again I will not hesitate to put a bullet between your eyes." Rip threatens.

The guy puts his hands up and throws his head back laughing. I look at him, confused, he's completely crazy. I know Rip would most certainly do it. That wasn't just a threat, that was a promise.

"Easy, I get why you would be protective of her, I've seen what's under her clothes. She looked deliciosa." The big guy smiles licking his lips, his eyes never leaving me.

I frown in confusion.

"I've never seen you before in my life." I point out.

"You didn't see me bella, but I saw you, all of you, dripping wet in the shower." He states smiling.

I gasp, realising.

"The front door." I whisper. I shiver at the thought.

"You want to tell me what the fuck is going on?" Rip growls low.

"After you left yesterday I went for a shower. When I came back downstairs the front door was wide open. I just assumed you didn't close it properly when you left." I say shuddering, feeling violated.

Rip doesn't speak, he simply turns to face

the big guy who is smiling, knowing he's got to him. Rip doesn't even blink. He pulls the trigger, hitting the big guy right between the eyes.

I scream and watch as his lifeless body falls to the floor.

"You go back to Luis and take that piece of shit with you. This is my message to him. I'm just getting fuckin' warmed up." Rip growls out.

I stand here shaking, stunned at what I've just witnessed.

"Make sure this fucker clears up and leaves." Rip orders.

He turns and scoops me up in his arms, walking us back to the clubhouse. My whole body trembling. He takes us through a back door and to his office, avoiding everyone. He sits me on his desk and pours me a drink of whiskey.

"Drink it." Is all he says.

I don't back chat. I don't argue. I down it and gag as the liquid burns my throat. You'd think I would be used to it by now.

"Why the fuck did you have to go against what I told you and come out? Did you not fuckin' think there may have been a reason I told you to stay the fuck behind? No, you just have to go against my orders." Rip seethes, pouring himself a whiskey, knocking it back and slamming his glass down.

"I am not one of your club brothers or a whore you can just order around. I was worried about you. I wanted to know exactly what it is that is going on and what you have to face." I argue back.

"Well now you fuckin' know! That little scene would have been avoided if you had just stayed the fuck inside like I told you to." Rip barks back.

"I'm sorry, okay! But you're the one that just killed a man! Can I just deal with that please?! I just watched the man I love shoot someone dead like it was something he does every single day! Can you please just give me a damn second to process that?" I fire back.

Rip freezes, his hands balled into fists at his side.

"Did it occur to you that I never wanted you to ever see that side of me? I was protecting you from seeing that. You weren't ever supposed to see it." Rip states, turning away with his hands on his hips.

I watch his body and his movements. He looks resigned, like he's giving up.

"I will get the guys to get your things. Then when it's safe to do so you can get a flight home." He sighs.

I blanch at his words.

"What?!" I ask .

"Fine, stay at your sisters, whatever you want." Rip answers, walking past me.

I put my arm out stopping him.

"I am not going anywhere, why the hell would you think that?" I ask.

Rip turns to me, placing his hands either side of me on his desk and leans in.

"You just saw me kill a man. I shot him dead without a second thought, right between the eyes. If you're expecting me to feel any remorse for doing it you'll be waiting a long fuckin' time. I liked killing him, he deserved it. I don't regret it in any way." Rip states.

His face just an inch from mine. His eyes are watching me, waiting for my reaction. I know he's deadly serious. I knew he had killed before. I knew he was beyond capable of killing and seeing him do just that was a shock, but not because he did it. It was a shock because I've never seen anyone get shot before. I don't speak. I reach up and pull his mouth down on mine hard, taking him by surprise.

Rip groans, his hands go under my behind, pulling me closer to him.

Both of our hands are fast and frantic, desperately removing clothes.

In one swift movement Rip fills me. He

doesn't pause or give me time to adjust, he fucks me hard and fast. It's what I want, it's what we need. He grips my hips, continuously pounding into me. Without building, without warning, my orgasm crashes over me, hitting me hard.

"Fuck! Rip!" I scream.

Rip lets out a low groan when his orgasm hits. We are both panting hard and fast, our bodies covered in a light sheen of sweat. I am about to speak when there's a knock on the door, Khan walks in and halts when he sees the sight before him. I tense and lean into Rip, using him to cover my body.

"Get the fuck out!" Rip barks.

Khan smiles and winks at me.

"Sorry Pres." Khan says holding his hands up in surrender.

I smile and hide my face in Rip's chest. Once I hear the door shut I place a kiss on his chest over his Satan's Outlaw tattoo.

"I love you for you. For the light and the dark. I accept all of what makes you, you. I am not going anywhere. You never have to hide any part of yourself from me." I say looking into his beautiful ice blue eyes.

Rip cups my face and leans in, gently kissing me.

"I would never hurt you or Caden, you

know that right?" Rip asks with concern in his eyes.

I smile and roll my eyes.

"Duh, I know that." I say teasingly.

"There she goes giving me fuckin' sass. God I fuckin' love you." Rip says smiling. He kisses me again before we both put our clothes back on.

Before we leave his office, I stop and turn to him.

"Do I look okay?" I ask, hoping I don't look flushed.

"Fuckin' perfect and freshly fucked." Rip answers opening the door and forcing me through it before I can protest.

CHAPTER EIGHTEEN

Rip

As we walk into the bar of the club-house it's complete chaos, there are kids running around everywhere, food all laid out and all of the brothers and their families standing around chatting. I stand for a moment and take in my club, my brothers, my family. Pride fills my soul seeing them all together supporting one another. I love the loyalty they give to the club and each other.

I find Khan, his eyes meet mine and I give him the nod to get the guys to emergency church.

Khan is one of the biggest jokers I know, and he's always saying the wrong thing, but he's my right hand man. He's a good brother and good at what he does for the club.

I take my seat at the head of the table and wait for the rest of the guys to follow. I didn't want to shout it out and cause worry or panic amongst the families. Truth is, me losing my cool has forced our hand, and now we need a new plan and quick. War is coming for us and we need to be fuckin' prepared.

One by one the guys fall in, Wes, Blake and Carter join us too. They are Satans' family and we need all the men we can get.

I bang my gavel to quieten the guys and start the meeting. All eyes fall to me.

"You know why I called y'all for emergency church. Things have changed. So that means our plans have to change. What happened earlier is on me, I shouldn't have lost focus and let them get inside my head." I state.

"I would have fuckin' blown his brains out too Pres." Rubble comments.

"I second that." Mammoth agrees

"Damn straight, that cunt crossed the line. It's only right he should meet his maker." Fury spits.

The rest all nod and continue to mumble

their agreements.

I'm not surprised by the support of my men. No matter what, they're by my side. I know Fury would understand being happily married for many years, there is nothing he wouldn't do for his old lady.

"I appreciate that, but it has forced our hand and now we need to up the security and protection for our family. Not only that, we have to take the war to Luis and we have to do that now. He's going to get the news of what's happened, and he isn't gonna take it lightly. I plan we roll out tonight, Luis wouldn't be expecting us so soon." I suggest.

I take a cigarette from Khan's pack and light it, taking a long pull. I'm not a smoker. I only smoke when times are tense or when I'm shitfaced. I watch as the guys exchange looks, clearly knowing how bad things are because I'm sat here smoking.

"I'm in, makes sense to attack under the cover of darkness. The trucks are fuelled up and ready to go. I can get the prospects to load them." Khan agrees.

The guys grunt in agreement.

"Get the prospects to do it discreetly, I don't want to cause panic amongst the women and kids. We leave at ten. Enjoy what time you have with your families. Pa, I want you and Big

Papa staying behind with the prospects. I need you guys to keep an eye on things here, just in case any of those fuckers decide to try their luck." I order.

"Sure son, you contacted the other chapters? Louisiana and Arizona?" My Pa asks.

"Yeah they are all ready to come if we need but it'll take them a couple of days to get here. We don't have a couple of days to wait for them. We need to act now. I told them I would know by morning if they're needed." I answer.

"Good." My Pa states.

"Go be with your families, prepare, and we'll meet at ten out front." I say banging the gavel.

The guys one by one get up and leave. I sit here deep in thought, finishing my smoke.

"You okay son?" I look to my Pa, there's concern written on his face. I nod and give him a tight smile.

"You know these men have your back, and so will I. This isn't like before. Back then the club was divided, the club was at war with each other. There is no way we were ready or even capable of war. It will not end up like that, I promise you." Pa affirms before wheeling himself out of the room.

I sit here running over earlier events in my

mind. I think about the darkness that took over my soul hearing that the fucker had watched Rose in the shower. The threat, that I knew would be a promise, from his mouth. His eyes said everything his mouth didn't. I would kill anyone before I would let harm come to her. She completely consumes me, I knew the moment I saw her curled up asleep that I was in fuckin' trouble. Then meeting her properly, her sass, her don't give a shit attitude which I could see was a front. She cares, maybe too much. There isn't anything she wouldn't do for her family that's for damn sure. She's fierce and loves with everything she has. Rose is fuckin' perfect for me.

That's why I can't shake this feeling in the pit of my stomach, the feeling of dread, of fear. I've never felt this way going into any dangerous situation before and I know it's because this time I could actually lose her. Whether it be me getting killed or worse: the thought of losing her. It's a feeling I don't like and one I can't fuckin' shake.

I stay seated for I don't know how long, until there's a little tap on the door and my Ma enters.

"Hey, we are all sitting down to eat. You should come and join us. I know Rose and Caden are looking for you." She says perching on the edge of the table next to me.

"Yeah sure, I'm coming." I answer, still deep

in my thoughts.

"Honey, listen to me. I know what's going through your mind, you need to use those thoughts and focus. I know you love Rose, I know you're scared of losing her. You have that feeling in the pit of your stomach and it won't go away until you hold her in your arms afterwards. I know that feeling well, I get that with you and your father. I'm so proud of the man you've become but god, between you and your father you scare the ever loving shit out of me. It's any wonder I'm not grey." Ma tries to joke.

"What I'm trying to say, son, is that this feeling, no matter how awful it feels, it means you're in love. It means you have something to fight for and I will tell you, she will be feeling it too. So go out there tonight, lead your brothers and put a stop to this war so you can come home and feel the good...because it far outweighs the bad." Ma finishes.

She stands gives me a kiss on my cheek and goes to leave.

"Thanks Ma." I say, she turns and give me a small smile.

I stand with determination to kill this war. My Ma and Pa are right: if I don't fight this and put a stop to it, then I'm forever going to have this bad feeling in the pit of my stomach. The sooner this is over, the sooner I can get my happy ending.

I pour a whiskey and knock it back, I smile as I stand there and think of ways I can tear Luis limb from fuckin' limb. The Mexican Cartel will face my blade. They will face my wrath and they will be left in a sea of blood.

CHAPTER NINETEEN

We are sat down eating and there is so much food. The kids are all sitting together and the club members that have wives are together. I sit with an empty chair next to me, waiting for Rip. Trudy said he was just sorting something out and then he would be out.

Truth is, I know something is eating at him, because I'm pretty sure it's the same thing that's eating at me. I have such a fear that he won't make it back to me. The whispers between wives is that they leave tonight. I can't help the dread I feel. I wish I could beg him not to go and to stay, but I know he has to do it.

I poke food around my plate when the chair next to me is pulled back. I look and see Rip sitting down, he grabs me by the nape of my neck and brings my mouth to his.

He pulls back slightly.

"You feel it too." He states.

I nod.

"I will be back, sweetheart, and this feeling will go. I promise." Rip says as he kisses my forehead and sits back in his chair.

"Eat." Rip orders.

"Don't tell me what to do." I snap back.

Rip just smiles, knowing his words have riled me. I smile knowing he was just doing it to distract me and lighten the mood.

We eat with everyone talking and laughing and it reminds me of a big family Christmas. It brings back memories of home, pasting tables, family members sat on all sorts of different chairs at different heights, but no one would care, because everyone was just happy to be with each other and spend time together celebrating Christmas with the people they loved.

I've always missed those Christmases over the years with the family now all over the country. It's been years since I've sat at a table like this. It fills me with warmth and proves although they are not related by blood, they are a family. It's a family I'm now a part of. The Satans' family, and I couldn't be happier.

"You okay sweetheart?" Rip asks holding my hand, bringing me out of my memories.

"Yeah, just reminds me of our family Christmases from years back. Although at least these are proper tables, and everyone is sitting at the same height." I laugh. Rip smiles and kisses my hand.

I look over to Daisy and Lily. Their eyes meet mine and they both nod, obviously feeling the same as me. With this, something that is simple like all sitting around like we used to for our big family Christmas, I know I will be happy. I know I have found our home. This is home.

After we've eaten and cleared away, the kids run out back to play and all of the club members go in for a strategic meeting. Me, Lily and Daisy are sitting on the bench outside watching the kids play.

"You know they will be okay, they will come back." I state.

"Who are you convincing, us or yourself?" Lily mumbles.

"Both." I answer honestly.

Daisy grabs both mine and Lily's hands. We look to each other and sigh.

"You rang Mum and Dad and told them

what's going on?" Daisy asks.

Lily and I both snort back our laughter.

"Good god no, could you imagine? Mum wouldn't still be in London if she knew, and she would probably go with them and demand to talk with this Luis' mother. She'd then proceed to tell them how would their mother would feel about what they are doing." I laugh.

"Or she'd want to put them on a time out." Lily adds laughing.

"God, they're both going to lose their shit when they find out about all of this. We are going to get such an ear full when they find out we kept it from them." Daisy points out.

We all nod in agreement.

"Dibs, I'm not doing it!" Lily shouts.

"I second that dibs." Daisy calls out straight after.

I look at both of them and roll my eyes.

"I guess that means I'm the one that has to tell them. I don't see why you can't Lily, you're pregnant. They won't go completely crazy at you as you're giving them a grandchild." I say poking her round bump.

"Stress is bad for the baby, I'm trying to avoid it." Lily rushes out.

"Yeah you're doing a bloody great job of that." I say sarcastically.

We all chuckle and go back to just sitting in silence, watching the kids play.

Maddie is running around laughing and chasing Caden. I smile and watch my boy being cute and sweet with her. An older kid walks over and purposefully trips Maddie over, making her cry. All three of us immediately stand up ready to give this kid some shit for hurting sweet Maddie, but we stop when Caden walks up to him and shoves him as hard as he can, taking the boy by complete surprise and making him fall over.

"Yeah Caden! Kick some arse." Lily mumbles under her breath.

The boy, clearly embarrassed to be taken down by a kid that's at least two years younger than him, stands and walks away ducking his head.

"Your boy is certainly following in Rip's footsteps." A woman says next to us. We turn and look to her. She's a beautiful petite blonde woman, wearing a cut that says property of Fury. I've seen her around but never actually met her.

"Hi, we haven't met. I'm Rose, and these are my sisters, Daisy and Lily. I'm not sure Caden is Satans' material." I laugh.

"Hi, I'm Bonnie. Yeah, I know who you all are. Don't be so sure, he stood up to my boy there and that takes guts. You need to stand up and make yourself heard in this family." She smiles.

"Oh my god I am so sorry, I didn't know that was your lad." I apologise, embarrassed.

"Oh honey don't be worrying about it. I saw what my boy did, and he deserved it for tripping up little Maddie. I was about to give him a piece of my mind, but I think your boy has done that for me." She giggles.

I sigh with relief that I don't have to apologise for Caden. Although I do have it down to a fine art. I had to do it enough to parents from his school.

"Oh look how sweet Caden is being." Daisy points out.

I turn my gaze back to them and watch as Caden puts his arm around Maddie's shoulders, comforting her. I feel so proud watching him be so caring towards her.

"Well excuse me ladies, I'm off to get my boy to his bed and find my man before they all head out. It was good to finally meet y'all." Bonnie says waving over her shoulder.

"She has a point, it's eight. The guys should be done by now. It would be good to spend some time with them before they leave." Daisy says.

Agreeing I call in Caden and Maddie comes running over with him.

"Hey did you see?! Caden came to my rescue! He pushed that smelly Braden right over on his bum. He is my pwince." Maddie says excitedly.

"We did see, and I'm super proud of him too. He was being a real prince rescuing a princess!" I say pinching Caden's cheek.

He groans in protest. Lily smiles and Maddie giggles.

"Come on princess Maddie, let's go find your nana and get you to bed, it's getting late." Lily says holding out her hand to Maddie.

Maddie smiles and before Caden can do anything about it she jumps up and kisses him on the cheek. She giggles taking Lily's hand and skips off. Caden acts annoyed but I catch his little smile, it's hard not to like Maddie, she's too sweet and adorable.

"Mum, do I have to go to bed?" Caden moans as we walk back to the clubhouse.

"Yes. You can watch a movie in bed, but yeah buddy, it's time for bed." I compromise.

"Fine. Wait, a movie? Does that mean I'm not going to school tomorrow?" He asks in confusion.

"No school tomorrow bud, there are some things going on. That's why we are all staying here for a little while, hopefully you'll be back at school soon." I say and kiss his head.

"Oh I know, the Mexicans right? They are

causing us problems." Caden sighs like he knows all about it.

I stop and hold his shoulders, making him look at me.

"How do you know that?" I ask.

"Heard some of the guys talking." Caden shrugs.

I sigh, he always has a habit of being where he shouldn't be and listening to conversations that he shouldn't know anything about.

"Where did you hear them talking about it?" I ask.

Caden starts to fidget and I know that means he was somewhere he shouldn't have been.

"I didn't mean to, I just wanted to see what it's like in there, that was all, and then all the guys came in and I had to hide and wait until they were finished."

"You sat in on their meeting?!" I screech.

I'm trying to shield Caden from everything that is going on. I don't want him hearing any of the undoubtedly scary, horrific things that the guys may or may not have been talking about.

"It's cool Mum. The guys are doing it to protect us. Plus they are totally badass, they will kick their butts and win." Caden states nonchalantly.

"That's not the point Caden, you do not do that again, alright? They have those meetings to talk about grown up things, things that are private. You don't ever creep in there to ease drop!" I chastise.

Caden hangs his head.

"Sorry Mum, it's just I want to be just like them." Caden apologises.

I sigh and bring him in for a hug and kiss the top of his head.

"Maybe when you're an adult, okay? But not until then."

"Fine." Caden huffs.

I smile and ruffle his hair.

After I've settled him down, I go off in search of Rip. I find him in the bar with Mammoth, Khan and Rubble. As soon as he spots me he smiles, grabs me and pulls me to him so I'm standing in between his legs.

"Caden go down alright?" Rip asks.

"Yeah he's just watching a movie. He told me something earlier." I pause, hoping Rip doesn't get to angry.

"He, um, well, he snuck into your meeting, hid and listened to the whole thing. I've told him off, and he won't do it again..."

Rip interrupts me.

"He hid in our church? Sweetheart there were things said that no child should hear. Is he okay?" Rip asks.

"Yeah, he's absolutely fine. He said he wanted to be like you, well, like all of the guys, that you're all total badasses. I told him he would have to wait until he was an adult to be like you." I say smiling. The guys grunt with laughter behind me.

Rip laughs and shakes his head.

"Telling you now Pres, that boy is made to be a Satan's Outlaw." Khan adds.

"You ain't fuckin' kidding." Rip agrees.

I look up at the clock and know they will be loading things up soon and getting ready to leave. I sigh and bite my lip, nerves swimming around in my stomach. I can't shake the feeling, no matter how positive I try and be.

"Boys, fuck off a minute will you? I will meet you out front in a bit." Rip orders.

They get up and leave, not saying a word, leaving just Rip and I.

Rip tucks my hair behind my ear and cups my jaw, his thumb stroking my bottom lip.

"I promise you I will be okay. By tomorrow morning I will be home. I won't leave you, not ever. Now kiss me so I can go and organise shit." Rip promises.

I kiss him, slow and passionately, part of me never wanting to break this kiss because I don't want him to go. Reluctantly I stop, wishing I could take him hostage and keep him safe with me. Rip kisses my forehead and moves me so he can stand, still keeping me in his arms.

"Fuckin' love you sweetheart." Rip rasps, emotion thick in his voice.

"I fucking love you too biker boy." I whisper, trying to keep my emotions under control. I move aside and Rip walks out the door to see to the guys loading up the trucks.

I sag on a stool and signal for the prospect behind the bar to get me a drink. I down a shot of tequila, coughing from the burn as it travels down my throat.

"God I wish I could neck a couple of them right now." Lily says, pulling up a stool next to me.

"I will have a fucking orange juice thank you." Lily says in mock pleasure.

"Just pass the bottle and another glass please. There's a good lad." Daisy says, sitting down on the other side of me.

"You just said your goodbyes too?" I ask, knocking back another shot of tequila.

"Yup. Feeling like utter shit, actually you know what, I know I can't wallow in drink, but

I can wallow in ice cream. Young lad, could you be a diamond and grab me a big tub of ice cream from the freezer, any flavour, I'm not fussy at this point." Lily asks the poor young prospect. He doesn't seem to mind, he smiles and wanders off to get it for her.

"God damn I forgot how much this stuff burns your throat." Daisy coughs next to me.

I snort back my laughter and rub her back.

"I swear to bloody god that if anything happens to them, I will go down there and kick the Cartel's butts." Daisy says angrily. Well I say angrily, it's Daisy, it's like watching Snow White get angry. She just doesn't have a bad bone in her body.

"They will be okay, Rip promised me, and we all know Rip is a little psycho. He can, and will, scare the shit out of anyone that tries to hurt one of his men." I state again, downing another shot.

I refill our glasses and hold mine up in a toast.

"To the Satan's Outlaws and family, may they go unharmed and kick some serious Cartel butt!" I shout.

"To the Satans'!" Lily and Daisy both shout and clink glasses in unison.

CHAPTER TWENTY

Rip

Once we've loaded up the trucks we head straight out. No emotional goodbyes. We need our heads in the game. We need to be focused.

I know I told Rose that we would be home, and all would be fine, but this is the Mexican Cartel. They are organised, and if we were hitting them on their home turf, we would be outnumbered three to one.

A shooting pain hits through my chest at the thought of Rose. I rub my chest. I've never had this feeling or worry before. It's completely foreign to me. The only way I'm going to survive this and get through it is to channel those feelings into killing and ending this shit with Luis.

"You're not alone in that feeling. We fucking end this tonight, for them." Wes states.

We all grunt in agreement. I pause and look at Wes, wondering how he's feeling the same as us. He has always been shady about a woman that was in his life in the past, but more and more recently he's become more distant. I'm now wondering if there's someone in his life that he hasn't introduced us too. He will tell us when the time is right.

As we drive through the deadly quiet roads, the atmosphere in the truck is tense with rage. We all know what faces us isn't going to be easy, but we are the fuckin' Satans' and we are to be feared. Even though they aren't Satan's Outlaws, Blake, Wes and Carter are all capable and have valuable skills that would make any man piss their pants. Our man power combined with the element of surprise, the Cartel won't know what's fuckin' coming for them.

I move my neck, trying to ease my tension. That's one thing I worry about, losing one of my men, losing one of my family. Blake, Wes and Carter are not official Satans', they didn't have to come, they could have stayed behind. They chose not to, they chose to fight alongside us as brothers.

"How much longer?" Blake asks from the back of the truck.

"We're about twenty minutes out. We will park up a mile out, keep the trucks out of sight. I will go over the plan and then we will make the rest of the way on foot." I say.

"Gottcha." Blake answers.

"No one is to touch Luis. He's mine." I growl.

I feel my blood boil at the thought of him. What he's done, trafficking women, young women, abusing their fear and desperate situations to fill them with false promises and hope. In reality they are becoming slaves for the sex industry, sold to the highest bidder. The thought makes me fuckin' sick to my stomach.

We arrive at our location and park up down a side dirt track, keeping the trucks out of sight.

I gather the men for a final briefing.

"Stay low, keep hidden until the very moment when we ambush. You will need to watch your back, and do not let your guard down at any point because the Cartel are trained. They know what they are doing. Keep it quick and swift, we are outnumbered so be smart. Finally you make it out of there alive, no one leaves anyone behind. We get in and get out. Now lets go make it rain fuckin' red." I growl.

The guys grunt in agreement and we make our way through the bushes and trees, keeping out of sight.

A large house comes into view. I spot two men, armed, patrolling the front. I signal to Mammoth. He nods and moves forward and the rest of us stay where we are, crouched low.

Mammoth moves quietly to the side of the house without being seen by the guards. For a guy so big he's light on his feet.

He creeps quickly and grabs one of the guards from behind. In one quick movement he slices across his throat. The guard falls to the floor, blood pouring from his neck.

Mammoth quickly moves across to the other one and does the same. Both guards lay dead in a pool of their own blood.

We move quickly to the house. I send Fury, Khan and Rubble around the back.

Mammoth, Blake, Wes and Carter and I move to the front of the house. We peer inside. There are two guys snorting blow and watching tv.

"Other window, lights out and I can't make anything out." Blake says coming to my side.

"Two guys, getting high. We take them out quickly and carefully, then we'll clear the other rooms." I order.

We make our way up the steps to the house,

with Blake, Carter and Wes watching our backs. Mammoth and I approach the two men in the lounge. I look to Mammoth, my blade in my hand, and smile.

I reach out and grab his head, my hand covering his mouth. I push my blade against his neck. He's shocked and completely frozen still. I lean in close to his ear.

"Ready to meet your maker?" I whisper quietly.

He tries to shake his head.

"Like you had a fuckin' choice." I sneer.

In a clean, quick movement I slice through his neck from ear to ear. My sharp blade slices through like butter. I watch as he tries gasping for breath, blood overflowing as he suffocates and bleeds to death.

"Rip, he's dead. Let's go." Mammoth states.

I shake out of my daze and look to the other guy now slumped forward, dead. I nod and follow Mammoth out of the room.

We clear the rooms, all except the one with the light off as it's locked.

"We will come back to it. First we need to clear the rest of the house."

As we make our way to the kitchen, Khan, Fury and Rubble come through the back door covered in blood.

"Five of them. Sat around the fire pit. Some fucker stabbed my leg." Khan points to his thigh.

There is a blade sticking out of his thigh.

"I gutted the fucker, gonna have to get Flo on this when we get back, fucking hurts like a bitch too." Khan moans.

"You good walking?" I ask.

"I got stabbed in the thigh, I'm not missing a fuckin' leg." Khan states.

I snort, he would have to be missing every limb of his body to step aside.

"It's just upstairs left to clear. Khan, Fury there's a locked door just there. Get entry to it, I wanna know what's behind it...but be quiet and careful. The rest of you, lets get this shit over with." I order.

With Khan and Rubble seeing to the locked room, we make our way carefully upstairs.

Creeping down the hallway, slowly and quietly, checking each door as we go. So far: no one. We reach the door at the end of the hallway, we can hear moaning coming from the inside.

"Well at least he's gonna die happy." Wes smirks.

The guys all quietly grunt. I slowly open the door and take in the room and sight before me.

Luis and one of his goons, fucking the same

girl.

The girl looks thin and very young. I have no doubt it's one of his trafficked girls.

My blood boils and I grip my blade tight in my hand, needing blood.

"Evening gentleman." I sneer.

They both stop what they're doing and look my way, the young girl looks on, terrified. I walk into the room followed by the guys.

"You wanna put your dicks away. I will at least give you a little dignity before I fuckin' kill you." I threaten.

Luis and his goon both move, pulling on their pants. They don't say a word and their eyes never leave us.

"Cover yourself darlin', and leave." I order the girl. She just looks at me wide eyed and petrified, shaking. She doesn't move.

Luis' goon speaks fast in Spanish and back hands the girl across the face. She cries out and runs from the room.

Before I can say anything or blink, a gun shot is fired.

I watch as the guy's head flies back. His blood and brains splatter on the wall and he falls to the floor.

I turn around and look to Wes holding his

gun.

"What the fuck man?" I ask.

"Not apologising, fucker deserved it. We were gonna kill him anyway." Wes answers.

"Agreed, but next time give me a heads up." I state.

I turn my attention back to Luis, his eyes keep flickering to the open doorway.

"Oh, I wouldn't run if I were you. I have men downstairs. If it's your men you're expecting you'll be waiting a long fuckin' time as they're all dead." I inform Luis, smiling.

"Now, I hope you're listening this time because it's clear you have a problem with listening." I state pacing the floor, trying to calm the rage within me.

"Eres un hombre muerto caminando." Luis sneers.

I turn to Wes as I know he understands some Spanish.

"Dead man walking." Wes translates.

I throw my head back and laugh.

"There is a dead man walking in this room but it ain't me and it ain't any of my men. If you hadn't noticed, there are five of us and one of you. So it's you who will be meeting your fuckin' maker and it will be by my fuckin' hands!" I roar, losing what hold of my rage I had.

I storm forward hitting him hard across the face. He stumbles slightly, but he is quick and hits me hard. I lick my lip and taste blood. I smile and before he can do anything I surge my blade straight into his stomach.

His eyes go wide and his hands try to grip my shirt, but he's smiling.

"You idiota, you think killing me it will be the end? It will never be over, I am the fucking rey!" Luis spits.

I twist the knife and he lets out a groan.

"You think you're a fuckin' king? Well consider yourself overthrown. This is my fuckin' kingdom, it never was yours and now you know what happens to anyone who tries to take it!" I roar.

I feel the rage boiling in my veins. I want nothing more than to tear him limb from limb.

"I will take your reina even in muerte. You will pay. I will have venganza." Luis rasps through his pain.

"I will take the queen, you will pay. I will have vengeance." Wes translates behind me.

The thought of him harming a single hair on Rose's head has me losing what little hold I had on my rage. I growl and pull my blade from his stomach. He groans in pain and doubles over, grasping his gut. I throw my blade to the floor and take him to the ground. With him pinned underneath me I hit him over and over, his head whipping to the side with each blow.

I stop and sit back, panting. My shirt is covered in blood, my knuckles are split and raw. Luis groans and coughs, spitting out blood. He turns to me and smiles, his eyes barely open, his mouth full of blood.

"You are weak. You show weakness." He coughs.

"I think you'll find you are the one sat in a pool of your own blood, with no one coming to your rescue." I growl back.

I find his stab wound and jab my thumb inside it. Luis howls out in pain.

"I was gonna beat you until your last breath but now I think I'll leave you like this, to die a slow and painful death on your own. Then while you're led here dying, your only thought will be of me, taking down your precious Cartel, your kingdom." I grit.

One final hard jab of my thumb into his wound. He howls out in pain. I stand.

"Check for any phones and smash them. Lock all the doors and windows, and..."

Before I can finish, Fury sticks his head around the corner.

"Sorry Pres, but we got a situation." He says.

I sigh and tell the guys to keep an eye on Luis and do as I've asked.

I follow Fury downstairs and into the room that was locked.

"Holy fuckin' Christ!" I say stunned. There are floor to ceiling shelves filled with weapons on one side, and on the other is what looks like cocaine.

"Carry what you can of the weapons, leave the fuckin' drugs. We will…" Again, I don't get to finish.

"Um Pres, there's more." Khan says behind me.

I turn and follow a hobbling Khan down into the basement, there's a strong smell of urine and excrement as we make our way down. The smell is so bad that I have to cover my nose.

Khan switches on the dim light and my eyes take in the sight before me. Women. Four women and a small child. They are filthy and dangerously underweight, with cuts and bruising on them. I spot the young girl from upstairs. She is standing in front of the young child protectively. The others are all huddled behind her, shaking in fear.

I look around the room. There are just a few thin blankets and a bucket in the corner. I feel my blood starting to boil again, I turn to Khan.

"Ring Wes. Get him down here to translate, now." I growl low.

Not wanting to frighten them further, Khan pulls out his phone and tells Wes to get his ass down here.

"What is it now? Sweet fuck! What is that smell?!" Wes shouts from the stairs.

He soon shuts up when his eyes adjust and he takes in the sight before him.

"Fuck me." Wes seethes angrily, his fist clenched at his side.

"Wes in a calm way, can you tell them they are safe with us, we will look after them." I ask softly, trying to keep any harsh tones out of my voice. I don't want to scare them.

Wes translates. The one at the front shakes her head, then whispers an answer.

"What does she say?" I ask.

"She said that's what the man upstairs promised them. They are his. He said he will kill them if they try to leave." Wes translates.

"Wes, give her your gun." I order.

"What?! Are you fucking crazy? She could shoot us and fuck off." Khan says from behind me.

"She won't." I affirm.

Wes takes out his gun. They all hold up their hands in surrender, shaking more.

"Now what?" Wes asks.

"Tell her she can hold this gun and if at any point she thinks we're going to cause her or any of them harm, she can shoot us." I tell him.

I watch her face blanch in surprise at Wes' words. Wes holds out the gun to her. She very shakily takes it.

"Wes, go with one of the guys and bring the trucks here." I order. He nods but before he takes off he tells the women that it will all be okay.

"Khan, go and help getting what weapons we can from that room ready to load onto the truck." Khan nods.

I hold my hand up to signal one minute. I walk upstairs to the kitchen and open the fridge. I grab some bottles of water. I take them down to the women and they take them happily, clearly dehydrated.

I walk back to the top of the stairs, the smell getting too much. I pull out my cell and ring Rose. She answers on the first ring.

"Rip?! Are you okay? Oh god please say you're okay, you're not hurt are you? Do you want me to get your mum?" Rose rushes out.

"Sweetheart I'm okay, so calm the fuck down..."

Rose interrupts me.

"Dick, that's what you get for being bloody caring. Charming!" She huffs down the phone. I can't help but hold back my smile, even with all of the shit going on she still gives me her sass.

"Okay sweetheart, I need you to listen. There are trafficked women here, and a child." I say down the phone.

Rose gasps. She's horrified.

"I need you to make up a room for them. I don't care where but they will probably want to be together. There are four of them and the child. Any clothes you can gather would be good. Also you'll need to check them over and Khan needs some treatment." I say down the phone.

"How old is the child? Girl or boy? What happened to Khan?" She asks, I can already hear her moving around, getting organised.

"To be honest, the state they're in, I'm not sure. Maybe like four? The kid has long hair but dressed in dirty shorts and t-shirt. They don't speak English, so I don't know. At this point they need to be checked over, they need food, water and clean clothes. They are not in a good way, they've been treated like shit." I sigh. My fist clenches at my side, resisting the urge to hit something.

"Khan has been stabbed in the thigh. The blade is still in there, but don't worry, he's fine."

I add.

"Okay right. I'm on it. I will put my hospital scrubs on, it might make them feel a little more comfortable, seeing I'm a nurse. I'm gathering some of my clothes now, I will also grab some of Caden's and Maddie's. I will get the others to help set up beds and food, but Rip, if Khan's wound is too deep it might need surgery. You need to prepare him for that." Rose says banging and moving around.

This right now is one of the reasons I'm gonna make her my wife and old lady.

"Fuckin' love you sweetheart." I say into the phone.

Rose pauses what she's doing and goes quiet.

"I fucking love you too." She says and I can hear the smile in her voice.

I smile and disconnect.

The trucks pull up out front. The guys load the weapons in the back of one while the women and child are helped into the other. I walk up the stairs while the guys are all waiting for me at the trucks.

I walk into the room, seeing Luis is now tied to the bed post, blood pouring from his gut and his head hung low. He's drifting in and out of consciousness.

"You sick son of a bitch, not only women, but a child. A fuckin' child! You're gonna burn for this Luis, slowly and painfully." I shout angrily.

I rear back and hit him hard one more time, but not hard enough for him to be knocked out. I want him awake for his slow death. He deserves to be in pain until his last breath.

I shut the bedroom door and lock it. I'm not taking any risks.

Walking out of the house I nod to the guys. They walk around the porch which wraps around the house, pouring gas as they go. They chuck the canisters and we all lean back against the trucks.

I spark up my cigarette and take a long pull, feeling a weight being lifted from my shoulders. I walk up to the house and flick my cigarette.

It lands and flames immediately roar to life. Rubble, Mammoth and Fury walk around the sides and back of the house and throw petrol bombs, smashing through the windows. We step back and watch the house engulf in flames. I smile and turn to the guys.

"Lets get the fuck out of this place." They all grunt their agreements.

Wes and Khan jump in the truck with the women, while the rest of us squeeze into the other.

I cannot wait to get back and hold Rose in my arms. I need her like I need my next breath right now. Seeing what those women were living in, what they had to endure, has made me want to hold her and never fuckin' let her go.

CHAPTER TWENTY-ONE

It's near three in the morning, but the club-house isn't quiet and peaceful with everyone sleeping instead, everyone is working together to prepare for the guys coming back with those poor women and the child.

I prepped and cleaned my now medical room. We have an array of clothes for the women to try on and some clothes for the child, as well as cuddly toys.

I walk into the kitchen. Trudy insisted she was making up a huge batch of her mac n cheese as it's the best American comfort food. I wasn't about to argue, I love mac n cheese.

The smell coming from the kitchen is mouth watering.

"Hey, good timing. Can you take out the plates and set them up on the long table?" Lily asks waddling over with a large stack of plates.

I take them from her and stack them at the end of the table. I stand back, amazed that they've managed to pull off this in such a short amount of time. On the table are bread rolls, salad, chips and dip, fruit, and pies. At the end are bottles of water and juice boxes.

I hear engines close by and look out the window. I see the trucks pull up.

"They're here!" I shout.

I don't wait for anyone, I run out of the door as fast as I can to the trucks. Rip jumps out of one and sees me, he smiles. I jump wrapping my arms and legs around him. He grunts, catching me. I don't say anything or even give him a chance to say anything. I kiss him, hard, fast, hungry and desperate. It's like I haven't seen him in days not hours.

"Thank fuck you came back to me. You must always come back to me." I whisper across his lips.

I try to sniffle back my tears, relieved that he's back safe. Rip wipes them away.

"I will always come back to you, I fuckin' love you sweetheart." He says smiling.

I giggle.

"I fucking love you too." I say back.

"This is all very sweet and like something out of some chick flick, but if you don't mind I do have a fuckin' blade sticking out of my leg." Khan grumbles from the side.

I bite my lip, smiling. Rip puts me down and sighs. He turns his attention to Khan.

"Quit your damn whining, you're waiting your turn. The women and child need to be checked over first." Rip orders.

I spin around and look for the women and child. They are getting out of the car and are all huddled together, the little child nestled protectively behind a woman holding a gun.

"Um, Rip, she has a gun." I state.

"Yeah. I gave her it so she felt safe. I wanted to prove we weren't going to harm her." he states.

I look at him wide eyed.

"She could have got scared and shot you." I point out.

"She didn't and she won't. She could have shot us and stole a truck earlier and she didn't. We are her only hope." Rip says shrugging.

He's got a point. I didn't think of it that way.

Wes speaks to them in Spanish and points to me, all eyes come to me. I smile and wave. I gesture for them to follow me. They do, warily.

As we enter the clubhouse their eyes are everywhere, taking everything in. Lily, Daisy, Trudy and Raven are stood together. Their eyes widen in shock at the state these poor women and their child are in. They quickly mask their reactions with warm smiles.

"Girls, I'm going to need your help. Wes you're going to have to translate." I state.

We walk into my makeshift medical room. I have clothes for them folded on a table at the far end. Luckily there is a shower room attached. I show them the shower room and point to the clothes, Wes translates for me. I get Wes to tell them I will check their health after they've washed and dressed.

They all huddle in the little shower room together and I can hear faint voices whispering to each other.

"They are so underweight...and the marks on them...God my heart breaks for what they must have been through. All for the promise of a better life." Trudy say solemnly.

"Do we know if the child is a little girl or boy?" I ask.

"Girl, she's five. She hasn't been sexually abused. Her older sister is the one with the gun, she promised she would do anything they wanted as long as they didn't touch her." Wes states.

"How old is the sister?" I ask pain in my voice.

"Seventeen." Wes grits out.

We all gasp. That poor girl. You can see Wes is holding down his anger and I completely understand and feel the same.

We all stand in silence for a moment, the severity of what these girls have suffered leaves us speechless. There are no words that can describe the level of hell they've been through. My heart bleeds for them. I hope to god they stay with the club and end up overcoming this and living the life they deserve.

The door slowly opens a while later and they huddle out together, freshly showered and in clean clothes. The clothes hang off of their tiny malnourished bodies.

I stand and guide them to the gurney.

"Wes can you ask if any of them are in any pain anywhere on their bodies? If they are, can they point it out to me?" I ask.

Wes translates, the women all look to each other and the girl with the gun nods. It's as if they are asking her if it's okay to tell me their problems.

The woman from the back steps forward nervously, she's holding her hand. I hold out my hands for her to show me.

Tentatively she lets me examine her hand. No wonder she's in pain, her little finger and ring finger have clearly been broken.

"Wes can you translate please?" I ask.

Wes nods.

"I'm going to do my best to straighten out your fingers. I will put a splint in that will hopefully help mend your fingers. Is there any pain in your hand?" I ask pressing gently on her hand.

She doesn't flinch and shakes her head.

I wrap her fingers using a splint, mentally noting that I need to speak to Rip about when he got all of this equipment in. This is better stocked than some practices.

When it's all done, I look up and smile.

"Any other pain?" I ask.

She shakes her head and walks back behind the others.

"Gracias." She says so quietly her voice is barely a whisper.

The other women step forward and have a few cuts that need cleaning. One has angry welts on her back where she was belted. I treat her as best as I can. While I'm doing this Lily, Daisy and Trudy are showing the little girl some toys and teddies. They are trying to coax her out of her shell but she won't leave her sisters side.

Finally I get to the girl with the gun. She steps forward and places the gun down, a sign that she trusts us. She points subtly her intimate area.

"Wes, translate." I croak.

I cough and take a deep breath.

"I can check that for you, would you prefer to do it privately? Also, can I ask if any of the other girls were abused sexually? Do you know if protection was used?" I say softly.

I catch Trudy's gaze flicker to mine, but I ignore her and keep my attentions solely on the girl in front of me.

Wes translates.

"Si, condon." She answers in Spanish.

I sigh, thankful that protection was used. She tells her sister and the others to go for food. Wes goes with them.

She nervously lays down for me to examine her. She winces in pain. She is badly bruised down there and there are deep bruised finger marks on her inner thighs. I have to step back for a moment, the evidence of what this poor young girl has gone through is too much for me to handle. All these poor girls wanted was a chance at a better life, but instead they faced the worse kind of treatment any human could endure.

A hand touches my shoulder. I spin round and she has sat up and is looking at me.

"I'm okay." She says, although I'm not sure if she's asking or telling me.

I nod anyway.

"Yes, you are okay. It will heal." I say, not knowing if she understands me or not.

She takes me by surprise and hugs me. I swallow back the lump in my throat and hug her back. She leans back and smiles.

"Safe." Is all she says, and I nod in agreement.

"Yes, safe." I say smiling.

I take her hand and lead her back to join the others who are all sat down, their plates piled high with food from Trudy. Their eyes are wide, taking in the amount of food before them.

The girl sits down next to her sister and smiles. She leans across and says something to them all. They look up and slowly, each one smiles and the little girl's face lights up how a child's should.

She stands and does a clap to get all of our attention.

"Me llamo Catalina, mi hermana Ana." She introduces herself and her sister. Then she tells us that the three other women with her are Carla, Valentina and Daniela.

We introduce ourselves just as the guys come in with Khan hobbling behind.

"Will you slow down you fuckers?! You're supposed to help an injured brother out." He moans.

"Khan watch you mouth, there are women and a child present." Trudy chastises.

We all laugh. I'm surprised when Catalina walks towards Rip and hugs him, she does it to all of the guys then steps back.

"Muchas gracias, nos salvaste la vida." She says smiling.

We look to Wes for translation and he has a big smile on his face.

"Big thank you, you saved our lives." Wes translates.

"Wes, tell her she is welcome. They can stay here as long as they want. We will help them." Rip tells Wes as he walks to me, wrapping me in his arms.

Wes translates and she just smiles bigger and sits back down.

Rip kisses me.

"You doin' okay darlin'?" I nod.

"Yeah, those women are incredible and you doing this for them makes my heart swell with love. I can't even breathe. I am so incredibly proud of you. You may think you're the darkness, but you are the light for so many, including me."

Rip's eyes bore into mine, his hands come up and he cups my face.

"Fuckin' love you sweetheart." He whispers across my lips.

"Fucking love you too." I reply smiling.

He leans in and takes my mouth, taking control and making me forget we are in a room full of people.

"Hello! I'm stood here with a fuckin' blade in my damn leg! Yo Flo, drop the pres and come stitch me up." Khan yells.

"Language!" Trudy yells.

I smile and break the kiss.

"Later pres." I say smiling and pat his chest and walk away.

Rip spins around.

"Khan. You speak to my woman like that again I will give you a matching fuckin' blade in the other leg." Rip shouts.

"Ripley! Language!" Trudy shouts again.

Everyone bursts out laughing. Even the women who don't speak a word of English, but understand the mocking and the love in the room.

Sat in my medical room with Khan laid out on the gurney, I put on gloves and prepare a few things.

"You know when I pull this blade out, you could bleed out and you may need to be rushed to hospital." I say setting up my tray.

"No hospitals Flo, hospitals lead to questions and questions lead to police. Just do what you gotta do." Khan states.

"Khan, I've only been in surgery like ten times through my nursing career, if the blade has cut through a main artery you could die. I don't have the equipment to deal with that. So I am sorry, but I will be getting your ass to hospital if that happens because I don't want you dying on me." I say finishing the tray.

"I knew it! It's because I'm hot isn't it? All the ladies love Khan. Don't worry Flo, I won't tell pres." Khan winks.

I poke him next to where the blade is.

"Arrgghh! What did you do that for?!" He cries out.

"Just making sure you're still with us and

not losing your sanity." I say smiling.

Khan grumbles under his breath about women being a pain in the ass. I choose to ignore him and concentrate on the task.

"Okay, so this is going to hurt. I don't have any anaesthetic, so do you want me to get you some whisky from the bar? I don't want you tensing up or moving, okay? I need you to keep still." I ask.

"Sure, get me a bottle of Jack." Khan answers.

I open the door and shout for a bottle.

I get started. I slowly and carefully remove the knife.

"Arrggh! Fucking son of a bitch!" Khan shouts.

Rubble comes in with the jack and hands it to Khan.

Blood pools in the wound. I try to clean it away so I can see what I'm dealing with, but Khan keeps moving his leg.

"Khan I need you to keep your bloody leg still." I state.

Rubble moves around me and holds his leg down.

"Thanks Rubble."

Happy that he's not about to bleed out and die, I get stitching.

Once finished, I cover it with gauze and bandage it up.

"There, all done. Go careful, don't get it wet and they should be ready to take out in about two weeks." I say taking the tray away.

He gets up and sways on his feet a little. Rubble's hand reaches out to steady him.

"Flo, you are the fuckin' man. You know that." he slurs.

I giggle, looking at the bottle. He has drank over half already, there's no wonder it hit him hard.

"You're welcome Khan." I say smiling.

Khan shuffles towards me, his jeans around his ankles, and wraps me in a tight hug. I awkwardly hug him back, patting his back slightly.

"What the fuck do you think you're doing with my fuckin' woman?!" Rip bellows from the doorway.

Khan drunkenly laughs and opens his arms wide.

"Hey! Pres, she's the best, you know that. She fixed me up. Nothin' else happened, I swear." Khan defends.

"I know nothing happened, but you have your arms around my woman with no pants on and your dick out." Rip points out.

"What?" I ask.

My eyes instinctively look down and sure enough, his t-shirt is just covering his junk.

"I thought you hand boxers on!" I shout.

"Nah, it restricts Vlad." Khan shrugs.

"Vlad?" I ask.

"Vlad the impaler." Khan states proudly.

I burst out laughing.

"Laugh all you want, you'll shut up when you see it." He says lifting up his t-shirt and flashing me his cock.

I choke on my laughter. Fair enough, he's hung like a horse.

Before I know what's happening Rip hits Khan straight in the face and knocks him out.

Rubble bursts out laughing, it's only then I notice he's holding his phone up.

"You recording this?" I ask.

"Fucking right, the guys will love this." Rubble chuckles.

"Why did you knock him out?" I ask Rip.

"You're kidding right? He just flashed my woman his junk. Sweetheart, he will know when he sobers up that he overstepped the line." Rip points out.

I bend down and check he's okay and not

bleeding from his head or anything.

"Rubble, get Mammoth and move this dumb ass to his room." Rip orders.

Just as I stand Rip takes me and drags me down past everyone into his room. He shuts the door and starts taking off his clothes.

"Get your clothes off sweetheart or I will take you in the shower as you are." Rip orders.

"Do not boss me around." I answer back.

Rip walks towards me completely naked. My eyes drink in his beauty.

"Get in the shower, last chance, or I will take you in like that." Rip warns.

I smile and try to run around him. His arm reaches out and grabs me around the waist. I squeal and burst out laughing.

"No, put me down!" I giggle.

Rip puts me down in the shower and switches it on, getting me soaking wet. Caging me in. I'm not about to complain. With the warm water running over us Rip makes quick work of removing my clothes and making passionate love to me, we need each other after today's events.

CHAPTER TWENTY-TWO

With Luis gone and the Cartel no longer a problem everyone was able to return to their normal lives and the club was no longer on lock-down. It was a relief. As much as it was nice to be around everyone, being there like that for more than a couple of days would have driven me insane.

Rip is sorting out fake papers for the women so they can start their lives over here, go to schools, get jobs. I've just dropped Caden at school and now I'm hitting the mall with Lily and Daisy, in need of some sister time and retail therapy. We're buying clothes for Catalina and the rest of them.

"God my feet are killing me. How does carrying one little baby make your feet balloon like elephant's feet?" Lily complains.

"Stop your moaning. Your feet aren't that bad. Come on, you love shopping. I promise this will be the last shop, then we can go sit down and get some lunch." Daisy says picking up more clothes.

"Can we get done now? I'm ready for food. We have like ten bags of clothes for them." I state.

I just want to sit down now, eat and chill out.

"Okay, let's pay for these and then we can go and get some food." Daisy says walking to the checkout.

"How long you have you got left now?" I ask poking Lily's bump.

"Eight weeks, and stop doing that or I will pee all over the floor." Lily says as she slaps my hand away.

After Daisy has paid for the items we head to an Italian restaurant.

Lily orders us a huge pizza with sides to share.

"So I have some news and I want you guys to know first." Daisy says.

"You're pregnant." Lily states with a mouthful of pizza.

"No." Daisy answers.

"What?! We found out that your psycho ex-husband was a lying shit bag, so you never know." Lily shrugs.

"Lily, shut up and let her speak." I sigh.

"Alright, pissy pants, geeze." Lily says rolling her eyes.

"Okay, well, we've decided to get married in six months, but that's not all. I'm going to meet with a doctor who is going to check me and test my fertility so we can potentially start IVF treatment. Carter is fine and who knows, it could work. I wanted to tell you before telling Mum and Dad because, well, you know how excited Mum will be, she won't shut up about it." Daisy says smiling.

Lily and I both reach over our food and bring Daisy in for a hug. Sitting back Lily wipes her eyes.

"I am so happy for you Daisy." Lily sniffles. "Stupid hormones."

"This is the best news, I'm sure it'll work out. This time next year you'll be just as fat as weeble here." I say pointing to Lily.

"Hey! I may be a weeble, but I am not fat. Do not piss me off or I will sit on you. This weeble will crush you." Lily threatens.

"Calm yourself and eat your food." I laugh.

We finish eating and Lily demands dessert. We are sharing, well, Lily keeps batting our spoons away every time we go to take some. I ask them something that's been really bothering me.

"What's going on with Wes?" I ask.

Daisy and Lily look at me confused.

"Okay, well, since when does he speak fluent Spanish? Rip mentioned that he thinks he's seeing someone but keeping it quiet. It's not just that, out of all of the guys he finds it the hardest to deal with women that have been mistreated by a man. Which is great, he is so protective, but what on earth happened to make him that way. Do you think he has anyone?" I ask.

"No idea, Wes has mentioned a woman in the past, but never said anymore about it. He's always been very tight lipped about it and never told anyone anything." Lily says with a mouthful of tiramisu.

"Same. He mentioned someone to me but not in any detail. When I was staying at Bessie's place he said he was in the area visiting a friend, but no one we know lives around that way so I have no idea who that was." Daisy shrugs.

"It's just he's been there for all of us right?

One way or another he's helped us. It would just be good to see him settle down with someone special. I think he deserves it." I finish.

Lily and Daisy both nod their heads and agree.

Once Lily has finished we head out. As we are walking to the truck in the mall parking lot the hairs on my neck stand on end and I feel like I'm being watched. I stop and look around. I don't spot anyone looking this way. I shake my head and ignore it.

"What's up?" Lily asks.

"Nothing, just being stupid." I wave her off.

She shrugs and gets into the truck.

On the way back my cell rings, I see it's Rip calling.

"Hey biker boy, we are on our way back now."

I don't finish because Rip interrupts me.

"Your folks are here." He states, and I can hear the smile in his voice.

"Oh shit." I sigh.

"Yup, your mum and dad are currently trying to talk broken Spanish to the girls." He sniggers down the phone.

"Good god, so they know what went down?" I ask.

"Yup, your mum spoke with my ma and here they are." Rip answers.

"Christ, it's like being checked up on when I was a teenager. Okay, I will brace Daisy and Lily and will see you in about twenty minutes. Do me a favour?" I ask.

"Anything."

"Pour me a large gin and tonic." I say pinching the bridge of my nose. I feel a headache coming on.

"Sweetheart, it's only one o'clock." Rip chuckles.

"Trust me, I'll need it, so do it please." I beg.

"Sure thing, see you in a while." He finally agrees.

"Thank you, yeah, bye." I say and hang up.

I groan in the back of the car.

"What is it?" Daisy asks.

"Mum and Dad have arrived. Apparently Mum spoke to Trudy, so now they are here." I inform them.

"Oh for the love of God, Mum's going to have kittens with her worrying and Dad's going to think he could have kicked their arses himself." Lily groans.

We all brace for ourselves for seeing our parents. This is going to be fun.

We pull up and Daisy barely gets the truck in park before Mum is running out to us.

"Oh my girls, I cannot believe not one of you called me! Are you sure you're all okay? I mean the Cartel are not to be messed with. I watched this documentary on the mafia and well, you know they are practically the same thing. They are just awful monsters, the violence! So much violence. Machine gun killings, beatings. and the language! Well it made you all look like nuns." Mum rambles on.

"Penn, that wasn't a documentary, that was the Godfather movie. Hello girls." Dad greets us.

We all roar with laughter at Mum's confusion.

"Well it was very realistic I'm sure." Mum mumbles embarrassed.

We all walk inside with all the bags, Dad taking and carrying most of them. When we get inside Catalina comes over and hugs Lily and Daisy and I. She tries taking the bags, but Dad declines and places them on the table.

"Wes about?" I ask the young prospect, thinking to myself that I really should learn his name.

"Which one of you hot ladies wants me?" Wes sings, walking in.

"Ahh. We all do of course. Can you translate

that these bags of clothes are for them? They should fit, and there are clothes for Ana too." I say, Wes smiles and kisses mine, Lily's and Daisy's heads.

"Angels, brace yourself. I don't think you'll expect this reaction for clothes." Wes states.

He calls them all over, including little Ana, he points to the bags on the table and explains that they are for them.

Wes was right, I don't think any of us expected the reaction to be like this. They start to cry, Catalina shakes her head.

"No, err, no um, too much." She stutters out.

I grab her hands in mine.

"For you, it's a gift. Please." I say.

Wes translates. Her eyes drop to the bags briefly before she lunges forward and hugs me in a tight hug.

"Oh god, I need my tissue, this is just so moving." Mum sobs beside me.

Catalina moves along hugging Lily and Daisy and so do the rest. I look at Ana, she's trying to peek inside a bag. I kneel down and pull out a cute little tea dress we picked out for her. Her eyes light up in excitement. I smile and hand it to her, she takes it and her face is full of amazement like I've just given her the world. I hold up my hand to tell her to wait. I reach in and pull out a sweet pair of ballet flats that match and a pretty little hair band. She jumps up and down with excitement, saying something in Spanish. She then jumps up, wrapping her little arms around my neck. I choke back a sob and squeeze her back. She skips off, dragging Catalina with her to try on her dress.

"God damn hormones, making me cry all the time." Lily sobs.

I turn and smile at her and squeeze her arm. Blake comes over and he wraps her in his arms, comforting her. Carter does the same with Daisy.

"Oh my, you are all adorable." Mum coos.

I turn and see Rip, leaning against the bar, his ice blue eyes fixated on me. My heart skips a beat from the heat in his stare and he walks towards me, not paying anyone else any attention. For him at this very moment only I exist, his walk is almost predatory.

"Oh my!" I hear Mum swoon beside me.

"Here we bloody go." I hear dad grumble.

I am too captured by Rip to pay them any attention. He reaches me and cups my face. He leans in, his lips brushing against mine so softly they are barely touching.

"Marry me." He whispers.

I smile.

"Ye..." I go to answer.

Rip crashes his mouth down on mine. His tongue sweeps against mine, his lips caressing mine. In that moment it's just us. He slows the kiss just nipping at my lips.

"My woman, my wife, mine." He rasps.

I hadn't realised I was crying. Rip wipes my tears smiling down at me. I smile up at him. Without warning he picks me up and spins me around. I squeal in surprise.

"She said yes! Meet the future President's Old Lady of Satan's Outlaws!" He roars to everyone in the club.

The guys all cheer and raise their bottles. He puts me down, and we turn to my parents.

"Ben, I'm sorry I didn't ask the traditional way, but I didn't want to waste another second. I love her, she is my queen, and I will give her the world. She is made for me. I know it would sure mean a lot to Rose and I to have your blessing." Rip states to my dad.

"Oh my!" Mum sniffles.

"If I didn't give you my blessing would you listen and honour it. Not marrying her until I gave it to you?" Dad asks.

"Dad, come.." Dad holds his hand up, stopping me from talking, his eyes fixed on Rip waiting for his answer.

"Fuck no! Sorry Ben, I wouldn't. She is my

world and there ain't nothing to keep me from making her mine permanently." Rip informs Dad.

"Oh my!" Mum swoons.

"For the love of god Penn, control yourself." Dad yells at Mum.

He turns his attention back to Rip. The whole room is silent, waiting for Dad's response, not that it matters, because I'd marry Rip anyway. But a daughter will always want their dad's blessing.

"Thank fuck for that. Then you have my blessing. If me not giving you my blessing was enough to keep you from marrying my daughter, then you ain't man enough for her. She needs a man that will fight for her and not give a shit about who he upsets so long as she's happy. Welcome to the family son." Dad says holding out his hand.

Rip shakes his hand and everyone cheers, hoots and hollers.

"Does this mean Rip is my new dad now?" I hear Caden say from behind me.

I gasp, feeling awful that I had just agreed without considering Caden and what he may want.

"Honey I am so sorry, I should have spoke this through with you. No it doesn't mean that

Rip will be your new dad, but it will mean that he will be a part of our lives permanently. Is that something you're comfortable with? Because your happiness is the most important thing to me." I say, crouching down in front of him.

He looks from me to Rip and around the room. Rip calls Mammoth over and Mammoth hands him something. He crouches down next to me.

"Caden, I love your ma, very much, and I want to spend my whole life making her happy and making her smile...but I will need you by my side, because you are the one that brings your ma true happiness. I may not be your dad, but I want to be an important part of your life. So that means you'll be my right hand man. You'll be an honorary Satan until you're an adult. What do you say little man?" Rip holds out a little leather cut with patches for the Satan's Outlaws. Stitched on it is 'Caden'.

Caden's eyes go wide. I am crying again and the room has gone silent, everyone awaiting Caden's answer.

"Caden?" I ask when he doesn't answer.

"Hell yeah! This is the best day ever! Of course I can't wait for you to marry Rip, he's badass! And now I am a badass just like him with my own cut! He makes you really happy mum, and that makes me happy." Caden says beaming.

I pull him in for a hug, kissing him until he pushes me off, wiping his scrunched up face.

"Rip, if you did decide to be like a dad to me that would be cool too. I know you're not my dad. But it would be cool to have you as one." Caden says to Rip.

Rip smiles and holds his fist out to fist bump with Caden. He helps Caden into his cut and pats him on the shoulder.

Holding up Caden's arm in the air Rip shouts:

"The newest and youngest honorary member of the Satans!"

The guys all cheer and Caden couldn't smile anymore if he tried.

"These bloody hormones!" Lily sobs next to me.

"I don't think this is your hormones Darlin'." Blake states.

Caden runs around the room fist bumping everyone. Rip smiles and comes to me, wrapping me in his arms.

"I will go out first thing and get you a ring. Sorry it wasn't all romantic and shit." Rip states.

"You giving my son a cut and making his day and proposing to me the way you did...it was perfect. It was all you. I wouldn't have had it any other way. So in your way, it was romantic and shit." I say smiling.

"Watching you with the girls and what you did for them, I knew I didn't want to wait another fuckin' second. I want to see you in my cut, so everyone knows you're mine. I fuckin' love you sweetheart." Rip says.

"Fuckin love you too biker boy." I reply.

I am pulled aside by my mum enveloping me into her arms.

"Oh honey, are you sure this is what you want? It's so soon." Mum asks.

I pause for a moment because that hadn't even entered my mind when I accepted Rip's proposal. It feels like we've been together a lot longer than what we actually have.

"I hadn't really thought about it. It feels like forever, not what it is, which is crazy because it's been like six weeks!" I say starting to have a little panic attack.

"Mum, for God's sake, you've made her think. Her and Rip are perfect for each other. It doesn't matter if it's a month or a year, Rose hasn't felt like this about anyone. She isn't going to love anyone like she does Rip, why can't you see that? Even Stevie Wonder can see that!" Lily yells at mum.

I hear Blake and Carter snort back their laughter. Lily takes my face in her hands.

"Do not do what I know you're going to do and use this as a reason to hide and build that bloody wall. You love him and he loves you. Caden loves him! You have your happily ever after. So don't be an idiot and throw it all away because of our daft mother's comment. For once just enjoy yourself and live your life. Be happy and stop ruining it for yourself." Lily says sternly.

She's right, I know she is. I need to shut down that cloud of doubt that I always let control my life and use to keep anything out that might turn ugly and hurt me. I smile and nod. Lily pulls me into a hug.

"Thank fuck for that, I thought I was going to have to kick your arse." Lily states.

Mum pulls me into her arms again.

"I am so sorry honey, I didn't mean to doubt your choice. Lily is right; go for it and be happy. Plus Rip is very handsome, your babies would be beautiful." Mum cries out excitedly.

I freeze, babies? I hadn't thought of that either. Do I want more kids? I don't know.

"For the love of God Mum! Zip it! Dad, keep your woman in check." Lily yells at Dad. She turns back to me and slaps me across the face.

"Rose, snap out of it. I'm giving her a grand-baby, don't stress about it. One step at a time. We will do therapy for that another time. Now I am sorry for the slap but the moment caused for it before you lose your shit and ruin this amazing moment for you and Rip." She chastises.

I rub my cheek and frown at her.

"It's a good job you're pregnant or I'd be taking you down. I am not freaking out, okay? And I'm not about to ruin the moment, but my family will if they don't shut their mouths." I grit through my teeth.

Lily smiles.

"Good. Glad to see you've finally got your shit together. In all seriousness, always here if you need it, you know that right?" Lily asks.

Sighing, I nod. Lily will always act the clown and tease, but she always has to know we're okay. Of course we know she is there for us/ She's our sister and she has been there for all of us forever.

Trudy and Max come over to congratulate me, I am not sure where Rip has disappeared to.

"You ready to take us on as your family darlin'? There is still time to run." Max teases.

"You guys are easy compared to my crazy dysfunctional family." I state.

"I heard that!" Mum shouts from behind me.

Both Max and Trudy laugh. I keep looking around for Rip but can't see him anywhere.

"Excuse me, I'm going to find Rip." I say walking off.

I'm a little peeved that he proposed and then rather than spend time with me and the others celebrating, he has disappeared. I see the side door is open, so I stick my head through to see if he's out there. I spot him, standing with Khan and Mammoth. They are all facing someone. Their bodies are rigid and they don't look happy.

I creep out to be nosey and see who it is they are talking to.

As I get closer, I see it's Darcy. My blood immediately begins to boil. I watch as she leans forward to touch him. Rip does nothing in return. His arms crossed over his broad chest. I keep walking towards them, no longer trying to hide. Trust her to show up now and ruin what is supposed to be a celebration. Now I just feel angry.

"Rip baby, you know you love me. I can give you what she can't. I doubt she would play with you and Khan like I do. You know how good it was between the three of us." I hear Darcy whine in an annoying brat voice.

I feel my body tense, is that what Rip likes? I don't think I could ever do that. A man or a woman in bed with us. I don't share and I'm not sure I'm comfortable sharing myself. I am definitely not comfortable sharing Rip.

Rip just throws his head back laughing.

"You really are a stupid bitch, I would never do that with Rose because I will never share her. She's mine. If anyone was to touch her I would kill them. You on the other hand I couldn't give a shit about, you are a club whore. So don't come to my club now claiming it was something it wasn't. You were happy doing all of my brothers, it was never going to be anything more. Yet you tried trapping me with a fake fuckin' pregnancy and now you have a fuckin' nerve turning up here causing a fuckin' headache for my brothers, wanting to see me. I will say this one more time because I am fuckin' nice. Get off my land, don't ever step foot near my club again. I am not going to threaten you. You know exactly how I can make your life hell, so fuck off." Rip growls.

Darcy pales slightly clearly knowing exactly what Rip is capable of, but something inside her changes. She straightens and pulls her shoulders back, clearly ready to fight back.

"Uh oh, this isn't going to end well." I mutter under my breath.

Rip and the guys clearly thinking they are done, turn and go to walk back inside. They all stop when they see me. Rip puts his hands on his hips and looks to the sky, swearing under his breath.

"Sweetheart, will there ever be a time you

won't be fuckin' nosey and will keep out of the whatever bad shit is going down?" Rip sighs.

I smile and shake my head.

"Sorry biker boy, you want me as your wife and old lady you're going to have to deal with me backing you up when shit goes down." I shrug.

Rip doesn't even try to fight his smile, he hits me with it full force, sparkling ice blue eyes and dimples. I don't think I will ever get used to how handsome he is.

"You're getting married?!" Darcy screeches.

Rip's beautiful smile falls and his face sets to stone.

"I mean, you've only just met her! She has baggage, and she's ugly. Seriously?! What do you guys see in her? Even Luis thought she was hot." She grumbles.

All of us turn rigid at her comment. It takes her a moment to realise what she said. When she does I can see the panic in her eyes.

"What were you doing talking to Luis?" Rip seethes, his voice low and deadly. It sends chills through me.

She doesn't answer, she just looks around, clearly looking for her escape.

"Answer me." Rip barks loudly.

She jumps, and for once she actually looks

sorry. Although I think it's more of a sorry for making the mistake of saying something and getting caught rather than actually being sorry for what's she has done.

By this point I've had enough and I storm forward, right up to her.

"Answer the damn question." I spit.

"I err, well I may have told Luis about you and given him Rip's address." She mumbles.

"You gave a dangerous deadly man from the Mexican cartel my name and told him where I was staying? Knowing I had a son?" I state calmly. Inside I feel anything but calm.

"Yeah, well, you took my man. I wanted you out of the picture." She shrugs.

All calmness now completely disappeared, pure anger descends. No one puts my son's life in danger.

I leap at her and take her to the ground, slapping her multiple times.

"You led the Mexican cartel to the place where I was staying with my son, all because you weren't getting your way? All because you wanted Rip! My son could have been hurt or worse! You put myself and my son at risk just so you could have Rip!" I yell at her.

She tries to throw me off, but I have her pinned.

"You are going to fuck off and never come back. We are getting married! I am going to be his old lady and we are going to be happy because you will never darken our bloody door again!" I say smiling.

Darcy snaps and swings at me hitting me right across the face. I fall to the floor and then she pins me.

"Get your skanky hands off of my sister!" I hear Lily yell.

I turn my head to see everyone standing outside watching, even Caden. Not wanting my son to see this I try pushing her off of me. She uses all her weight to stop me.

"Kick her butt Mum!" Caden shouts.

I smirk, thankful that seeing his mum scrapping hasn't scarred the boy for life. I buck and kick her off, standing over her.

"Leave and never come back, or next time it won't be me you have to deal with, it will be the entire club." I threaten.

I turn and walk to Rip, who pulls me into his arms. His thumb runs across my cheek where she hit me. I wince a little.

"Stop trying to fight my battles sweetheart. I've got you. I will always fight them for you, for us." Rip states warmly.

"That was our battle, and she put my son at

risk. I had to." I shrug.

"Get your fucking hands off me!" Darcy shouts as the two young prospects manhandle her off the compound.

Caden comes running up to us and wraps his arms around my waist.

"Mum you're a total badass! That was so cool." Caden says proudly.

"Fighting someone isn't something to be proud of. She just said some nasty things that made mummy very angry." I say kissing the top of his head.

Everyone, and I mean everyone, from inside comes and stands behind us, the guys cheering me on for having a girl on girl fight. The old ladies pat me on the back and my sister's promise to kick the crap out of her if she comes here again. I turn and face my parents, feeling like a scorned child. It's not something I ever envisioned doing in front of my parents, especially at my age.

"Mum, Dad, I'm sorry.."

"Super proud of you honey! Knew my girl could handle herself." Dad pulls me into a hug, taking me by surprise.

I pull back and look to Mum who is saying nothing.

"Mum?" I ask.

"She really did that tell that awful man where to find you?" Mum asks.

I nod.

"That's it!" Mum shouts.

She pushes past us and heads for Darcy.

"Let me at her! How dare she put my baby and grandbaby at risk!" Mum shouts.

My dad grabs her and pulls her back.

"Calm down Penn." Dad tries to calm Mum down.

"I cannot believe she would do such a thing, I mean, we've seen what that sort of man is capable of with those poor girls. Rose and Caden could have been seriously hurt." Mum rants.

"Calm down Penn, it's taken care of. Everyone is okay." Dad soothes.

"Oh Ben." Mum sighs.

"Save your feistiness for the bedroom later. You know I love it when you get all riled up." Dad says to Mum quietly. Unfortunately not quietly enough as me, Lily and Daisy all gag at the thought.

"I see where you get your sass from." Rip says in my ear.

I elbow him in the stomach. He lets out a grunt and laughs.

Trudy walks up to me. I go to apologies, but

she holds up her hand and stops me.

"I am so proud my son has found a strong, passionate woman. You can handle him and what club life can throw at you. You're perfect for him." Trudy pulls me into a hug.

"Everyone inside! We are fuckin' celebrating!" Rip shouts.

"Language!" Trudy shouts back, making everyone laugh.

CHAPTER TWENTY -THREE

I awake the next morning and my head is pounding. The party got a little wild last night; I lost count how many tequila shots I had. The thought of tequila has me gagging. I jump up and run to the bathroom, emptying the contents of my stomach.

I rest my head on the seat of the toilet, feeling like death.

"You struggling there sweetheart?" Rip asks.

He strokes my hair away from my face and

flushes the toilet.

"I'm never touching tequila again. I am dying. Please just leave me to curl up and die." I groan.

Rip chuckles. I hear him moving around. He hands me a bottle of water and places a couple Advil in my hand. I take them and sip the water.

I quick brush my teeth to get rid of the sick breath and crawl back into bed. Rip takes a shower, clearly unaffected by the amount of alcohol we consumed last night. The man is a machine, or a robot. He was barely drunk last night. Rip comes out of the shower dripping wet in nothing but a towel. My eyes drink in his body, every curve and dip of muscle, that delicious v that some men have. I lick my lips.

"Sweetheart, stop eye fucking me. You're hungover and just emptied your stomach. You're not well enough for me to do anything about it." Rip states.

"I may be suffering and ever so slightly hungover, but I can still appreciate my fiancé's bloody delicious body. I'm feeling rough but I haven't gone blind." I moan.

Rip laughs and gets dressed. Before he leaves, he leans over and kisses me.

"Rest, I've got to call church."

"Everything okay?" I ask frowning.

"Yeah sweetheart, just usual business to attend to." Rip says before closing the door behind him.

I curl up and drift back to sleep, hoping that when I next wake up I won't feel so vile.

Thankfully having an extra hours sleep helps a lot. After having a shower and getting dressed I'm ravenous. I go in search of some breakfast. I can smell bacon cooking my nose leads to me to it.

Walking into the kitchen, my mum, dad, Max and Trudy are all gathered around the table with coffees. They turn their attention to me and smile.

"There she is! You want some breakfast honey?" Trudy asks.

"Oh I'd love some. Is there anything left?" I ask pouring myself a coffee.

"Sit yourself down. I kept some bacon and pancakes warm for you." Trudy says moving around the kitchen.

I sit down with my coffee, all eyes are on me.

"What?" I ask.

"You were pretty drunk last night honey. Do you remember any of it?" Mum asks.

I frown and shake my head.

"Not a lot of it, my brain is a little foggy this morning." I answers sipping my coffee.

"Well don't panic. You didn't do anything too crazy, you just told everyone how much you loved them and how they are now your family. Oh, and that if anyone tried messing with your new family you would kick their butts." Mum says smiling.

"Oh god." I groan.

"Don't forget that she promised us grandbabies!" Trudy says, giggling from the stove.

My head snaps around to look at her, wide eyed.

"Oh god! Please say I didn't." I ask.

"Oh sorry honey, you did. You kept telling us that Rip's babies would so beautiful it would be a crime against humanity not to have them." Trudy says laughing.

"Well I hate to disappoint but I haven't even had that conversation with Rip yet, so ignore my drunken self." I inform them.

"Well my boy certainly seemed keen on the idea last night. What is it he said...oh yeah, once you're married he likes the idea of you carrying his children. He wants a whole damn football team of them." Max teases.

I face plant the table and the parents just erupt with laughter. Trudy comes over, places her hand on my shoulder, and puts my breakfast on the table.

"Max stop teasing the poor girl! Here you are honey. Eat up, it'll make you feel better."

"Thanks."

I tuck in enjoying every mouthful.

"So honey, me and your Dad have found a place. It is down the same street as Max and Trudy's house. Isn't that brilliant!" Mum claps excitedly.

"That's great Mum. Dad, when do you move in?" I ask.

"Well there's still a lot to sort out with visas and we have to wait for it to go through but hopefully in the next couple of months. It will be brilliant living down the same street as Trudy and Max! Just think, when we have the grand-babies over they can go between houses and have both nannies close. It's perfect." Mum sings happily.

I smile and look to Trudy and Max who look equally as happy.

The talk of visas reminds me that I need to sort mine out. The last thing I want is to be deported and be away from Rip for months.

After breakfast, I go off in search of Rip. I quickly drop Lily a message to see if Caden is behaving himself. Her and Blake said they would have him last night as Lily can't drink and join in the fun. She may as well look after Caden so I can let my hair down. She did make me promise to return the favour, which of course I agreed to. I cannot wait for cuddles with my baby niece or nephew.

As I walk up to Rip's office door I can hear the guys talking. I pause and stop just outside of the door to listen.

"You need to be out searching, you need to fuckin' find him, and when you do, call me. Not a word to anyone. I don't want a big panic or anyone feeling threatened. We are to act normal. Everything is just fuckin' normal. You keep close tabs and eyes everywhere, but you do it discreetly! I am not having him fuckin' everything up!" Rip roars angrily.

I freeze and the door opens. I quickly dive behind another door out of site, not wanting them to know I was eaves dropping again. I wait a second to make sure everyone is gone, and I creep out, take a deep breath and try to act normal.

I walk to the door and lightly tap before I enter. When I walk through the door Rip is at his desk. He's smoking, which I know means he is stressed.

"How much of that did you hear?" Rip asks, sitting back and looking at me.

I freeze.

"Uh! None, I just got here. I did not hear a thing, not a word." I say, doing my best not to show I'm lying.

"Sweetheart, come here." Rip orders.

I move to him acting completely natural, pretending I've not a care in the world. I totally have my lie under control. I deserve an Oscar for my performance. I'm looking around the room, being breezy.

"Sweetheart, what are you doing?" Rip asks.

I look to him and shrug. He pulls me onto his lap. I give myself a mental note to keep calm. You know nothing Rose, act cool.

"What's up babe?" I ask casually.

Rip throws his head back and roars with laughter.

He slows his laughter and pinches the bridge of his nose.

"Fuck me." He says under his breath.

"Sweetheart, I've just watched you walk across the room looking like you have a limp and are high on something. Your eyes were twitching all over the damn place. Then you sit down on my lap and ask me that, in a way you've never asked me before. So answer me again, honestly this time. What did you hear outside my office door?" Rip asks.

I bite my lip and look away.

"Sweetheart, just tell me. Don't make me bend you over my knee and spank you." He threatens.

My pulse kicks up a gear. I swing my gaze to his and smile.

Rip groans and kisses me.

"God damn it woman! Stop giving me sass and turning me on. Tell me what you heard. You're a shit liar and we all know you like to listen in and be in places when you fuckin' shouldn't be, so just tell me." Rip sighs, exasperated.

I pause for a moment because I saw how stressed and angry he was. He was clearly trying to protect us in some way but I guess my acting skills were not Oscar-worthy.

"Okay, well I was coming to find you and as I approached the door I heard you tell the guys to find him, to keep it quiet and avoid causing panic. Obviously not your exact words but that's pretty much it. So are you going to tell me what it was about?" I ask.

Rip sighs and shakes his head.

"Not fully sweetheart. I want you and all of the club members and their families to be carefree and not concerned. All of the brothers will be keeping close eyes on everyone to make sure everyone is safe. All you need to know is we are dealing with some shit, but we have it covered. Don't go anywhere without telling me. I want you to text when you arrive anywhere you are going if I am not already with you. Even if one of the brothers is escorting you. Got it?" Rip asks sternly.

I nod not saying anything, my thoughts at war. On one hand I want to demand to know what the hell is going on to make Rip so twitchy. On the other hand I know this is how club life is. This is the club's business, it's for the brothers to sort out. I have to trust that Rip will tell me what I need to know. I have to trust that he has this under control. I need to put my faith in him and the club.

"Sure, I can do that." I answer softly.

Rip pulls me in for a kiss.

"Now she's giving me her sweetness. I don't know what I fuckin' did to deserve you, but I thank fuckin' God every damn day for bringing you to me." Rip admits.

"You've said this before biker boy, yet somehow I still don't see you thanking God?" I ask mocking him.

"Hey sweetheart, what can I say? You bring out the godliness in me." Rip shrugs.

I burst out laughing.

Our time alone is cut short when there's a knock on the door.

"Yeah!" Rip shouts.

I am surprised to see Daisy stick her head in.

"Hi, I was wondering if I could steal my sister for a couple of hours. I want to take you to see the centre. I have something I want to show you." Daisy asks.

"Yeah, I'd love to. Just let me put on some proper clothes. You're okay with it, right Rip?"

"You don't even need to ask sweetheart. Go and I will see you in a few hours. You driving?" Rip asks Daisy.

"Yeah, Carter has to work." Daisy answers.

"I will have one of the guys escort you, okay? And sweetheart, text me when you're there."

"Okay." I answer.

I give Rip a quick kiss then jump up to go and change.

Once dressed Daisy and I head over to the site of her centre.

"What's with the escort?" Daisy asks.

"Oh it's just a precaution thing. Rip is not taking any chances." I say shrugging it off like it's nothing.

Once we hit the site I quickly send a text to Rip, letting him know we've arrived safely.

Looking around the site I'm amazed to see how much progress there is. The building is done and the workman are busy putting in windows and working on the inside. Daisy hands me a safety hat and leads the way. Walking around there is still lots to do but the main structure is done. I'm excited for Daisy. I feel so immensely proud of her.

We walk down a couple of corridors, Daisy pointing out suites that will be for the women to stay in. She turns again and stops in front of large double doors, she pushes it open and gestures for me to enter. I walk in and gasp.

It's a large room, painted a pale lilac. There are grey couches still covered in cellophane, and on the opposite side of the room is a floor to ceiling curtain, and a full size hospital bed. I spot boxes of equipment stacked high. There are white shelves and large units for storage. I walk in further, there is a white corner desk and a doorway to a toilet and wet room.

I turn to Daisy and grab her for a hug.

"This is amazing! It's better than any private care facility. I can't believe you've done this. It's truly a wonderful thing you're doing and I'm so proud of you." I sniffle back the tears.

Daisy squeezes me back and wipes her tears.

"I wanted it to be the first room to be done. It will be one of the most important rooms here at the centre and I want you to be happy working here. I want the women that come here to be comfortable and be able to relax." Daisy states.

"Well I think you've definitely achieved that. I think I'm going to be very happy here. What you're doing for these women...this centre is amazing. I am so proud of you." I croak back the tears.

"Don't start or I'll start." Daisy sniffles.

We take a walk around the ground and Daisy points out her aims for the gardens.

We head back to the truck and I notice the prospect that was escorting us has gone. I pull out my phone and see a text from Rip.

Prospect with me, business to see to. See you back at the clubhouse. Fuckin' love you. R x

I smile reading his message. I type a quick reply saying we are just heading back and will see him when he's done.

As we are driving home Daisy and I are singing along to a bit of Salt n Pepper. We notice a car broken down up ahead. There's a man with a walking stick, clearly struggling with his spare tyre.

"Daisy, pull over. Let's help this poor guy out." I suggest.

Daisy pulls the truck over and we both jump out.

"Hi, would you like a hand?" I ask walking up to him.

The guy is hunched over his stick with his back to me.

"Gracias belleza." The man says in a rasp Spanish accent.

I pause, the voice sounding familiar. I hear Daisy let out a scream behind me. I turn around to see her being held by some guy in a suit. His hand is clamped around her mouth and he has a gun to her head.

"Get off of my sister." I shout in a panic.

"He will let your sister go if you get in the car belleza." The guy with the stick states. I turn back to face him and gasp.

His face has suffered burns and I notice his hands have also. Even underneath the burns I can see who it is.

"Luis?" I gasp.

He just smiles.

"Si senora, please get into the car." He says, his voice coarse and gravelly. I'm guessing that's from the smoke inhalation.

"Let her go and I will get in the car." I demand.

Luis gives his man a nod, and the guy lets Daisy go.

"Rose don't go." Daisy rushes to me.

"It's okay, Rip will come for me. Go to the club and tell them. It will be okay. Go." I kiss her head and turn and get in the back of the car. Luis slams the door behind me.

I watch as Luis walks around to get into the other side, the guy with a gun still held on Daisy. Eventually the guy turns, leaving Daisy, and gets in the driver's seat.

We pull away. I turn back to see Daisy run to her truck and speed off in the direction of the clubhouse.

I release a slow breath to calm my panicking heart.

"Do not worry mi amor, you are merely a pawn in all of this. It's your man I want. Once he knows I have you he will come to me, but in the meantime while we wait we can have a little fun." Luis says reaching over. He places his hand on my upper thigh and squeezes.

I slap his hand away and in turn he back hands me across the face so hard my head whips to the side. I hiss in pain and hold my cheek.

I sit up straight, determined not to show that I'm secretly shitting my pants.

"I can see why you're single." I huff crossing

my arms.

Luis lets out a low rumble of laughter.

"I see what has Rip so enamorado, you have fire." Luis strokes my face with his burnt hand. I shrug him off.

"So where are you taking me, Cancun? I've always wanted to go there. Beautiful beaches." I say like I'm talking to a tour guide.

"Careful hermosa. I can get you out of this country and take you to my country. You will be sold to the highest bidder. You will never be seen again. Do not test me." He threatens.

I immediately shut up. At least if he has me captive in this country I might find a way of getting free and getting back to Rip...getting back to Caden.

"Good girl." Luis says, his voice eerily sweet, it makes my skin crawl.

We drive for what seems like hours, but in reality it's only been about forty-five minutes. The car turns off of the main road, I've been trying to read road signs and get an idea of where I am. We drive for at least another ten minutes down this lone quiet road. There are no signs, no houses, nothing. Up ahead is a big warehouse looking building.

We pull up to it, my heart is beating in my

chest erratically. There are three men walking around the building with machine guns.

"Oh shit." I say without thinking.

"Now you're getting it." Luis says getting out of the car.

The other guy opens my door and yanks me from the car.

"Ow! You son of a bitch, there was no need for that. Christ!" I say, giving him an angry glare.

Luis is just laughing and shaking his head. I'm glad I amuse him so much.

I am dragged into the warehouse. It's dark and my eyes take a moment to adjust. There are rows of shelves with weapons on and what looks like packages of cocaine.

I am taken down a dark hallway and pushed through a door to an office.

"Sit!" The guy manhandling me shouts and points to the chair. I do as he asks. He grabs cuffs and pulls my arms behind my back and places them on tightly, purposefully cutting into my wrists. He then gets rope, wrapping it around my middle and tying it tight to the chair. He yanks the rope hard making me grunt in pain.

"I am sorry for this...err...situation, but you understand I do not trust you. I need you secure. You, mi amore, are my bait." Luis whispers in my ear.

I rear my head back and headbutt him as hard as I can. It makes me dizzy.

Luis rears back, clutching his face.

"You stupid crazy bitch!" He shouts before hitting me hard across the face, so hard the chair rocks and I nearly go over. I can taste blood in my mouth and I can feel my face sting and swell. I spit out the blood and smile up at Luis.

"Don't underestimate me buddy. I am English, I am in love with a biker, and I am a mother. I will not make this easy."

Luis looks almost stunned and I see a flicker of respect. He perches on the edge of his desk, still holding his nose which is bleeding. I think I broke it, the thought that I've been able to hurt him brings me some contentment.

"I see you are not only a strong hermosa, but stupid too. I know you are a mother and I know your little boy is currently full of life. I know he is with your hermana. I believe they have just gone to the park to play and have ice cream." Luis sneers at me, blood still pouring from his busted nose.

My whole body runs cold, he has people watching my son, watching Lily. Fear and an overwhelming urge to protect Caden take over.

"Don't fucking touch my son or my sister. I will do whatever you want but you leave them the hell alone." I grit out.

"I knew you were smart underneath it all. Not like your biker who left me for dead. If he was smart he would have made sure I was dead. Now...now I have my revenge, no one gets away doing what the Satans' did to me. They will pay. All of them." Luis says angrily walking around the room, his hands clenched into tight fists at his side.

I swallow back my fear and refuse to let it surface. I will not give him the satisfaction. As if Rip can hear my thoughts I beg over and over again for him not to come. I would rather lose my own life than risk his. I know that Caden would be well loved and looked after without me, but I will not stop fighting for them.

Please Rip, don't come. Stay away. Stay safe. Look after my boy.

I repeat over and over again in my head, wishing Rip could hear me.

CHAPTER TWENTY-FOUR

Rip

After getting a tip off that Luis was hiding out in a nearby farmhouse, we all head over there to check it out. When we go there Luis had clearly already gone. Left behind were rags with blood on them, sleeping bags and takeout cartons.

Pissed off we had missed him, we ride back to the club house. I know he's out there and I know he will be planning his revenge. I need to stop him before he gets that chance.

We've just pulled in and parked up our bikes

and are standing around having a smoke when I notice a truck turn full speed into the compound, straight through the closed gates. All the guys brace, their hands on their weapons. It's then I notice it's Daisy's truck.

"Hold it! It's Wallflower!" I yell.

She slams it in park and jumps down, running frantically to me.

"Rip! It's Rose." She yells.

My blood runs cold, I already know what she's going to say next.

"Some guy...with a messed up face...he took her. I tried but the...the other guy had a gun to my head. She told me to come get you." Daisy pants.

"Luis." I grit.

"Where did he take her?!" I yell making Daisy jump.

"I err I don't know. They drove off and I came straight here to tell you." Daisy says panicking.

"Don't worry Wallflower, we will find her." Mammoth reassures her, putting his arm around her in comfort.

"Ring Carter, Blake and Wes. Make sure Lily and Caden are brought here now! Get all other club family here under lock down immediately, no excuses. Meeting in ten minutes." I shout and I storm inside.

I should have comforted Daisy, but all I can think about is getting to Rose. I know exactly what Luis is capable of. I walk straight into my office and grab the bottle of jack, downing a few long swigs.

How could I let this fuckin' happen? Fuck I am so fuckin' stupid I played right into Luis hands. The informant was a set up. The house! I was played!

I rear back and throw the bottle across the room. It hits the wall and shatters everywhere.

I brace my hands on my desk and hang my head. My blood feels like it's on fire, I know that when I find them I am going to tear Luis apart.

"Honey." My ma says from behind me.

"Not now Ma." I sigh.

"Honey, you will find her, and she will be okay. She's a fighter and I know she won't be making this easy for Luis. Don't lose focus or hope. You will get to her, and when you do, you make that sick and twisted cockroach wish he had never been born." Ma seethes.

I turn and look at her, my beautiful ma. Old lady and protector of her family. I don't answer, I just nod.

"They are waiting for you. I love you son." She says before turning and leaving.

I open the draw on my desk and pull out my

packet of smokes. Lighting one I take a long pull. I reach inside the draw and pull out the small velvet box. I went to the jewellers earlier and brought a ring for Rose. I open up the box and stare down at the princess cut sapphire, encased with diamonds.

I snap the box shut and put it in my pocket. Standing, I make my way to the brothers. I need to keep a level head, I can't let my emotions takeover. I need to be strong and think clearly to get my woman out of there safely. This isn't just about me, I would be destroyed without her in my life I know I would, but her son needs her. I cannot fuck this up.

With pain searing through my heart and gut, and the weight of what feels like the world on my shoulders, I enter the meeting. I'm determined to get my girl home.

Taking my seat at the head of the table I bang the gavel.

"Talk to me, tell me you know where she is. Tell me we've got the fucker pinned and that I can get my goddamn woman home!" I bark.

The brothers all look at each other, no one answering.

"Pres, we think we know where he is. The cartel have a warehouse not far from here, it's the only building that we have listed as theirs apart from the properties we've been to, which we know he isn't at." Khan informs me.

"Good. What the fuck are we waiting for?! Let's go." I bang my gavel and stand. Mammoth reaches out his hand and stops me.

"Pres, wait. Think about it. He already set us up so he could get to Flo. It's a trap. He's using her as bait. He wants you, he wants the club. We can't go in there all guns blazing." Mammoth points out.

I sink back into my chair and pinch the bridge of my nose.

"Fuck!" I yell.

"I know you're fucking right, but that's my woman he's got. You know exactly what that sick asshole is capable of. I cannot sit back and play this out and do nothing. That is not going to fucking happen. We are going in to get her whether it's a trap or not. We just have to be fuckin' smart about it." I slam my fist down on the table.

"He will have some men watching the area, we need to figure out a way in. They wont be patrolling. I've looked at the maps and there is high coverage here through the wood." Rubble says lying the map on the table. He points to the area he's on about.

"We can enter here and strike. You know I'm a trained sniper, I can take out as many as I can from that vantage point, if I need to." Rubble adds.

I look at the map then look at Rubble.

"Lets go now. Load up the trucks, we leave in ten. The longer we leave her the more danger she's in. I won't risk a single fuckin' hair on her head!" I stand and storm out of the room.

I load up the truck, Blake and Wes help me and the rest of the brothers load up the other trucks.

"Why the hell am I only just hearing about my bloody daughter being taking?" Ben shouts behind me.

I turn to face him, feeling a little bad that I didn't tell them straight away. My mind has been so consumed with Rose and wanting to kill Luis that I completely forgot about her parents.

"Sorry Ben, my mind has been all over the place trying to plan an attack to get her back, I just didn't think." I apologise.

Ben sighs, pain written across his face. I have to feel for him, all three of his daughters now have had their fair share of shit.

"I get it, but she's my baby girl. I am coming too. I don't give a shit what you all say, I will not sit back and wait. All I've done is wait around, I am done with doing nothing." Ben firmly states.

I nod, he may not be trained in any way, but

I get it. If it was my daughter I would be the same.

"Respect that Ben, but I will warn you now, I will not hold back. My brothers will not hold back. There will be bloodshed, apart from us there will not be a living breathing soul left. This isn't going to be pretty, we are not going in for a chat. I, along with my brothers, will kill anyone that gets in our way. You gonna be cool with that?" I stand and wait for his answer.

Ben set his jaw and gives me a brief nod.

"They've got my daughter and they did what they did to those poor girls. I'd say they deserve everything coming to them."

I nod and continue loading up the truck. Blake's hand claps my shoulder.

"She's a strong woman, she's probably giving Luis shit right now. You were there for me, now I'm here for you. I've got your back." Blake says. He squeezes my shoulder and climbs into the truck.

"Ready to go kill some drug dealing, human trafficking scum?" Wes asks.

"I am more than fuckin' ready. I am thirsty for it." I answer.

We all jump in the truck and start our journey there. My mind is focused on Rose. I wonder if she's running her mouth giving them shit. My lips twitch with a small smile, because I know she will be. Dark thoughts soon cloud my mind; she may give them mouth but it's what they will do to her that scares the shit out of me.

I grab my blade and run it through my fingers, I feel all of my muscles tense with eagerness to kill. I feel the anger I need to release, the urge to gut the fuckers. I will make every single one of them pay and I am going to enjoy every last second of it.

CHAPTER TWENTY-FIVE

I've been sat here in Luis office for about ten minutes on my own. He has a goon outside the door. I am dying for a pee.

"Hey! You! I need to use the bathroom." I yell.

He comes in and just stares at me. I tug on my cuffs.

"Well?! Are you going to untie me so I can

pee or what?" I ask.

He sighs, not saying anything and unties me. I stand up, still handcuffed. He places a bucket in front of me and points to it.

"Go." Is all he says.

"Uh, fine, but it's a bit hard to get my pants down with my hands cuffed behind my back." I say turning my back to him.

Again he sighs like I'm a huge inconvenience to him. He uncuffs my hands. I rub at my wrists from where the cuffs were so tight. The big goon stands a foot back and aims his gun at me. He gestures for me to go.

"No privacy? Fine, luckily for you I'm a nurse and a mother. I've had my gash out so many times it doesn't bother me anymore. Professionally that is, I ain't no slut." I say crouching down and relieving myself.

Once I finish I look around for toilet paper.

"No tissue?" I ask.

He doesn't say anything. I sigh and do a little shake.

"Fine, drip dry it is." I mumble pulling up my pants.

The door opens and in walks Luis. His eyes alight seeing me half dressed.

"I hope he's treated you well, I apologise for

the facilities." Luis smiles and sits behind his desk.

The big goon moves towards me and re-cuffs my hands behind my back. He ties me to the chair.

"You know mi belleza, I am not a monster. I think given time you might come to like me." Luis says.

I snort back my laughter.

"I doubt that, no chance of Stockholm syndrome from me buddy. I would still shoot you to get away. You can keep telling yourself that I will like you though, whatever makes you feel better and helps you sleep at night." I say honestly.

Luis surprise me by bursting out laughing.

"You really are a challenge mi querida, I like a challenge." Luis says running his tongue along his bottom lip.

My stomach recoils at what he might mean.

"Well, I will fight you on everything so brace yourself. I don't know what you think you will achieve by having me here. You must know that Rip will kill you." I point out.

"You seem to forget. He may want to kill me, but I have the one thing that he loves the most. Amor is a powerful thing, it makes even the toughest men weak, they lead with their heart instead of their head. When the heart takes control of your decisions is when you make mistakes. That's where I have complete control over this situation. My plan is calculated, and I will execute all of them." Luis says smiling.

My heart rate quickens and I can feel myself panic at his words, but I hide my fear. I trample it down deep inside, refusing to let it surface.

"You weren't breastfed as a child were you? Never had that nurturing love from your mother." I say in mock sympathy.

Luis's demeanour changes instantly. The smile falls from his face and pure anger replaces it. He storms towards me and grips my throat tight.

"Don't you ever speak of mi madre ever again. You think I don't see the fear in your eyes?! You run your mouth off like that again and I cut your fuckin' tongue out." Luis growls.

I try gasping for air, but he is squeezing too tight. Luis smiles and leans in close to my ear.

"I can think of many uses for that smart mouth of yours. Maybe I shall change my plan. Maybe I shall change my plans and keep you. I could taunt Rip for years taking what is his. Breaking him every time I fuck you." Luis whispers in my ear.

My body turns ice cold with fear. Luis knows this and smiles with pleasure.

"Fuck you, I would never let you touch me." I hiss.

Luis laughs shaking his head.

"My sweet amor, like you have a choice." Luis sneers.

He sits down, putting his feet on his desk and crossing them at his ankles.

He lights a cigar and inhales, smiling at me.

"Lets see. I think maybe the Satans' should be here in say, twenty minutes. Oh how I look forward to seeing the pain in his eyes when he sees me with you." Luis says excitedly.

"Sees you with me?" I ask nervously.

"All in good time mi amor, all in good time."

For the first time I feel pure fear, not just for me but for Rip. It's clear Luis is planning on using me in whatever way he can to break Rip. I can survive whatever he does to me, but I just hope that Rip doesn't lose his head. I will do whatever I can to protect him. I need to listen to them see if can figure out their plans. Only problem is I don't speak fluent Spanish. If I can play Luis, and in some way warn Rip when he arrives, I have to try. Even if it means risking my own life, I can't let Rip walk into an ambush.

"So what's the big plan then? You going to have me on display then hide in the shadows and shout 'surprise!' and then shoot?" I ask.

Luis looks slightly taken aback by my change in demeanour. That's what I want, I want to throw him off. I want to keep him guessing.

"It's not that simple." Luis answers.

"So I'm right, aren't I? I thought you were the scary Cartel, you know, not to be messed with. To me it just sounds like you're planning a five year old's birthday party." I shrug.

Luis get up and walks around his desk, he perches on the corner and leans in.

"What would you have me do mi amor?" he asks.

I can't tell if he is amused and mocking me or genuinely wants to know my input.

"Well, I'm not, you know, running my own illegal gang so ambushing people isn't really my forte, but I know Rip. He will be expecting you to do that. Do you know what is my forte?" I quickly change the subject.

"What is that?"

"I'm a nurse and whatever you've been doing to treat your burns, it isn't working. They look sore and angry and possibly infected. I could treat them for you. You don't want infection to set in, then you're looking at sepsis, which can be fatal." I advise.

I'm hoping that he accepts my offer. If I treat him for a while it might distract him long enough and with any luck Rip will come while I'm doing it.

Luis thinks for a moment, then he gets up and opens the door, speaking to the big goon on guard. I try to listen and catch any familiar words but it's too difficult.

"You will come with me." Luis says, taking his gun out of his draw, and putting it in his holster.

The big goon unties me and, keeping me cuffed, escorts me behind Luis.

We walk down the corridor, and out of the other side of the building. There is a little outhouse building behind the warehouse. Luis is taking me there. I look around and see at least four men with guns patrolling.

The big goon shoves me forward and I stumble, nearly falling over. I spin around and kick him in the shin.

"Don't you push me, you big freak. Didn't your mother ever tell you not to lay your hands on a woman?!" I yell, trying to get in his face, but my face only comes up to his chest.

Without saying a word, the big goon spins me around and grabs the handcuffs. He yanks them hard making me fall back. He then proceeds to drag me. I kick and scream, pain in my wrists from the cuffs cutting in.

"Let me go you stupid son of a bitch!" I scream.

He ignores me and drags me into a room. Then he just dumps me on the floor. Luis is laying out bottles of things and gauzes and he opens a cupboard which is full of medical supplies. I guess he wants me to help him after all.

"You know you could have just said, rather than have lurch over here drag me." I huff.

"My apologies mi amor." Luis says.

The big goon uncuffs me and I hiss out in pain. The cuffs have cut into my skin and are bleeding.

Luis orders the big goon to go out and stand guard. He then moves to the chair and takes off his shirt. He places it all down with his gun. My eyes immediately go to his gun, wondering if I could just pick it up and shoot him now. But then I would have the guy on the door and the others with their guns to take on.

I sigh.

"Realised that even if you shoot me you still have my men to face?" Luis asks.

My gaze quickly shoots to him in a panic.

"I am not stupid mi amor, and from the look on your face neither are you." He states smiling.

"Now, treat me." He smirks.

I look at him sat there in the chair shirtless, he has an impressive body. If you could overlook the fact that the man is pure evil, he's actually very attractive.

I walk to the cabinet and look at what I've got to work with. Getting out what I need, I walk to the sink and wash my hands. The cuts on my wrists stinging.

I lay everything out and go to treat his burns.

"I have to say mi amor, I've never had such a hermosa woman tend to my wounds before." Luis smiles.

I just nod and continue to treat his burns.

He hisses in pain.

"Sorry." I apologise.

I carefully treat his burns and wrap and cover them.

"There, all done." I say clearing up the rubbish.

"Gracias, you know considering I am holding you captive against your will and planning to kill your love and friends, you were gentle. You could have caused me a lot of pain but didn't, why?" Luis asks putting his shirt back on.

"I am a nurse, I've treated many wankers like you in my time but I always have to be professional and treat every patient equally. I guess I must apply those ethics outside of work too." I say shrugging.

I walk to the sink and wash my hands. Catching me off guard Luis comes up behind me, pinning me in place, I freeze.

He sweeps my hair off of my neck and runs his nose up and along to my ear. My heart feels like its about to burst out of my chest.

"Hmmm, you smell deliciosa. You are quiet a woman Rosa, I think I may keep you with me. I could give you anything you wanted, I'm a very wealthy man mi amor." Luis growls low in my ear.

"I'm flattered, but I'm not into drug lords or cartel leaders. Maybe try one of those online dating apps. You swipe right and all that, I've heard people hook up all the time on those." I rush out.

I'm feeling a little panicked now and really wishing that Rip and the guys would get here.

"I like that you're not afraid to speak your mind around me, I like that you challenge me. It is refreshing mi amor, it is arousing." Luis nips my ear.

I shudder and my stomach lurches. *Well done Rose you've managed to stop the bastard killing you but now you've made him want you.* I mentally chastise myself.

His hands reach around my waist and I instinctively elbow him hard in the gut, winding him slightly. Luis clearly not liking it grabs my hair and yanks my head back to his shoulder.

"You can challenge me, mi amor, but don't fight me because I will win." Luis whispers in my ear.

Fear crawls across my skin and my body starts to shake. Luis smiles against my neck, knowing and liking the fact he's caused this.

I close my eyes and take a deep breath, knowing I will have to do whatever I can to stay alive, for Caden and for Rip. Even if it means giving Luis my body.

CHAPTER TWENTY-SIX

Rip

Once we've parked up I send out the guys in groups to cover the area. We make our way through the wood quietly. As we near the edge, the Warehouse comes into view. I hold up my hand halting everyone and we crouch low.

I have Blake, Wes, Carter and Ben with me. I wait for the texts to come through to say that the rest of the brothers are in position. As we wait and watch we see the door to the ware-house open and out steps Luis, followed by Rose who is handcuffed. There is a big guy behind her pushing her, making her stumble, and it takes everything in my power not to shoot him dead right at that very moment.

We watch as Rose spins around and kicks him as hard as she can in the shin while giving him some shit. Blake and Wes snort back a laugh.

"Even now she's not afraid to speak her mind." Blake mumbles.

"Gets that from her mother." Ben grunts.

I don't say anything. I keep my eyes fixated on her. I jump to my feet when the guy drags her by her cuffs. Wes places a hand on my shoulder, holding me in place.

"Easy man, we will get her out. Think smart, remember. This is what Luis wants, he wants you to lose your shit." Wes says.

I shrug him off and reluctantly crouch back down. I know he's right, but seeing your woman being treated like that is hard to watch.

I get the texts and we slowly make our way towards the warehouse. The guys put silencers on their guns so we can take the men out one at a time without alerting the others.

I watch from the other side of the ware-house as Mammoth shoots a guy straight through the head. Rubble does the same to the other. We make our way to the Outhouse where I saw Luis take Rose while the other guys take and cover the warehouse.

As we creep low I peer into the window; a big mistake. I see Luis holding Rose by her hair, he is whispering something in her ear. I watch as Rose resides with her fate. The look on her face kills me.

Luis smirks and his hands start to travel over her body. I don't get a red mist descend over me, it's more like a red fucking tidal wave.

I get to my feet and I charge down the door. Taken by surprise the big guy isn't ready for me. Before he can shoot his gun, I throw my blade straight into his head. He falls to the floor immediately. I charge forward. Pressing my boot down on his head, I pull my blade from his skull, blood sprays but I don't care. I step over his lifeless body and kick down the next door.

Luis freezes and smiles, still holding Rose tightly by her hair. I notice marks on her face where she has obviously been hit. Every muscle in my body is tight with anger. It feels as thought my bones could snap at any point.

"So good to see you Rip, I've been getting to know your lady here. I see why you like her so much. I have to say I've become quite fond of her too." Luis smiles.

I take a step forward.

"Ah ah ah." Luis says shaking his head. It's then I notice the gun he has pressed into her side.

I don't move.

"You want me, you've got me. Now let her go." I grit out.

"Si, that was the plan, but now I'm changing my mind. I am quite liking the look of pain on your face right now. I know that you have probably killed my men already, and you plan on killing me. Why not destroy you first?" Luis says smiling.

Rose's eyes go wide with panic. My heart beats erratically. He has nothing to lose, whereas I have everything to lose.

"I am giving you a clear shot Luis, I won't kill you. Do not hurt her." I plead.

I throw my blade to the floor and hold up my hands.

"I treated your burns you son of a bitch, if I'd known you'd then kill me I would have made them sting." Rose spits.

If it wasn't for the situation we were in I would smile at my woman. Even with a gun pointed at her, she still comes back with sassy threats.

"Such fire, you could have had it all with me mi amor." Luis says.

Rose rolls her eyes, like she's tired of all of this shit.

"Told you already, not into drug lords and Cartel types. Anyway, you're about to kill me, so unless you're into necrophilia I'd say that plan is a no go. Wouldn't you?" Rose asks.

Luis tugs her hair hard and Rose gasps in pain and grits her teeth. I clench my fist. Having her so close to me and not being able to do anything is destroying me.

"Careful mi amor." Luis threatens.

"Sweetheart." I say as a warning not to push him.

I catch a glimpse of the brothers moving past the window. I wish they'd hurry their fucking asses up.

"You know, mi amigo, maybe I take her sassy mouth right here in front of you, make you watch as she chokes on my cock. Then I could slit her throat. Watching it destroy you would be the highlight of my life." Luis threatens. He runs his tongue along her neck.

"You fuckin try it Luis, I would slit your throat before you even undid your fuckin pants!" I yell.

Luis smiles and bites Rose's neck.

"Hhmm deliciosa." Luis goads.

I watch as a tear falls down Rose's cheek. She

is panting in fear.

"Fuck you and your tiny dick. You put that anywhere near my mouth, I would bite the little pecker clean fucking off!" Rose threatens.

Luis yanks on her hair and jabs the gun hard into her side. Rose cries out in pain.

He starts to move, keeping hold of her hair and keeping the gun aimed at her.

"Get on your knees mi amor." Luis growls out.

Rose looks to me with tears in her eyes. Shaking with fear she starts to do as he asks. I am running out of time. I need to do something. I look around the room for something. Anything that would stand a chance of getting that gun away from Luis. Something catches my eye. It's Rose. As she settles down on her knees she does a fake wobble and picks up a pair of scissors off of the floor. Luis doesn't notice, the sick fuck is too busy getting off on the power he has over her.

Rose's eyes flick to mine. I try to tell her with my eyes to not do it. But of course the stubborn woman ignores me.

I look for my blade, it's just a few feet in front of me, but if I go for my blade I risk Luis killing Rose. One wrong move and she's dead. The turmoil waging inside of me is near killing me. My hands twitch, eager to wrap around Luis's throat and kill him. I just want my woman safe and in my fucking arms. I've never wanted blood more than I do right now.

Luis lets go of her hair and undoes his pants. My stomach lurches. I can't let this happen. I can't watch her go through this, I fucking can't.

Luis frees his cock, Rose's eyes come to mine, wide.

"In your mouth mi amor. You even try biting it I will blow your pretty brains everywhere." Luis threatens.

She mouths the words 'I love you', looking me directly in the eyes. She starts to lean forward, and I have to look away.

"Rip, now!" Rose yells.

I swing my gaze to her and watch as she shoulder barges Luis making him stumble and fall. She twists and stabs the scissors into his thigh as hard as she can. Luis roars in pain. He kicks her hard across the face, sending her across the room. I move quickly, I don't have time to grab my blade. I tackle Luis to the ground, releasing my rage and anger. I continuously hit him, blood splattering across his face.

I'm briefly distracted, trying to see where Rose is. Luis takes advantage of that. Bringing the gun round he hits me hard over the head. Luis gains the advantage and takes aim at me. I pause, not scared to be looking down the barrel of a gun. This isn't the first time and it won't be the last. I would happily take a bullet right now if it meant Rose was safe.

Before I can do anything, Rose dives towards Luis. She jumps in front of him, using her body to knock him off of me. I reach out for my blade and rear back and stab him in the chest with all of the strength I have.

Luis' gun goes off. I freeze for a moment, thinking I've been shot. I haven't.

"You okay Rip?" Rose asks, panic and worry in her voice.

"Yeah sweetheart." I watch the life drain from Luis' eyes.

I get off him and turn to Rose, she smiles a small smile. I go to smile back but stop as her smile falls from her face and her eyes roll closed. She slumps forward. I charge across the room to her and see she has been shot in the stomach.

"Rose! Shit! Stay awake." I shout.

The rest of the guys charge in.

"Get the fuck out and get us to the hospital now!" I yell.

I pick Rose up in my arms and run from the building through the woods and back to the trucks with the guys following behind me.

Ben keeps close on my heels. I dive into the back of the truck with Blake, Carter and Ben.

We speed all the way to hospital and Ben rings Penny.

"I know love...just get there...she will be okay, this is Rose we're talking about. She's far too stubborn to ever stop fighting. We will see you there. Love you." Ben disconnects.

He turns to me in the back seat. I've taken my top off and I'm using it to apply pressure to the wound. His eyes flicker to his baby girl, pain slicing through them.

Rose's breathing is laboured, she keeps flickering in and out of consciousness.

"Stay awake for me sweetheart, for once just do as I ask."

"Don't...tell me...what to do." She breaths out.

She tries to smile, but her eye lids become heavy again as she loses consciousness.

"Rose! Rose sweetheart, please wake up." I beg.

I place my fingers on her neck, feeling for her pulse. I can barely feel it, it's so weak.

"Fuck! what's taking so long?" I shout.

"Just turning into the street now." Blake answers.

The truck speeds through the parking lot to the entrance. There are people shouting and moaning and cars honking their horns. I couldn't give a shit. The truck has barely stopped but I jump out and run in, shouting for help. A group of nurses come running over with a bed. I lay her down and kiss her head. They rush her off to the doctors.

I run my hands through my hair, gripping it tightly. She got fucking shot because she was helping me. She's in there fighting for her fucking life because of me.

"She'll be okay Pres." Khan says from behind me.

I spin around, anger building inside me.

"Where the fuck were all of you?! I was in there, he had a gun to her head. I had to go unarmed! He was going to fucking rape her. She saved me from getting fuckin' shot! That shouldn't have fuckin' happened! We were supposed to be saving her! Where the fuck were you?" I yell, not caring I'm in a waiting room full of patients.

"There were more than we thought. It took us longer to get through them all than we thought it would. We are fucking sorry Pres." Khan apologises.

It's then I notice Khan's busted lip. I look around: Mammoth has blood on his shirt and Rubble has a cut down his face.

I sigh and rub my face.

"Fuck!" I yell.

"Do you mind! There are good people here and they don't need to listen to your fowl mouth." I hear behind me.

I spin around and see some weasel of a man with his hands on his hips.

"What?" I growl.

My tone and stare are threatening. I almost want him to start, needing to beat the shit out of something.

The guy falters a little before responding, clearly seeing the threat in my eyes.

"I said stop swearing. It's bad enough that you're stood there like you are, not even dressed properly with blood all over you. People like you throw your weight around expecting to bully your way through life. That poor woman is probably in there because of you. You're all the same you lot, don't consider the consequences of your life choices." The guy says shaking his head.

I am gone before anyone can stop me. I grab him by the scruff of his neck and pull him close to me.

"You really should have kept your fuckin' mouth shut." I whisper.

I watch as pure fear washes over his face. I rear my head back and head butt him hard. The guy's nose makes a loud cracking sound and he cries out. I chuck him to the floor and storm out of the hospital.

Walking around the side of the building I punch the wall over and over, releasing my frustration and anger. My knuckles split and bleed. I welcome the pain. I stop and brace myself against the wall, hanging my head.

"Better?" Blake asks.

"I had to watch the fear in her eyes, I had to stand there and watch as she was fucking held by that son of a bitch. I should have just taken him out, I should have stopped him sooner. Fuck!" I roar.

Blake clasps me on the shoulder and hands me a packet of smokes and a light. I take them and slump down on the ground.

Blake sits next to me.

"You did what you could. If you charged straight in she would be dead. She will fight, she's a strong woman, and trust me, she's stubborn. It runs in their damn family." Blake nudges me.

"Now, as some asshole said to me a few months back, you've had your moment, now. Man the fuck up and be strong for her. She needs you. You need to stay strong for her, brother." Blake smiles and stands.

He holds out his hand. I grab it and he pulls

me up and slaps me on the back. He is right, I can't break now. Rose needs me now more than ever.

"I can't believe you remembered that little speech." I say as we walk back to the hospital.

"Ingrained in here." Blake says tapping his head.

We are shown to a waiting area on a different floor. Rose needed surgery to remove the bullet and stop the internal bleeding.

Penny comes to me as we enter. Ma brought me a T-shirt. She hugs me and pats my face.

"Thank you for getting her out of there. Ben told me what happened, believe me I will be having words with her when she wakes up. She really can't stop that sass, even with a gun pointed at her." Penny says, trying to lighten the mood.

"Trust me, you won't be the only one." I add.

We all sit down and wait. Wait to hear from the doctor.

"No I am not moving my car, do you have any idea how much I've been to this god damn hospital in the last six months? I should have my own damn parking space. I am heavily pregnant, and my sister is here because she's been shot. Now if you even think about towing it I will personally ring every newspaper in the area and inform them of your treatment of a pregnant woman while her sister was fighting for her god damn life!" Lily shouts.

We exchange a look and smile. I look to Blake who sighs and rolls his eyes. He gets up to go and try to calm his wife down.

"Now you all know why I'm bloody grey. I swear, don't have daughters, they only age you." Ben mutters.

It occurs to me that Caden isn't here.

"Who's got Caden?" I ask.

"Daisy. Carter has gone to get them and bring them here when Rose wakes up. We don't want Caden sitting here worrying about his mum." Penny answers.

I pray to Christ she does wake up. I don't voice my thoughts. Penny and Ben seemed convinced she will. I wish I had their hope, I just want to hold her again.

I go to the vending machine to get a coffee and Mammoth joins me.

"Pres, I just wanted to say...there were a lot of weapons on the site and a lot of blow. We took the weapons and burnt the blow with the rest of it. Burnt Luis and his men too. The whole site is ash...one good thing is it was far enough out in the sticks that no one called fire department...

Flo will pull through, she's a Satan." Mammoth claps me on the shoulder and walks back into the waiting room.

A little while later a doctor and nurse come in the room.

"I won't ask for immediate family, I remember from last time so unless you tell me otherwise I will just update you on Miss Rocke's progress." He says with a small smile.

"Appreciate that doctor. Please tell us how is she?" Penny asks.

He smiles. She is doing just fine, she came out of theatre about forty-five minutes ago. She's awake and groggy and, well, letting our staff know she wants to see you."

Everyone in the room hoots and cheers. I tell Lily to ring Daisy and get her and Caden here.

Penny, Ben and I make our way to Rose's room. As we approach we can hear laughter. We walk in and see the nurse laughing. Rose is smiling. Her eyes come to mine and her smile falls and tears form in her eyes. I walk straight to her, past Penny and Ben.

I cup her face in my hands and kiss her, feeling her, knowing she's okay. I break the kiss and lean my forehead against hers.

"I fuckin' love you sweetheart." I rasp. I'm trying to fight back my emotions.

"I fucking love you biker boy." She sniffs.

I wipe her tears away and kiss her head. I step back a moment so her parents can see her.

"Oh honey, I am so proud of you. I heard what happened; you are so brave." Penny sniffs.

"Don't be so bloody stupid next time, if a man has a gun to you don't give him your bloody lip. Usually if someone has a gun aimed at you, you should do as they say, not answer him back." Ben chastise her while kissing her head and holding her.

He pulls back and sighs.

"Honestly, you girls have really aged me these last few months. From now on me and your mum will be living closer to keep an eye on you. Clearly when giving you girls too much freedom, all you do is run your mouths off and get in to bloody trouble." Ben grumbles.

"I learnt from the best old man." Rose says smiling.

Penny laughs and shake her head.

"Come on, let's give these two a minute before Caden arrives." Penny tugs Ben's hand and they leave.

I sit next to Rose and stroke her hair from her face.

"I swear watching you go through that and not being able to do a damn thing was the hardest thing I've ever done in my life. Fuck. I am so sorry sweetheart, you have no idea how much. He's dead, I made sure of that this time. I burnt the site down to the ground. I swear I will not let anything happen to you again." I say raw with emotion.

Rose cups my face.

"You have nothing to apologise for, you did everything you could. If you had tried to intervene sooner he could have killed me. Anyway, I held my own until you got there." Rose smiles and winks.

"Fuck! I swear when you're better I am putting you across my god damn knee. Your dad is right, if someone is holding you at gun point it's not the best time to give them your sass." I say, running my finger across her lip.

Rose kisses my finger.

"You love my sass, and it was fine in the end. I learnt my boundaries. By all accounts he didn't like the mention of his mother. That's how I got this." Rose says pointing to the mark on her face.

I grit my jaw, feeling the anger run through me again. Rose takes my chin in her hand and tugs lightly.

"Hey, stop doing that, okay? I am fine. I am alive, and I am breathing. Luis is dead. Just focus on us, and when I'm better you promised me a spanking." She says smiling.

"You're fucking incredible, you know that? I swear I'm the luckiest son of bitch to have you as my own. We're not waiting to get married, we are doing it as soon as you're better. The sooner you have that damn ring on your finger, the better." I say, my chest aching with love for this incredibly strong minded, stubborn ass woman.

CHAPTER TWENTY-SEVEN

With Rip declaring that we are to get married as soon as I'm better, I can't wipe the smile from my face. Usually that would have made me build up those walls and hide away; not anymore. I don't care that it's going to be a rushed wedding, I'm not scared. I want nothing more than to be Rip's wife. I've found a place I belong, Caden too. I feel free to be me, no judging from my dick of an ex, or the teachers and parents at Caden's posh school. Rip loves and accepts me for me and so do his club and family.

I smile to myself.

"What you smiling about sweetheart?" Rip asks.

"That I don't have sex for six years, I push away any guy that tries to get near me, then I meet you and within weeks you destroy my barriers. Now I'm going to marry you. I think you have some kind of Pussy magic going on. It's voodoo." I state smiling.

Rip throws his head back laughing.

"Sweetheart, maybe just maybe it's because I am meant to be with you, and you are meant to be with me." Rip says smiling.

"Wow! That's some cheesy romantic shit. You feeling okay?" I tease.

Rip just growls back at me.

The door flies open and Caden comes running in. His eyes are red from crying. He dives on me making me hiss in pain.

Rip goes to move him a little, but I shake my head. Caden is cuddling me tight and sobbing his little heart out. I soothe him, stroking his hair.

"It's okay buddy, I'm here." I comfort him.

Caden lifts his head up and wipes his eyes.

"I thought I'd lost you Mummy. I don't know what I would do without you. I would never want to go with dad. He doesn't love me like you do. Don't leave again please." Caden sobs.

"Oh buddy, I'm not going anywhere. Never. I promise that you will never end up with your father, okay? I love you buddy." I say kissing his head.

Rip kisses my head and gives me and Caden a minute. I hold him in my arms. His quiet sobs fill the room and break my heart.

He lifts his head, his red rimmed eyes staring at me.

"Mum?"

"Yeah buddy?" I answer with a smile and stroke his hair.

"You're a badass." Caden says straight faced. I smile.

"You think so?"

"Yeah, totally! You've been shot. That means you're a real badass. Does it hurt?" Caden ask curiously.

"Being shot?" I query.

Caden nods.

"Yeah, it hurts a lot, but I feel a lot better now because the doctors and nurses are taking good care of me. I've got medicine to help take the pain away." I say.

I smile, thankful that Caden is getting back to his inquisitive self.

"Mum?" Caden asks again.

"Yes buddy?"

"Will you and Rip ever have kids?" Caden randomly asks.

A little surprised by his question and the random timing of it.

"Err, honestly buddy, it's not something we've talked about properly. What do you think? Would you like a baby sister or brother?" I ask.

Caden looks thoughtful for a moment. He turns to me and nods.

"Yeah I'd like a baby sister so I can look after her and if anyone is mean I can kick their butts. Then I'd like a baby brother so I can teach him stuff and he can be my best friend in the world. We will always have each other's back." Caden states.

I smile and fight back the tears. My beautiful sweet boy has the biggest heart. The thought of him with siblings makes my heart swell.

I spend a few days in hospital, by the end of it I'm driving Rip crazy. I feel a lot better. I just want to go home and things to go back to normal. I hate not being able to do anything. I hate being useless.

"Sweetheart, will you sit your ass down?!

You're gonna pull your damn stitches out." Rip moans at me.

I give him a death glare.

"Don't tell me what to do biker boy. I am just putting my slippers on so I can go for a little wander. The doctor says I'm allowed to." I bite back.

As I bend to get my slipper my stitches pull, causing me to gasp in pain.

"God damn it woman! Will you stop being such a stubborn ass and just let me help you? You know I've lost count how many time I have to spank that ass of yours." Rip states, shaking his head.

"Ever wonder if I'm playing this to my advantage? Hhmm." I ask smiling.

"I don't doubt it sweetheart. You've told me once or twice you're looking forward to it." Rip says, as he pulls me gently to my feet.

He leans in kissing me. I give it all I've got, teasing him with my tongue and nipping his bottom lip. Rip groans low in his throat. That makes me smile.

"Sweetheart, you need to calm it. You're not well enough so stop being a dick tease. Now let's take you for a little walk." Rip chastises me.

I grumble and moan under my breath. This just makes Rip shake his head and laugh.

Caden, Daisy and Lily come to visit me for lunch. We sit all around my bed eating taco bell.

"Are you guys okay with what went down?" I ask.

Lily and Daisy exchange a look.

"Yeah, well Carter and I know the others feel the same, that they blame themselves. They feel they should have got to you quicker, then maybe you wouldn't have got hurt." Daisy says.

I turn to Caden and hand him some money.

"Hey buddy, can you go to the vending machine just outside and grab me a drink?" I ask.

"Sure thing Mum." Caden says as he jumps off of the bed.

Once I know Caden is out of sight, I start talking.

"Listen, they couldn't have helped what happened. Luis was a nasty piece of work and yeah, you know I got shot, but I'm okay. You need to tell Carter and the others that I do not in anyway blame them and so they shouldn't blame themselves. Okay?" I finish by taking a big bite out of my taco.

Daisy and Lily both nod and smile.

"So you're getting married in what, three or four weeks? You know Mum and Trudy are out there overexcited and organising shit." Lily states.

I smile and shake my head.

"I am not surprised, but I honestly couldn't care less. I mean I did the whole big white wedding and look how that turned out. I will be happy if it's just me, Rip, Caden and family in the back garden with a BBQ. I just hope Mum and Dad can get Nan over okay. I don't know if they can even get hold of Ax." I shrug.

Lily and Daisy look at each other in a way that doesn't sit right with me.

"What? What is it?" I ask.

"Okay no one wanted to tell you for a little while because, well, you have obviously been through some tough shit these past few days..." Lily pauses.

"It's Axel." Daisy says.

Panic and dread take over. Please let him be alright.

"He's okay. Well...we think he's okay. Truth is, no one knows where he is. He's gone AWOL." Lily states.

I'm stunned, Ax has always been about the army and the pride he got from fighting for his country. This is not like him. Something serious must have happened for him to do this. The army is his life, there is no way he would just give it up.

"But...but that's not Ax." I add.

"We know, we have Blake's contacts trying to locate him. If he doesn't turn up soon with a bloody good reason he could go to prison. And when I say a reason, I mean you know he's been held captive somewhere, been unconscious, or had severe memory loss. God forbid the worst." Daisy states.

She's right; he could end up in serious trouble. I just hope he's safe wherever he is.

"Maybe I should ask Rip as well? He has a few contacts too. Well that's if Blake hasn't already got him involved in looking." I say biting my nail anxiously, worried for Axel's wellbeing.

Caden comes running back in with my drink and we all stop talking immediately. I don't want him worrying about Ax.

"Mum, I just seen Owen. He said to say hi and that he hopes you're doing alright." Caden says eating some sweets he clearly helped himself to from the other vending machine.

"Oh, why didn't he come in himself and say hi?" I wonder.

"I asked him to, said you're just there go say it yourself. He just shook his head saying he didn't have time. He just kept looking at Rip, like Rip was scary." Caden shrugs shoving more sweets in his mouth.

"Wait, Rip's here?" I ask.

"Yeah, he brought me the sweets and your drink, said he will be in to visit in a second. He had business to see to first." Caden shrugs then takes the money I gave him and hands it to me.

I look to Daisy and Lily who both shrug.

I wonder what the hell he is up to now. Poor Owen. I hope Rip isn't threatening him because Owen is such a nice guy, he doesn't deserve it. Owen respects my decision to be with Rip.

The door opens and Rip walks in with a white box and flowers. I furrow my brow in confusion.

Caden jumps off of the bed and goes to Lily and Daisy.

Mum, Dad, Trudy and Max come into the room. Followed close behind by Blake, Wes and Carter. The room is packed with family. I smile and look at them all confused.

"What's going on? Why the hell are you all here?" I ask.

Rip walks to my side. He places the flowers and the box down on the bed.

"Sweetheart. I proposed to you and I didn't have a ring for you, well, now I do." Rip gets down on one knee and holds a small velvet box in his hand.

He opens it and I gasp when I see the beautiful sapphire ring.

"Rose, sweetheart, my life would be nothing without you. You make me a better man. You make me laugh, you test my patience, and you drive me insane. You're fuckin' perfect for me. So, what do you say? Will you marry me?" Rip asks.

I wipe my tears and smiling, I nod.

"Yes." I sniffle.

Rip stands and places the ring on my finger. He kisses me passionately. He stops and pull back.

"There's more. You have the ring, but there was one more thing you needed to make you mine, one more thing that shows the world you belong to me. I'm not talking about the wedding and you becoming Mrs King. This shows the world who your family is and who has your back." He hands me the white box.

I smile a tearful smile. I bite my lip, anxious to see what's in the box.

I open the lid and remove the tissue paper. I can't wipe the smile off of my face.

"Oh my god this is amazing." I breathe.

I reach in and pull out a cut, clearly made for me. It has the Satan's Outlaws emblem on the back with Property of Rip written on it. I run my fingers over the writing and sniffle.

"Sweetheart?" Rip asks concern in his voice.

I look up and wipe my tears. I hold the cut out and put it on. Slowly I get up and kneel on the bed with Rip supporting me.

"You have no idea how much this means to me. I thought I knew where I belonged and then I found you and the Satan's Outlaws. Now I know I was always meant to be here with you with the Satans'. To be your wife, to be your old lady. I fucking love you biker boy."

Rip grabs the cut in his hands and brings me to him, crashing his mouth down on mine. I get lost in Rip, lost in us.

"Woohoo skin and blister! Wow! It's getting hot in here!" Lily says behind me, breaking our moment and reminding us that we are not alone.

I pull back from Rip just a little and smile up at him.

"Fuckin' love you sweetheart." Rip growls low.

"Christ, a father did not need to see that." Dad grumbles.

I laugh and Rip smiles.

I turn slightly and do a model pose for Lily and Daisy.

They applaud and cheer.

There's a knock at the door and Mammoth, Rubble, Fury, Khan and Big Papa walk in.

"Holy hotness, looks like we missed the surprise but fuck me that Satans cut was made for you darlin'." Khan says smiling.

"I'm a Satan's Outlaws mother fuckers!" I shout excitedly with my hands in the air.

Everyone cheers and Caden runs around the room fist bumping everyone.

"Language Rose!" Mum chastises, fighting her own smile.

"Perfect for each other." Trudy says smiling.

This has to be one of the happiest moments of my life, surrounded by people I love and who love me.

A few days later I am finally discharged from hospital, to say I'm happy about it is an understatement. I've been dying to sleep next to Rip again. I'm not going to lie, I'm so horny I feel I could jump Rip's bones at any given moment.

Being so horny is making me snappy. I went six years with no sex, it has been like ten days and apparently now I can't survive without it.

The worst part is that Rip is treating me like I'm going to break at any moment when all I want is to be thrown on the bed and fucked. It's driving me insane. I'm in the laundry room loading the clothes for washing when Rip walks in.

"What the hell do you think you're doing?"

I look to him then the washing machine.

"Well, I am doing this amazing magic trick called laundry, have you heard of it? It magically makes clothes clean again." I say sarcastically.

Rip grunts and moves closer, pinning me against the washing machine.

"Stop sassing me woman, you know you're supposed to be taking it easy. If the laundry needed doing you should have told me."

"For the millionth time, you love my sass. You love my mouth." I say smiling sweetly.

"Don't. I know what you're trying to do and it won't work. The Doctor said you have to take it easy for at least two more weeks." Rip reminds me.

I don't say anything. I lift my top off and chuck it in the washing machine. My eyes are on Rip the entire time. Next are my shorts and underwear. Finally, my bra. I turn and purposefully bend, pushing my behind into his crotch.

Rip moans and I smile to myself. I turn back round to face him and go straight for the button on his jeans. I undo them, reaching in I take hold of his thick hard cock in my hand. I stroke him up and down. I watch his jaw clench. His eyes fall closed and his head rolls back. I clench my legs together, feeling beyond turned on watching him.

"See, you want it just as much as me." I whisper.

Rip groans in response.

I stop suddenly and remove my hand. Rip's eyes fly open and come to me. I carefully lift myself on the washing machine. I spread my legs and pull Rip closer, so he's nestled between them. I yank his jeans down freeing him and place him at my entrance. Our eyes are focused on each other. I lick my lower lip.

"Fuck me Rip, please." I beg.

His eyes drop to my bandaged stomach and his hands run very lightly over it, concern and sadness washes over his face. I take his jaw in my hands and bring his focus back to me. I take his cock in my hand holding and positioning him perfectly. I wrap my legs around him slowly push him forward inside me. I let out a low moan, loving the feeling of us connected. I've missed this.

"I am more than fine, just watch me. Watch what pleasure you bring me. No pain, I promise. I need you, I've missed this so much." I breathe as I move my hips slowly.

Rip's hands move to my hips and his grips them firmly. His eyes on me he thrusts forward. We both let out a moan. He does it again and again. He leans forward and cups his hand around the back of my neck, crashing his mouth to mine. His tongue invades my mouth, playfully stroking my tongue. He breaks the kiss and rests his forehead against mine. Watching me, watching us. Slowly moving in and out teasing in blissful torture.

"You're my fuckin' world, my everything. You have me." Rip growls.

He thrusts harder this time.

"You have all of me. I'm all yours." He breathes.

Thrusting in harder again making my head roll back, the pleasure building.

"Mind, body and fuckin' soul. It's you, sweetheart. You have it all." Rip says as he thrusts again, this time we both moan.

"Say it sweetheart, say you have me. Say that you belong to me." Rip grits out, holding back, waiting for my answer.

"I have you Rip, I am yours. I completely belong to you and you belong to me. I love you biker boy." I breathe.

Rip stops moving and leans in and whispers in my ear.

"Fuckin' love you sweetheart."

Then he grabs hold of my behind and slams into me over and over. We are both panting, our pleasure building. I know I'm close. Rip can feel it too.

"Sweetheart, come for me." He growls low in my ear.

His pace is relentless and I soon fall blissfully off of the edge. I bite down on Rip's shoulder to stop myself from screaming out his name.

Rip buries his face in my neck and groans a low throaty groan, finding his release.

I stroke the back of his neck. He lifts his face up and looks into my eyes.

"Who knew sex in the laundry room could be so romantic and so fucking hot." I say smiling.

Rip chuckles, he leans in and kisses me.

"You sure you're feeling okay, I didn't hurt you?" He asks concerned.

I shake my head.

"I'm fine. Actually, I'm more than fine."

"MUM!" Caden yells.

"Shit!" I say wide eyed, looking around for my clothes and then remembering I put them in with the washing.

"Bollocks!" I panic.

Rip just chuckles, shaking his head and doing up his jeans. While I turn the laundry room upside down looking for anything to put on.

"Why are there no clothes in the pissing

laundry room?!"

"Mum! Where are you? Nan and Grandad are here." Caden yells again, this time his voice sounds closer.

"Fu-u-u-c-c-k!" I say with my head in the tumble dryer desperate to find anything.

"Maybe she's out here doing some laundry, I'll check." We hear Mum say from the other side of the door.

In that moment I freeze, it's like all time freezes. I watch the door handle turn and suck in a breath, bracing for the humiliation of my mother seeing me stark bollock naked. Rip is fighting back his laughter.

Mum opens the door, steps in, and gasps. I jump behind Rip using him as a human shield.

"Oh my!" Mum gasps.

"Erm, hi Mum. Wasn't expecting you." I state.

"No, I'm guessing you weren't." Mum's lips twitch, fighting a smile.

"Hey Penny." Rip smiles and winks.

"Hey sweetie, good to see you managed to get dressed." Mum says smiling.

"Um hey, here's an idea, how about someone grabs me a robe or you know, some form of bloody clothing?! So I don't have to walk naked past my son and father. That would scar them for life." I grit through my teeth.

Rip is finding this whole thing very amusing. Mum smiles.

"Well darling, maybe you should have thought about that before you decided to get frisky in the middle of the day with your son down the hall watching TV. Now don't get me wrong, I know it's hard to get what you want when there are kids about, but that's what play dates at a friend's house are for. Although there was this one time I had your father cuffed to the bed and I could find the key..."

"Mum! Focus! Please can you get me my robe? It's on the bed upstairs." I interrupt.

Mum rolls her eyes.

"Fine." She turns and leaves, shutting the door behind her. I sigh. Rip is still laughing. I whack him across the back.

"Stop laughing! This is not bloody funny." I huff.

Rip pulls me into his arms.

"It is sweetheart."

"Right, no more sex for you. You are on a ban for taking pleasure from my humiliation. No more good times for you, no banging, bonking, shagging, hide the sausage, sexy time, fucking or what ever you want to call it! You sir have lost all access to my punani." I threaten.

Rip throws his head back laughing.

"Sweetheart, I'm just going to point out that you got shot, have just come out of hospital and it has only been seven days since we last fucked. You can try and put me on a ban, but you know you won't last." Rip says smiling.

As if to prove a point he leans down kissing and nipping along my neck. He doesn't play fair. He knows the neck kissing is my kryptonite. I go from zero to horny in less than a minute.

Rip stops and pulls back, smiling.

"Bastard! You don't fight fair." I groan.

"Never said I did. That's why you love me, sweetheart. The dirtier the better." Rip teases.

"Ooo cheesy line." I mock.

Rip growls. His hand cups my behind and he lifts me. I wrap my legs around his waist and let out a squeal.

"You sassing me woman?" He asks. His eyes are playful.

"I have no idea what you're talking about; I am a total angel." I say sarcastically.

"There it is again, sass. If you're not careful sweetheart, I will give that sassy mouth of yours something to keep it quiet." Rips eyes dilate, and I feel his words straight to my core.

I lick my lower lip at the thought of tasting him and having him in my mouth.

"Err, I will just leave your robe here. I'll put the kettle on." Mum says from behind us, and quickly shuts the door.

We both look to each other then burst out laughing.

"Fuckin love you sweetheart."

I smile "Fucking love you too." I reply.

After I've gotten dressed I walk to the kitchen where Mum is making everyone lunch.

"Oh honey, I got you some bridal magazines. I put them on the counter. Might give you some idea of what colours you want, oh and themes." Mum says pointing to them.

I roll my eyes and flick through the magazines.

"Mum, I've told you I don't care. As long as the important people are there I couldn't care less. I'm marrying Rip and that's all I need." I repeat to her.

"I know you said that, but I just want to make sure you're happy with your wedding day. At least pick a dress you like? We can go shopping and get one for you tomorrow." Mum suggests.

I roll my eyes, I'm not a massive fan of shopping and I don't want a big wedding dress. I just want to keep it simple.

I pause looking through the magazine. I see the perfect dress.

It is a plain, simple, satin dress. It has thin spaghetti straps, a sweetheart neckline, it is form fitting, and then it just flows straight. It has button detailing all the way down the back. It's not white or ivory. It is almost a soft champagne colour.

I check to make sure Rip's not looking in or listening.

"Mum! This is the dress." I call her over.

Mum quickly runs over and takes a look. She smiles and nods.

"Yes honey, it's perfect. It's all you." Mum give me a side squeeze on the shoulders.

"What about the bridesmaids?" Mum asks.

I hadn't thought about bridesmaids, but I suppose it will be Lily and Daisy, if they want to, that is.

"I will ask Lily and Daisy, see if they want to. I'm not sure that Lily will, being so close to her due date. She said she feels like a beached wale as it is. Oh and I'm not having a hen party or anything. It's literally going to be a small and quick wedding. Please, nothing big and fancy." I inform Mum, with a warning look. I do not want her to go overboard and make this a big over the top wedding.

"Cross my heart." Mum swears.

I roll my eyes because there will be something, whether it's releasing doves or a firework display. It will be something. She just can't help herself.

I put down the magazine as my thoughts travel to my brother Axel. Is he okay? Will he be able to make it? God I really hope he's okay. What's stranger is that no one is talking about it, like it's normal and he's just on deployment somewhere. Is there more to it? Do they know something I don't?

"Mum, what's going on with Axel?" I ask getting straight to the point.

I watch Mum's shoulders tense. This can't be good. She dries her hand on the towel and turns to face me.

"Okay, well. He's no longer AWOL. I got a call from him last night. He's safe." Mum says, giving me a small smile.

I know she's holding back something.

"What are you not telling me?" I ask.

"He's being discharged from the army." Mum states.

"What? For going AWOL? But I'm sure he had a very good reason for doing it. He loves every second of the army! He is the army! Did he say why he disappeared?" I ask.

Mum shakes her head.

"No. He said that he can't say where he was, or what he was doing. Not even to the army. For his years of service they said that his punishment is to be discharged. He's lucky he's not facing worse. He will find his way, I'm just glad he's alive and well. I couldn't give a toss what the army say about him, he's served his country and done them proud. That's enough for me." Mum says, but I can see the worry behind her eyes.

Axel is the army. Ever since he was little that's all he wanted to do. He worked his way up quickly through the ranks. So I know why Mum is worried: he can't be handling this well.

"Is he coming over?" I ask.

"Yes he is, he will be here next week with Nan." Mum smiles.

"Good, he will need his family around him right now. I'm sure Blake can sort him a job at the Den or something." I squeeze Mum's hand and she smiles.

"You're right. Now that's enough worrying, you don't need it. You're trying to recover. Although you seemed to be recovering very well in the laundry room earlier." Mum winks.

Mum and Dad spend a couple of hours with

us, and we make plans to go to the bridal shop in the next couple of days.

Shutting the front door behind them I lean against it and sigh, exhausted.

Rip moves to me. Without saying a word he picks me up in his arms and carries me upstairs.

Once upstairs he lays me down and pulls the cover over me.

Leaning over me his eyes roam my face.

"Two weeks today, you'll be Mrs King."

"What?" I ask surprised. I knew we were doing in the next few weeks, but we hadn't actually booked anything yet.

"Yeah, I've got someone to marry us, got it all booked. Well, thanks to my ma and your mum." Rip rolls his eyes and smiles.

A huge smile spreads across my face.

"I fucking love you biker boy."

"I fuckin' love you sweetheart." Rip leans down and takes my mouth.

The moment is broken by loud footsteps running into the bedroom.

"Mum! Look what I can do." Caden says excitedly.

He then proceeds to burp the alphabet.

"An-n-nd the romantic moment has died." I

say laughing.

Rip lays down next to me and Caden dives on top of him, laying between us.

Cuddling in I watch as Caden's eyes start to get heavy. It's not long until Rip is joining him. Looking at them both fast asleep, I realise I may have had my walls up keeping every guy out. But it wasn't a bad thing, it was a good thing. Over time those walls had become a fortress that the weaker guys couldn't break. That fortress could only ever be broken down by the one that was strong enough, the one that would do anything to have me, the one that could handle me without trying change me. Of course there was only ever one man, and that man was Rip.

I had finally fucking found my happily ever after with my biker boy. My happily ever after with the President of the Satan's Outlaws. There will never be a predictable or dull moment again and I cannot not fucking wait.

THE END

EPILOGUE

Two weeks of hell leading up to this moment. I'm getting married again. I'm having my hair done and I think there are enough products in it that if I was to pass near a naked flame my hair would catch fire.

"Ughh I'm so hot. I need to pee again and my feet are swelling." Lily moans from behind me.

"Sorry skin and blister, I didn't make the weather this way. I promise the service will be quick and every fan we can get our hands on will be switched on. As for the rest of your problems, go for a pee, then lay down on the bed and keep your feet up." I shrug.

"Fine. I'm getting a snack while I'm up, you better have good food in your fridge." Lily grumbles and waddles out of the room.

I roll my eyes and Raven just laughs and carries on doing my hair.

Maddie and Caden come running in.

"Caden! Do not touch my special pwincess dress. I can't get messed up. You can't get messed up either, you look smart like a handsome pwince." Maddie smiles and spins around, making her dress float out.

"I do not! I look like a badass not some dumb prince!" Caden moans.

"Oi! Watch your mouth." I snap at him.

Maddie shrugs and smiles.

"Okay, okay, you're a badass pwince." Maddie sighs.

Caden giggle at her saying badass.

I am sorry Raven, my son is corrupting your granddaughter." I sigh.

"Don't think that's the worst she's heard." Raven snorts.

"Damn right I'm a badass prince, come on princess Maddie let's go see what snacks we can eat. I'm starving." Caden runs out of the room.

I sigh and roll my eyes. That boy will have cute little Maddie swearing like a sailor by the end of the day. I look at Maddie who is grinning from ear to ear.

"He called me pwincess Maddie." She beams and then skips out of the room.

"Uh oh, I think a certain little princess is taking quite a liking to Caden. We could have an interesting few years ahead of us." Raven says laughing.

There is a knock on the door and Khan sticks his head in.

"Special delivery." He sings carrying a box.

"Woah! Looking foxy! You know it's not too late back out and run away with me?" Khan teases.

"Stop saying that. You couldn't handle me and you know it." I say getting up and taking the box from him.

"Darlin' I think it's you who can't handle me." Khan says laughing and holding his crotch suggestively.

"For goodness sake, Khan. Piss off and take your sexually infected crotch with you." Lily snaps, walking back in the room with a sandwich.

"Hey! That was a long time ago and I got it

treated!" Khan fires back as he leaves the room.

We all burst out laughing. Daisy and Lily come over to see what's in the box. I lift the lid and move the tissue paper. I pull out a cropped leather biker jacket. I turn it over and beautifully on the back it says just married with a little rose on it. Putting it on I walk to the mirror. It's perfect.

"Oh my! Who would have thought that a wedding dress would go so perfectly with a biker jacket." Mum smiles brightly.

I take a deep breath and turn to face them all.

"Right, let's do this." I say picking up my bouquet of flowers.

"You look amazing. Rip won't be able to keep his hands off of you." Raven says kissing my cheek.

"Where are Dad and Axel?" I ask.

As soon as I've said the words they both walk in.

"You look beautiful baby girl." Dad says kissing my cheek.

"Yeah, looking good sis." Axel smiles.

Axel has been with us for a week now and ever since he came back he hasn't been himself. I get that being forced to leave the army is a massive thing for him, but there's something more.

There is a darkness behind his eyes that wasn't there before. There's a sadness that runs deep within him. No matter how many times, Lily, Daisy and I have tried to talk to him, he won't tell us anything. He's keeping it all locked up tight, and it's breaking our hearts. We can't seem to help or fix him.

"Maddie, come with me sweet girl. It's time for Rose to get married." Daisy says holding out her hand.

Maddie skips to Daisy and her face becomes sad all of sudden.

"Hey. What's the matter princess?" Lily asks.

"I wish my mama was here to see me in my pwetty dress." Maddie states sadly.

We all exchange a look, Maddie's mum, Patty, hasn't been in her life lately. No one is sure what's going on, only that it has something to do with her boyfriend. I know Raven is worried out of her mind about it.

The Merricks' have kindly lent us their house and land to get married on. With the rolling fields of crops it really is beautiful.

We reach the bottom of the isle made up of simple garden chairs placed with seasonal flowers. At the alter waits Rip, he's looking unbelievable hot. He is wearing light grey fitted suit trousers, a white shirt with the sleeves rolled up to his elbows. He has a few buttons undone from the collar, showing off some of his tattoos. Oh and of course he is wearing his cut. Standing with him are his best men Blake and Wes. My eyes land on the person who is marrying us and a giggle escapes my lips.

Khan is standing there with a robe over his shoulders. He wiggles his eyebrows at me. Rip kept it quiet, all he said is that he had booked someone. What Rip doesn't know is I have a little surprise of my own.

My entrance music starts, and everyone starts giggling and shaking their heads. My dad looks at me, raising his eyebrow. I laugh and shrug.

Lily, Daisy, Caden and Maddie walk down first, dancing and laughing.

The song I chose is one of my favourites and it always makes me feel good. The words are perfect. It is James Brown's 'I got you' (I feel good).

It is my turn to walk down the aisle, with Dad on one side and Axel on the other.

"Just have fun and dance. Let's go." I say laughing at their faces.

I dance and shake, moving my hips. My dad busts out some of his best moves and Axel just does a cool guy walk with occasional head bobbing. I can't stop smiling. I catch Rip's eyes watching me, they are alight.

When I finally reach him, he takes my hand in his.

"You're a fuckin nut, you know that?" He says smiling. I nod in reply.

"One of the many reasons I fuckin' love you sweetheart." He says before kissing me.

"Woah! Pres! Easy, we're not at that point in the ceremony yet. Put your woman down and let's make her your wife." Khan laughs.

We get on with the ceremony, and I can't stop smiling.

"Are there any reasons why any of you fuckers don't want these perfect two to get married? Speak now or forever hold your peace, but if you are a dick and do speak now we can't promise that you'll be able to speak again." Khan threatens.

Thankfully everyone laughs. I'm worried my nan may have a little heart attack over that statement.

"Good! Now to the good stuff, do you both love each other, promise to only bang each other, look after each other when you're sick and live life to the max until you meet your maker?" Khan asks.

Rip rolls his eyes and pinches the bridge of his nose. I giggle.

"Hell yeah I do." I say laughing.

Rip's eyes come to me, looking a little shocked that Khan hasn't upset me by speaking like that at our wedding.

"Rip?" Khan asks.

"Yeah, damn right." Rip says, his eyes never leaving me.

Khan gets us to exchange rings.

"Ladies and gentlemen, boys and girls! I would like to pronounce Pres Ripley King and Flo Nightingale Rose Rocke as man and wife. You may now kiss your hot bride!" Khan shouts.

Everyone cheers as Rip takes my face in his hands and kisses me.

We turn to face everyone who is still cheering and shouting.

"I give you Mr and Mrs King, aka The President of Satan's Outlaws and his Old Lady! Now let's get wasted!" Khan yells behind us.

The party is in full swing. It's basically a biker cookout, just with decorated tables and everyone is a little more dressed up. It's perfect.

I spot Axel standing away from everyone and staring out at the fields. I go over to him, his behaviour is still worrying all of us. I tap him on the shoulder. Axel jumps and spins round to face me. Before I can even say a word his hand reaches out and grabs my throat, gripping it tightly. His eyes are black with a mixture of rage and fear.

"Aaa-xx." I rasp.

I try tapping his arm, but it doesn't work. His grip on my throat just tightens.

"What the fuck!" I hear shouted.

Rip approaches and grabs Axel, throwing him off of me. I stumble and fall to the ground. I gasp for air and hold my throat.

Rip crouches down in front of me. He looks to my neck and his face sets to stone. I grab his hand and shake my head.

"Please don't." I beg.

Rip helps me to my feet and Axel stands, he looks to me with pain and sorrow in his eyes.

"Rose I...I'm so sorry...I just...I'm sorry...I can't." Axel says walking away.

"Ax wait." I call after him, but he just carries on walking away.

Rip puts his arm around me and pulls me in tight.

"Leave him sweetheart. He has some serious shit going on right now. Just give him space and time." Rip says kissing my head.

"Okay, but don't tell my parents about this. They don't need any more to worry about." I cuddle into Rip.

I watch my baby brother walk away, I know whatever it is he is fighting is big. The man I saw just now was not my brother. Axel would never lay a hand on me or any woman. He clearly has some serious demons he has to face. I just hope he has the strength to do it, to find himself again. I hope he knows he's not alone.

THE WAR WITHIN BOOK 4 OF THE ROCKE SERIES

(Axel's Story)

Coming spring 2020.

Thank you so much for reading my books. If you wish to find out more about upcoming releases, teasers and competitions, follow me on Facebook, Instagram, Twitter, Amazon and Good-reads.

Printed in Poland
by Amazon Fulfillment
Poland Sp. z o.o., Wrocław